The Billionaire's Muse

AVA LORE

ISBN: 1482795833
ISBN-13: 978-1482795837

DEDICATION

For everyone who got me into *la cosa nostra.*

CONTENTS

1

I hung back from the press of people, lingering at the edge of the crowd. The women were all dressed in onyx and ruby and sapphire and emerald dresses, brilliant birds of paradise, while the men stood with them, all black and white and staid and stolid as penguins. I scrutinized the assembled throng and pondered a very important question.

Which of these men is Batman?

I hadn't found him yet, because most of the people that attend these terrible 'charity' functions are old and boring because you have to be old and boring to be invited. No one with less than ten million dollars is allowed in, unless you're part of the support staff. Which would be me, I suppose. And usually if you have ten million dollars you are either old and boring or young and that particular sort of country club inbred that just screams *I have a trust fund and have never done my own grocery shopping!* Except Anton Waters, my employer, who is handsome, rich, sexy, self-made and young. Or I guess his wife and my best friend,

Felicia, is my employer, but ever since they were married a second time they've been so joined at the hip they might as well be one person.

I sighed. Thinking about Felicia reminded me of how much I missed her. I knew her before she married Anton, which is how I landed a job as her personal assistant, though recently it had expanded to include other duties as well. To my deep despair, I seemed to have a talent for this type of thing. Otherwise I'd still be drinking watery piss beer and smoking some dank nugs on my Friday nights rather than organizing a dumb charity auction for a bunch of people whose shoes cost more than whatever they'd spend on 'charity' tonight.

God. If only.

I sighed again and grabbed a flute of champagne from a passing alcohol jockey. I downed it in two gulps, feeling the alcohol warm me all the way down to my toes, and resumed looking for Batman, my favorite mental pastime at these events.

I didn't really expect to find him, of course. I know he's got a secret identity.

I scanned the men. *Too old. Too short. Too bald, although I guess Batman does wear a hood, so he could be bald under that outfit. But probably not. Too old. Too old. Too old* again. *Too thin. Too goofy. Wearing glasses. Wait, doesn't Batman wear glasses? No, that's Superman. Clark Kent. Whatever. Too blind, anyway. Batman would have laser surgery. Too old. Too inbred. Too old. Too...hot? Is that a thing? Wait a minute...*

I pulled up short, my eyes widening. Not twenty feet away stood a tall, sinfully handsome man, dressed to the nines. His sandy hair swept back from his temples in slick, perfect waves, highlighting his fine cheekbones and rich brown eyes. His mouth was a perfect, delicious pout, and the hand that held his flute of champagne was elegant and poised. An artist's hand. And I should know. Before I landed this sweet gig I'd spent most of my waking hours buried in my art, and this guy was making me want to pick up a pencil and sketch him. Naked.

His deep brown eyes bored into mine. Despite myself I felt my cheeks stain with color under his scrutiny, and his perfect, pouty mouth slowly broke into a suggestive smile.

Batman is staring at me, I thought. *What a creeper.*

His eyes flicked up and down my body, as though appraising me. It wasn't a comfortable feeling and pissed me off, so I returned the favor. Narrowing my eyes, I took in his broad shoulders and barrel chest, his trim waist, his narrow hips and the muscled thighs barely poured into his tux pants. I pursed my lips and tried to assess him from a cold, artistic perspective.

It wasn't working.

My god, he was hot.

I flicked my gaze back to his, hoping he couldn't see the hammering pulse in my throat and quirked my mouth at him. A *seen better* to his casual objectification. And I had seen better. In my dreams.

He held my eyes for a long moment, then lifted his brows and this time his smile was knowing.

Oh, really?

A hand on my arm thankfully tore me away from his arresting gaze, because who knows what kind of subtle semaphore we might have started engaging in across the crowded ballroom? I turned with a flash of gratitude, only to have it die in my chest as I realized it was Arthur, Anton's personal assistant.

Great.

I like Arthur. I really do. I think he's smart and motivated and actually pretty kind to people in general even though he doesn't have to be. But I think he simultaneously wants to fuck me and wants to fuck *with* me. Seeing as how he had to claw his way up from the rank of lowly intern to be Anton's assistant and all I had to do was be Felicia's best friend to become *her* assistant, I think he resents the ease with which I landed my job. I can't tell him that I've been putting up with Felicia's willful stupidity in the realm of her own personal affairs for the entirety of our acquaintance and I didn't even get paid for it. Felicia would be lost without me. It's a position with many drawbacks. Such as now. Second-in-command on the personal assistant totem pole is like coming in second place in a shit-eating contest.

And I was about to have to shovel turds.

"What?" I said. It came out a little sharper than I meant it, but I knew that look on Arthur's face. He'd found a shit job for me to do and he couldn't wait to pass it along.

He flashed me a smile, all business and propriety. One of the many things about being a personal assistant that I am total balls at. I can keep Felicia in line and do damage control, and bark orders with the best of them, but everything else? Might as well hire a Golden Retriever to handle the crowds. It'd be better and more coherent.

Arthur's eyes glinted. "Mrs. Glasscock is on the floor of the ladies' room in a pool of her own vomit," he said. "I'm going to go see if I can't locate Mr. Glasscock, but I need you to see if you can't get her on her feet and cleaned up."

I groaned. Of course. And to be fair, this wasn't a job he could just do himself. The *ladies room* is an inviolate sanctuary. Only a *lady*—and I hardly qualify, but if someone checked I'd have the biological bits, I suppose—may enter. Tossing back my champagne, I looked around for a place to put it, and finally just set it down in a nearby potted plant. Someone would find it. "Fine," I said. "I'll have her up and running in ten."

"Great. And then I need you to go make one last check on the auction items, okay? Ta!" And with that, he was gone, disappearing into the melee of well-dressed assholes.

"Wait!" I cried. One last check? Seriously? We'd checked the auction items at least five times already. What the hell was I supposed to be checking *for?*

But he was already gone. Cursing, I slipped between the milling people, my sandy-haired Batman all but forgotten. I had a drunken society maven to attend to. And what could be more important than that?

ꕥ

Mrs. Glasscock took fifteen minutes to get up off the floor. I took great satisfaction in slapping her awake, knowing she wouldn't remember it. They were purely therapeutic slaps anyway. Therapeutic for me, I mean.

By the time I had mostly cleaned the vomit from her hair and made her as presentable as possible, *I* was a mess. My cocktail dress stank of regurgitated champagne, and I was red-faced and sweaty from the exertion of holding her up and maneuvering her out of the ladies room and into the arms of her grateful husband. Unfortunately I didn't have any time to straighten up—the auction was about to begin, and I still had to do my *one last check,* whatever the hell that meant. I could only suppose it meant making sure none of the staff had contracted a case of sticky fingers, or that nothing had become broken in transport from Anton and Felicia's house.

I knew Felicia didn't like charity events, but I'd organized this one especially for her. It was an art auction among New York's upper crust, and not a boring silent auction, but one where people actually had to raise their little numbers and everything. The snobs probably thought it was very droll, and it's great fun to watch drunk rich people try to outbid each other, so of all the mandatory functions Felicia was obliged to throw at least twice a year this, I had decided, was the least painful. Plus, Felicia could probably buy some nice pieces she wouldn't otherwise have access to.

Me, I was just hoping for a fist fight to break out.

I checked myself one last time in the mirror, making certain I didn't look too much like a vomit splash-guard, then grabbed my dumb beaded clutch bag—the one with my phone in it, the portal to all my plans and people—and stalked out of the bathroom, hurrying toward the backstage. The Edison Ballroom is an old Depression-era hotel-turned-theater, and it's pretty much perfect for an auction. There's a bar and a lounge and its dim and crowded so everyone can get all intimate with each other, whether they want to or not. The auction was about to begin, and I had to make certain everything was in place.

I arrived, out of breath, to inspect the pieces one

last time. Two handsome young men who probably did bouncer work as their day jobs were lingering near the first lot, joking about some girl they both knew. *Gross.* I stomped up to them and waved their bow-tie-wearing asses out of the way before grabbing my phone from my purse.

The pieces had been donated by the audience, and it was essential that they be in the same condition they arrived in. After all, people were here to be seen, and also so everyone could know just how expensive their tastes in art ran. That the money went to Felicia's favorite charity, an inner-city arts program for disadvantaged kids, was probably irrelevant to these people.

It didn't matter. I just had to make sure it ran smoothly, and to that end I had photographed every piece before it left storage in Anton's basement art gallery. I pulled up the list and began going down the line.

Lot one, an Andy Warhol. Pristine condition, still pristine. Good. You never knew when someone was going to smoke a thousand cigars right under their modern masterpiece. Next!

Lot two, an Andre Masson painting. Lot three, another one. Both fine. Lot four, a piece of facade from some Greek temple. Awesome. Let's just rip it all up. Lot five, a... really cool modern Aboriginal painting from Australia. Shit, I wish I was rich. Lot six, a bronze Chinese mirror. Lot seven, an ugly Edwardian brooch worth, like, nothing, haha, someone was doing spring cleaning. Lot eight, a white porcelain Chinese vase, Qing dynasty... and not here.

Why is it not here?

Out on the stage, the emcee, one of the inbred country-club set who fancied himself a comedian, tapped the mic. "I'd like to welcome you all to the First Annual Waters Charity Art Auction..."

Panic seized me. The auction was starting and we were missing lot eight, one of the more expensive pieces in the auction. Its spot was empty. Empty! It was a beautiful piece, too, exquisite and smooth and fine. For a long moment as the emcee started babbling, I stared at the picture of it on my phone, then at the spot on the table where it should have stood. Empty.

Phone: vase.

Table: empty.

Phone.

Vase.

Table.

Empty.

Oh, shit.

And that's when I somehow managed to fuck *everything* up.

Filled with ire, I took a step back, my voice already rising in my throat. "Where the *fuck* is that white vase?" I hollered at the top of my lungs as I pivoted smartly on the balls of my feet and set off to find out whose ear to chew. Instead of striding purposefully through the backstage area, my laser focus honed in on locating the missing vase, I collided violently with someone rushing in my direction.

I saw it all, in that perfect moment of stillness before disaster strikes. A young man, his eyes wide and horrified, reeling backwards. Our mutual momentum sent us both careening out of control, struggling to regain our balance. We both lost the battle.

And so did the white vase in his hands. Gently,

gracefully, it rolled from his fingers and began its fateful descent toward the floor.

Horror speared me straight through the heart as I fought to regain my footing, knowing I had only a split second to launch myself forward and catch the falling vase, but it was a pipe dream from the beginning. Still stumbling backwards, my ass hit the edge of the table holding the to-be-auctioned art, sending a shock of pain up my back, and I tumbled forward to my hands and knees. My phone hit the floor the same time as the vase. My phone, swathed in rubber, survived the fall.

The vase didn't.

With a terrible sound, it shattered into a million pieces on the hard floor. Bits of white porcelain skittered across the wood, some spinning off under the assembled tables, others content to stay where they landed in the initial blast.

Silence descended upon the assembled throng of my fellow peons. The kid who had been carrying the vase stared at its broken corpse, his face going green.

I knew that vase was worth probably five thousand dollars, if not more. Perhaps ten to the right collector. There was no way this kid doing grunt work for the elite had anything like that kind of money. He was probably living paycheck to paycheck in a six-story walk up apartment with three other roommates. In fact, I knew he was. I could see it on his face. The utter, abject *fear* of someone already deep in debt just about to head further into it. I knew it because I'd been there.

Shit.

"Fuck," I said out loud, breaking the silence. "That was my fault."

It wasn't. It was the kid's fault. The breakable pieces had been packed in well-insulated boxes for a *reason,* but it was too late. I'd been really fucking poor once. I wasn't gong to let him take the fall.

He looked at me with eyes full of gratitude, but I had to look away. *How the hell am* I *going to pay for this?* I thought. I mean, I had a good job. But I also had gobs of debt. Anton's accountant helped me consolidate it, but I'm still kind of cruising along, unable to save much. I expense everything I can, but frankly, this was not something any amount of expensed meals could save up for.

I scrambled to my feet and pointed at the culprit. "You," I said, "sweep this up. *Carefully.* I want you to have every single piece of this vase in a bag by the end of the night. And I mean *every piece.*" He nodded, and I gingerly picked my phone up from the floor and studied it, making certain it was still in one piece.

Thank god. No cracks on the glass, and it flashed to life when I hit the button. Pulling up my catalog of art, I found the entry again. Seeing the beautiful vase, still whole and healthy on my phone, made me feel sick inside, but I pushed it down. I had to find the vase's owner, and fast. I glanced at the name.

Malcolm Ward.

All right, I thought. *Sounds like an old guy.* I reached up and adjusted my little black dress so that my breasts—such as they were—pushed up over the top. Maybe I could knock a couple hundred dollars off my debt with some cleavage. Grabbing a passing stage jockey, I gave him fierce, whispered instructions and then swiftly strode out of the backstage area and to the lounge. Behind me I heard the emcee pause in his monologue, and then say: "Malcolm Ward, please meet Mrs. Waters' personal assistant, Ms. MacElroy, in the Edison Lounge." A chorus of whistles and whoops went up from the drunken crowd and I rolled my eyes as I exited.

The lounge was dim and mostly abandoned, the gaudy zebra stripes of the booths shining white and ghostly in the dark. I moved to one of them and sat down, crossing my legs at the ankle and sitting up straight so my breasts would thrust out. I had to look like the quintessential Personal Assistant, the one who would Do Anything to Make Her Employer Happy. I wanted Mr. Ward to think I was lovely and pliable, even though I'm anything but, on both accounts. Getting a thousand dollars or two knocked off my debt was worth it, though. What's a little exploitation among unequals?

In an attempt to look nonchalant, I turned my phone on and casually swiped through my catalog. There were twenty-five pieces in all—well, twenty four, now—and each of them was slated to bring a decent price in. If we were lucky we'd end up with at least fifty thousand dollars for the charity, and I had to be content with that. That I was going to have to turn the heat off in my apartment for the next three years was simply the natural consequence of my own partial fuck up.

I sighed, watching the beautiful pieces of art pass me by, slipping up the screen, and I wished I was out of debt. And better paid. I'd have given quite a few pesos for some of these pieces...

A clearing throat had me looking up. For a moment, I was blinded by the flash of my screen still scored across my vision. Then it cleared, and I found myself staring at my blond Batman.

He towered over me, staring down at me with his weird, mischievous smile plastered on his face. He was scoping me out. I hate feeling like meat.

"May I help you?" I asked him icily.

"Miss MacElroy?" he said. "I am Malcolm Ward. You... wanted to see me?"

Even his voice was full of suggestion. Here was a man who liked to get what he wanted, and I was almost glad his pretty vase was smashed.

I stood up so he wouldn't be towering over me any longer, but that was a miscalculation, because he was very, very tall. He still towered over me. But I'm not a shrinking violet. *Project,* I thought. *Don't let this jackass think he can walk all over you.*

I looked him directly in the eye and ignored the little shiver that ran up my spine at the contact. "I am sorry to inform you, Mr. Ward, but your donated lot has met with an... incident."

He quirked a brow. "An incident, Miss MacElroy?"

"Yes," I said. "Specifically, an incidental floor. It has met with an incidental floor. I apologize, but it did not survive the meeting. I, of course, take full responsibility for this. Please tell me how much I owe you so we can work out a payment plan."

His eyes narrowed. "Are you saying the vase was destroyed?" he said at last.

No use beating around the bush about it. "Yes," I said. "It has been destroyed. Like I said, I take full responsibility. If you would like to sit down, we can work out a plan to resolve this debt, and then we can go on our way."

He didn't respond immediately. Instead he tilted his head and studied me. Again I felt the cool appraisal of his gaze, slipping over my face, lingering on my lips, traveling down to my cleavage—my damn cleavage! why did I think it was a good idea to show it off, again?—and then further down. Where his gaze touched me, I grew hot, then cold. His frank assessment gave me the willies, as if he were deciding just which part of my body he should... *do something to* first. I was only forty percent curious as to what that *something* was. The other sixty percent of me was telling me to run very fast in another direction.

And I was in this guy's debt.

I sure do know how to pick 'em.

Out in the ballroom, the emcee was announcing the third lot. The third lot, already! I needed to rush backstage to assess the rest of the lots and make sure everything was in place. Annoyance flared in me.

"Stop ogling me and let's get this done with," I snapped. "I have a lot of work to do." See? I'm terrible at public relations.

Mr. Ward raised his brows again. "Very well, Miss MacElroy. I will be quick. The vase, while beautiful, held little importance to me, and its monetary value has most likely been recouped already by my vast investments, so the money is, for lack of a better word, immaterial to me."

Was he letting me off the hook? Oh my god, I wasn't going to have to pay him thousands of dollars? I couldn't stifle the relieved smile that broke across my face and I opened my mouth to thank him, but he held up a hand.

"The chief value of the vase was in what it would have fetched for the charity tonight," he continued. "Where I had placed a piece on the auction block to be auctioned off, there is now... nothing. Something must replace it."

I blinked in confusion. "What do you mean?" I said. "Do you have something else you can auction off?"

That quirky smile returned. He looked quite devilish when he smiled. "I believe," he said, "that since you are in my debt, that I may now auction *you* off."

I blinked at him. He smiled back.

"What?" The word erupted from deep in my chest and I barely recognized it as my own voice. "What the hell are you talking about?"

He held up a long, beautifully tapered finger. The sort of finger useful for sculpting, or shading, or... *other* things. "Let me be clear. You *owe* me. Therefore *I—"* he pointed to himself, "—own *you."*

My blood boiled. "I don't think it works that way any more. Slavery was banned."

He shrugged. "In name," he said. "Now, lot six is up. I believe my lot is listed as number eight?"

I froze and listened. Yup, sure enough, the bronze mirror was going, going, and soon to be gone. I'd taken responsibility for the vase and now I was going to pay for it.

"Are you sure you don't want to just put yourself up there?" I said, trying to keep the pleading from my voice. "I mean, no one will argue that you don't own yourself. And besides, who would buy *me?* I'm not exactly high society material." This much was true—I didn't even try to hide my tattoos and piercings, even though plenty of people turned their noses up at them. But even more I wanted to know: *what would anyone buy me* for?

"If you don't want to go up on the auction block,

then I will simply have to set the price of the vase at one million dollars."

I paled. "No one would uphold that amount," I said.

"But who can afford the lawyer to argue that?" he asked me.

Ruthless. Not one of the old money set, and not one of the inbred country clubbers. A self-made man, just like Anton. Anton, who still gave me the shivers, though Felicia had softened his approach to other people somewhat. And this man, Malcolm Ward, had me in a bind. A drunken cheer went up from the crowd as someone won the mirror. Rich folks get randy at too much champagne and money changing hands.

"Lot Seven..." the emcee began. I knew that lot seven was pretty worthless. I wondered who would pay money for it. And after that...

"Fine!" I said. "I'll go up there. But no one gets to buy me for weird sex stuff!"

"Of course not," he said. "That would be illegal."

And with that, he gave me a bow and a smile, and turned around and walked out of the lounge.

"Anyone? Anyone?" the emcee was saying.

"Shit," I muttered under my breath, turned my heels, and ran back to the backstage area. The lackey who'd dropped the vase stood by its empty spot, looking agonized and awkward. I ran up to him and quickly told him the change in plans before ordering him onstage. What the hell, right? He'd already ruined my night and possibly more. Might as well make him do something useful.

He scurried back out onstage and whispered furiously to the emcee as lot seven—unwanted, it seemed—was taken away, numberless. Nervously I smoothed my skirt and hoped I didn't look too much like something the cat dragged in. The stress of this job was seriously getting to me. I deserved a vodka and vodka with a shot of vodka on the side after I was done being sold.

I had no idea why anyone would want to buy a person, but people sold at auctions were usually sold for dates. I had no desire to date any of these people. Although if a woman bought me I'd probably go lez for the night just out of gratitude for whisking me out from under the noses of the leering elite. Rich guys were the worst for that sort of thing. Guys period, actually.

"Now, ladies and gentlemen, the previous lot eight, listed in your programs, has met with its demise. That exquisite china vase, dating from the seventeenth century, sadly went to the great foyer table in the sky a few moments ago." He laughed at his terrible joke. "But we have a replacement lot, just as exquisite."

In the shadows of the side stage I rolled my eyes so hard I think I saw my brain.

"May I present to you the replacement lot eight, Mrs. Felicia Waters' personal assistant, Miss Sadie MacElroy! Let's give her a big round of applause!"

I knew my cheeks were flaming, but I plastered the biggest smile on my face that I could. It was this, or paying an unscrupulous business guy way too much money for no reason at all. I hated everyone in that moment, but you never would have known it as I strode out onto the stage, my head held high and my shoulders thrown back, showing off my still fluffed-up tits for the world to see. I mean, they're not B cups or whatever, but like my mom's boyfriend always said, *More than a mouthful is too much.* God, he'd been creepy.

The spotlights blinded me as I stopped by the emcee and turned, tossing my hair over my shoulder, then cocking a hip and putting my hand on it. I hoped looked sufficiently saucy and fiery to deter the older crusty guys from bidding for me.

The applause died down. "Very good," the emcee said. "I believe this lot is a date with Miss MacElroy. A meal of your choosing, or some other activity, negotiated between you and this ravishing woman."

Ravishing? More like ravaged.

"Let us open the bidding at a thousand dollars!"

A thousand fucking dollars? I tried not to let my shock show on my face, but then again the pieces selling here were worth two thousand minimum.

"I have a thousand. Good, do I have two—I have two thousand. Who wants—three thousand. Four thousand. Five! Five thousand..."

The blood drained from my head. I forced myself not to squint against the bright lights, seeking out who was bidding on me. It wouldn't have worked anyway. I could see nothing, blinded and dazzled and being auctioned off like an object. My smile hurt my face.

"Six thousand. Wonderful. Seven. Eight. Eight thousand. Do I see nine? Nine thousand? Nine thousand! And how about ten? Ten? Ten? All right. Going once. Going twice. Sold, for nine thousand dollars!"

Nine thousand, I thought numbly. That was almost two months salary. *Nine thousand dollars.*

Who the fuck has that kind of money? I thought. *Who*

the fucking fuck has nine thousand dollars to throw away on a date with a downtown tramp?

"Congratulations, Mr. Malcolm Ward, for purchasing your own property," the emcee said. The room erupted in laughter as the emcee turned to me and handed me the number of my buyer. Malcolm Ward. Stunned, I waved at the crowd and then walked off stage, my legs shaking.

Bought by Malcolm Ward. The guy who wouldn't stop staring at me like a creeper and told me that because I owed him, I had to go up on stage and be sold. And who then bought me. What a shithead.

Why, then, did my heart pick up its pace at the idea of going out on a date with him?

Maybe I just hoped he'd give me an opportunity to throw a glass of wine in his face.

Yeah. That was it.

2

Felicia found me before the auction even ended.

"What happened?" she cried, running into the Edison lounge where I was gulping down my well-deserved vodka and vodka with a vodka chaser.

"Only the most terrible thing that possibly *could* happen," I told her, slamming back my chaser. I smacked the shot glass onto the bar and shuddered. The liquor sent warm fingers through my stomach, making the muscles of my body unclench at last, though given what I'd been through tonight I wasn't so sure that was a good thing. I rarely indulged on the job because I'm a pretty dramatic drunk. And I was feeling pretty damn dramatic right then.

"I'm being serious." She stomped her foot. Her long, pale golden evening gown, overlaid with black lace, shimmered with the movement. "Why didn't you tell me something had happened to one of the pieces? Why didn't you tell me you were going to end up on the auction block? I wouldn't have blown my money on that Warhol if I'd known!"

"Well, I didn't even know until about three seconds before I ended up on stage," I told her. "Someone was carrying the vase barehanded, I bumped into them and... I took the fall for it. And the guy who owned it told me to auction *myself* off since I owed him!"

"Yeah," she said, giving me a funny look. "Malcolm Ward."

"That's the one."

Her mouth twisted. "You don't know who he is?"

I don't know who any of these people are and up until I have to remember someone's name I don't care. I shook my head.

"The guy who just bought out NovaTech," Felicia said.

I stared at her blankly. I don't follow the world of business and I try to forget anything I do learn as soon as possible. I'm just here for the free food and the job.

"*Billionaire* Malcolm Ward. Warden Industries. Don't you remember the guy who forcibly French-kissed the Italian Prime Minister last summer after the PM made those remarks about rape?"

Holy shit, I thought. "*That's* the guy?"

"The one who did donuts in his limo in Central Park? The one who performed an impromptu and totally filthy rendition of *Drop It Like It's Hot* on Letterman? The one who conducted a hostile takeover of his former best friend's company and then fired everyone and put a clown college in their old building? Yeah. *That's* the guy."

Okay, I *had* heard of Malcolm Ward, although, to be honest, I thought he was just a movie star who'd recently taken up a coke hobby and was just flaunting it around. This guy actually owned a company? Or compan*ies?* And made money off of them despite the fact that he was patently nuts? Perhaps my initial assessment pegging him as Batman wasn't too far off. I wondered if he liked to dress up in rubber.

An eccentric billionaire. Well. At least our date wouldn't be boring?

"So you said you'd auction yourself off and he bought you?" Felicia said, breaking into my thoughts. "I don't like that."

I shoot her a glare. "So?" I said. "It's better than having to pay him ten thousand dollars that I don't have. Unlike *some* people, I had to take out loans to go to art school. I'm just now getting back on top of them and I really can't afford to pay ten grand to some guy who wouldn't have even noticed it was gone."

"I know, I know," Felicia said. She held up her hands, clearly trying to placate me. "It's just that it's a little weird and manipulative."

"You started out with Anton as an arranged marriage," I said. "What if lightning strikes twice? We both get bought by secretly wonderful guys and have true love and happily ever after and all that shit."

"Anton didn't really *buy* me..."

"Yes, he did," I told her.

She looked chagrined for a moment, and then sighed. "Okay, fine, he *did,* but it was different. There was a contract. And it was for marriage. And he didn't have a reputation for being bugfuck crazy."

"No, he just had a reputation for being a sociopath. That's *way* better than bugfuck."

Felicia sighed. "Look, I'm just worried about you.

Anton and me... that was really hard on me. I don't want you to go through the same crap. Rich guys are assholes and I'd never forgive myself if something happened to you while you were on your date or whatever..."

I blinked at her. "Are you... are you afraid he's going to rape me?" I said.

She threw her hands in the air and sat down next to me at the bar. "I don't know what I'm afraid of," she said. "Just be careful, okay?"

"Where were you to tell me that *before* I broke a ten thousand dollar vase?" I asked her. "Some friend you are."

Felicia gave me a little knowing smile. "I was getting head in the coat closet," she replied serenely.

I turned away and stuck my fingers in my ears. "*La la la la la!*" I sang. Anton had a real *thing* for public sex, and Felicia seemed to have caught the fever from him. It was gross. Although I couldn't help but be curious about it. Would I ever have sex in public for a guy? Would I like it?

Maybe if that guy has billions of dollars, I thought to myself. *And* isn't *named Malcolm Ward.* I had enough crazy in my life without dealing with rich crazy, which is a whole other kind of crazy than poor crazy. I just had to get through my date with him so I could relegate this whole debacle of a night to the past and move the hell on.

I lifted a hand and was about to signal to the bartender that I needed another vodka injection, but just then Felicia elbowed me in the side, hard. I swayed and nearly fell off my bar stool. Perhaps I *didn't* need another vodka injection. "What?" I snapped at her, irritated.

She gave me a disgusted look. "Fine then," she hissed. "I won't tell you that Bugfuck Billionaire is at nine o'clock and heading this way."

Peeking from the corner of my eye, I spotted him striding toward us, looking handsome and formidable. I winced. Time to get the arrangements over with.

I hate first dates.

ৎ

Malcolm Ward arrived at the bar just as Felicia's phone buzzed at her, and she gave me an apologetic look before sliding off the stool. No doubt Anton required her presence for some reason or another, and I just rolled my eyes as she bolted from the lounge, not looking Ward in the eye.

Coward.

I met his gaze head on. The smile on his face was dazzling, his teeth a brilliant white in the gloom of the lounge. The sound of people milling in the next room told me that the auction had ended and now there would be dancing for anyone who felt like it. Pulling up alongside my chair, he gazed down at me, tilting his head as though he were assessing me... again. He just didn't give up.

"Like what you see?" I asked him, feeling snide.

"I do," he said. "I'm very pleased with my purchase. I have received something far more valuable than a vase, which, just between you and me, was destined to collect dust until the end of its days anyway."

I arched an eyebrow at him. "You didn't like it?" I asked him.

He shrugged. "I liked it well enough. It made me

very happy when I first purchased it, but the pleasure of it has waned over the years." His eyes swept over me once more. "Perhaps more impermanent pleasures will prove more lasting."

I couldn't take it. "Ew," I said. "Stop looking at me like I'm a piece of meat. It's seriously grossing me out."

His eyes widened and he took a step back. "I'm sorry," he said, "I did not mean to make you uncomfortable." He frowned. "Though I can certainly see where I've put my foot in it. I merely meant that while a vase is fragile, it also lasts hundreds of years, if not thousands with proper preservation. A woman—" he gestured to me, sweeping one of his lovely, slender hands up and down in the air in front of me, and I felt a strange thrill as his fingers passed close to my body, "—is more ephemeral. A beauty that does not last."

It took me a moment to comprehend what he was saying, and when I did realize what he'd said it sure as fuck didn't make me feel any better. I'd once semi-jokingly told Felicia I'd thought Anton might be a wife serial-killer because of his distance and his locked basement. This guy, though, was seriously weirding me out. Carefully I hopped off my bar stool, making certain to place it between us when I found the ground with my feet. "I'm sorry," I said, holding the stool in front of me like a shield, "but you sound like you're going to kill me and wear my skin when you talk like that."

To my utter shock, he threw back his head and laughed so long and hard that tears came to his eyes. After almost a full minute I started to seriously think about stomping my foot, one of Felicia's favorite gestures. "I'm not sure what's so funny," I told him. "You're creeping me out and that's not cool. Especially since you bought a 'date' with me." To emphasize my point I crossed my arms, the thumb of my left hand finding the tattoo on my inner right bicep and rubbing it, something I often did when I was discomfited.

He visibly calmed himself and wiped his eyes. "Oh!" he said. "Oh, wow. I'm sorry. I didn't mean to, er, give you that impression. What I meant was that I am an amateur artist, and I find you quite lovely as a potential subject for a piece."

...Okay, *that* threw me off balance. There's probably something wrong with me in that I seem to jump to the *serial killer* explanation for people's weird behavior instead of considering other viable explanations, but really. An amateur artist? This guy? From what I'd heard of him, his greatest talent was getting the media spotlight on him.

My incredulity must have shown in my face, because his smile grew. "You don't believe me?" he said. "It's true. I dabble in the arts."

"Oh," I said finally. "That's... great."

"In fact, it's the main reason I bought you."

Does... does this guy want art lessons? I wonder. "It is?"

"Oh yes. I knew from the moment I saw you from across the ballroom that I wanted to paint you. Or take your picture. Or perhaps sculpt you..." He took a step closer, and my hands tightened on the bar stool. He was so *tall,* and I caught a whiff of a very masculine scent underneath his aftershave. The hard muscles of his body filled out his tux, and I found myself praying that he was telling the truth, because if he tried to kill me I'd be no match for a barrel chest and biceps like the ones he was sporting.

"Wow," I said. "You, uh, work in a lot of mediums."

"I'm quite versatile," he assured me. "And that is what I have planned for our date. Or rather, for our several dates."

I scowled. "Excuse me? I never said anything about several dates."

He raised his eyebrows. "Oh? Well, I paid nine thousand dollars for you. I feel that I have procured your services as a model, or perhaps I should say as an *inspiration,* for as long as it takes to complete one masterpiece featuring you."

For an artist, this guy sure talked oddly about it. "I... I suppose we should see how it goes," I said cautiously. Nine thousand dollars weighed pretty heavily on my conscience, but I wasn't about to let him see that. "Let's stick with *one* and if I'm comfortable with you, then we can maybe negotiate more."

"A woman who drives a bargain," Ward said. "I like that. I knew you were different just looking at you."

"Yeah," I said. "I bet you did." He gave me a strange look and I shook my head. "Okay, fine. But here's the deal. No nudity unless we discuss things first. I won't have you doing that shitty creepy thing some male photographers do when they say, 'oh, just take a little more off, show me some nipple,' because that shit is gross and we are both professionals." I caught myself. "Well, I am, at least."

"I'm professional in many things," Ward interjected, sounding almost hurt.

"Uh-huh," I said. "Well, since you yourself said

you're an amateur, you'd better read up on the rules of engagement first."

In the dim light, I saw his eyes gleam and harden. He seemed to think I was presenting a challenge to him rather than giving him the benefit of the doubt and kindly instructing him on how civilized people behaved toward each other in situations such as these. "Hey," I snapped. "I'm not joking around here. This is how professionals behave."

"Of course," he said smoothly. "And I vow I shall behave quite professionally." From the depths of his jacket he produced a white card and held it out to me, pinched between two elegant fingers. Gingerly I reached out and took it, trying to ignore the sudden dark hum of my blood in my veins when our fingertips brushed together. I ripped the card from his grip as I snatched my hand away. His eyes glittered down at me, but he said nothing about my reaction.

"My home address and phone number," he said instead. "Are you available tomorrow afternoon?"

I swayed on my feet. I doubted I'd be available for anything tomorrow other than to try out any and all hangover cures, for science. However, a modeling gig wasn't so bad, and the sooner it was done the sooner I could cut ties with this guy. "Yeah," I said, tearing my eyes away from his and pretending to study his card under the dim blue light. "Yeah, I think I'm free."

"Excellent. Are you allergic to ferrets?"

My brain clunked.

"No?" I said. "I don't think so, anyway."

"Oh good." He beamed. "Because I have many ferrets. I might, perhaps, wish for you to pose with them. Nothing sexual, I assure you, but I think I could make an interesting composition from those elements."

Ferrets. Really.

Maybe this guy wasn't a PR juggernaut, using eccentricity to his advantage. Maybe he didn't have an unfortunate coke addiction. Maybe he really *was* as bugfuck nuts as I'd heard, and I suspected that I, virtuous woman that I am who owns no television, had only scratched the surface of his crazy.

I liked this deal less and less all the time. I don't like crazy. Crazy brings drama. Drama brings tears brings screaming brings fighting brings slamming doors brings makeup sex and the cycle begins anew. And I'd had enough of that bullshit to last me a lifetime. Longer than a lifetime. When I get reincarnated into, say, a deer herd, I'll totally be a loner deer who doesn't interact with the other deer just to avoid bullshit drama about who rutted with who, and who saw who rubbing antlers with who, and so forth.

That's probably why I stuck with my current job. It was a steady paycheck, and the drama was minimal, and always involved other people when it was there, people I could brush off and ignore and then when I got home I could just read a book and not think about it...

Oh, I thought. *Oh, crap.*

Am I getting boring?

I looked at Malcolm Ward again, really *looked* at him this time. Yes, he was quite handsome, extremely well-dressed, and very well-formed. But aside from that there was a certain... *something*... about him that called to me. A little thrill of attraction, stretching from him to me. I'd felt it when our eyes met across the room. I'd felt it when he had demanded I submit myself for auction.

I was feeling it now.

I won't lie. I've been a magnet for drama in the past. I'm used to handling it. The drama of my current job is piddling compared to the shit I've had to deal with in the art world. But I had to admit, life *was* getting rather dull...

I'm bad at avoiding drama. I'm good at resolving it, but I guess I've had a lot of practice.

"Great," I heard myself saying. "I'll be there tomorrow afternoon, ready to pose with ferrets. What time?"

"Shall we say four o'clock? That way we might catch an early dinner afterward..."

A date. Of course he wants a date from this. But whatever, if it took care of this, if it *resolved* this drama, I could do that. And it probably wouldn't be torture.

"Sure," I agreed. Because I'm an idiot who makes the same mistakes over and over again. "That sounds fine."

"Excellent!" He beamed at me, then reached out and put his delicate, long-fingered hands on my bare shoulders before leaning in to kiss my cheeks, European style.

The moment his skin met mine, a wave of dizziness swept over me, a slipping, falling sensation dropping straight through the center of my body. The warmth of his touch spread out over me, dripping along my skin like golden honey, and the scent of him, rich and masculine, invaded my head as he leaned in close. His cheek brushed mine—slightly rough with the growth of a day's beard—his lips barely grazing against my face before he moved to the other side.

As in a dream, I saw his mouth pass by my eyes as he traveled from one cheek to the other, and in that instance I saw his lips twisted and drawn, not in a devilish smile as I thought he might be wearing after wringing concessions from me, but in misery. Then the moment passed and he kissed my other cheek before drawing back, beaming once again, his hands still heavy on my shoulders.

"Tomorrow!" he bellowed, then swept past me, leaving me reeling.

Dazed, I watched him weave through the crowd, clapping his hand on backs, leaning in for more kisses. My face burned with his touch, my heart racing like a rabbit's in my chest, and long after he disappeared through the door to the ballroom I stared after him.

What a weird guy, I thought. And I was going to spend more time with him. The most interesting character to come out of these terrible events, and I'd pretty much fallen into his lap. A neat disruption to my dulling life.

Despite my better inclinations, I was looking forward to it, ferrets and all. But what I was most looking forward to was a chaser for my chaser.

I signaled the bartender and settled back in my chair, preparing to forget this stressful night ever happened, with the help of my good friend alcohol.

❧

My bid to contract amnesia didn't work, sadly. It only made me wake up at ten the next morning with dread and bile in my stomach, last night's clothes on, and one of my false eyelashes stuck to my forehead. Looking at the clock, I realized I had to be clean, presentable and preferably not sick in slightly less than six hours. I didn't know if I was going to make it, so I did what I always do when I wake up with a terrible hangover and guy problems: I took a cold shower and dragged myself over to Felicia's house.

"So," I said, when Felicia opened her door to my incessant knocking, "what do you know about Malcolm Ward?"

Felicia crossed her arms, and through my hungover haze I realized she was wearing only a waist cincher, a garter belt and some stockings. I clapped my hands over my eyes and lurched forward until I was well inside the house and she closed the door behind me. "*Must* you?" I demanded blindly from the middle of the foyer. "*Must* you insist on destroying my brain with your perversions?" It was mostly faux-outrage by now, but man. She and Anton just did *not* let up.

"Oh, come on," she said, "you know I do it all for you."

"Put a robe on. I can't look at your tits and think straight."

"I'm glad I have that effect on you," she said, and I heard her waltz off and ascend the stairs.

With a sigh, I lowered my hands and staggered into her kitchen for coffee. By the time she came back down wearing a black silk robe, I was feeling a little more chipper and ready to assess my contracted modeling gig-slash-date with her. She sat down across from me at the breakfast table, propped her chin in her hand, and grinned at me.

"So," she said, "you like Malcolm Ward?"

I glared at her. "I didn't say that. I asked you what you knew about him."

She shrugged. "Not much besides the stuff he does to get himself in the news and on the gossip blogs."

"But... he was on the list for *your* party," I said. "And you must know him well enough to have asked for him to participate in the auction... right?" Given my level of idiocy regarding the current state of who was *in* and who was *out* in the worlds of business, finance, and high society, Anton left the invitations to Arthur and the organizing to me. I had assumed that Anton would know the guy, and that Felicia, by virtue of being married to Anton, would sort of absorb the information by osmosis.

Felicia waved a hand. "Oh, you know, I don't have a lot of control over that stuff. I hate those functions. If you want to ask someone about Malcolm Ward, ask Arthur. He clearly thought Ward was a big enough player in the business world to invite him."

I groaned. "I don't want to ask Arthur. He hates me. Or likes me. I can't tell with that guy. He's always *smiling.*"

Felicia laughed. "I think he's a really nice guy."

"That's because he has to be nice to you. You guys pay him lots of money to be nice."

She pursed her lips. "I suppose that's true." Abruptly she stood and walked across the kitchen to where her cell phone sat, plugged in and charging. Turning it on, she selected a contact and held the phone to her ear.

"Who are you calling?" I asked her.

"Arthur," she said, though in a chirpy voice, and I knew that was my cue to lie low. "Hi! Sorry to call on a Saturday, but I was wondering what you knew about Malcolm Ward and why you invited him last night."

She listened as Arthur spoke on the other end of the line.

"Well obviously I'm concerned about Sadie," she said. "She's my best friend and she got sold off to him."

She listened for a while, nodding occasionally, then rolling her eyes at me. Finally she said, "Okay, well, that's all I wanted to know. Yeah, see you on Monday," and hung up.

"So?" I said as soon as she set the phone down. "What did he say?"

She shrugged at me. "Not much. Malcolm Ward is a self-made billionaire. He's thirty five. Comes from a good New England family, all that jazz. Before this past year he was known for being very severe and withdrawn, though he took insane risks with his businesses and he was a really brutal taskmaster for himself and his employees. That stuff paid off, which was good, but over the last year people have been saying he's going a little... crazy."

Ferret-crazy, I thought. "Yeah?"

She nodded. "He's still insanely rich and an incredible connection to have, so Arthur put him on the list and solicited a donation. He didn't actually expect Ward to show up, much less put something on the auction block. I think Arthur was hoping he was crazy enough to spend a stupid amount of money on something at the auction."

"He did," I said. "He bought me, remember?"

"I think Arthur was hoping more for something in the area of fifty thousand dollars. Nine thousand is still pretty good, though."

"So that's it? Nothing about what he likes or doesn't like or is famous for?"

"Other than being crazy and rich? No. I'm under the impression that up until last year he was extremely bland. I don't even know if he *had* much of a personality, to be honest." At my curious look she blushed. "I spent some time last night researching him on the internet for you."

I wanted to smack myself in the head, but I didn't because I was afraid I might cause myself to be sick. Looking shit up and handling things like that was usually *my* job. I'd been too drunk from my vodka chaser's chaser's chaser to even drunk-text an ex, much less actually do something useful, like research. "Anything interesting at all?"

She shook her head. "Not that I could see. Mostly it seemed like he was a workaholic for ages and now he's gone a little loopy in the head. Or so they say."

"Yeah, I bet," I muttered. He hadn't struck me as particularly nuts when I was talking to him, except for the ferret bit, but he *was*... well, definitely a little off. I sipped my coffee. "You don't think he'll, like, try to skin me and wear me as a hat, do you?"

Felicia laughed. "No. I totally don't. I met the guy last night after he talked to you at the bar. He was really... outgoing."

"Hmph," I said. I've known plenty of outgoing guys. They were all jerks.

"So what kind of date is he taking you on?" she asked.

"It's not a date. I don't think. He wants me to pose for him."

Felicia blinked. "Pose?"

"Like for pictures."

A horrified look crossed her face. "Oh, *Sadie—*" she began.

I made an irritated noise at her. "It's nothing illicit. He said he's an amateur artist and he wants to use me as a subject."

Felicia looked puzzled. "I'd never heard anything about him being an artist."

"I only know what he told me."

"Huh." She thought for a moment. "What kind of artist?"

We both knew what she meant, but unfortunately I had no idea what to tell her. "He sort of implied... everything?" I thought back on what he'd said. "Photography, sculpture, painting..."

Felicia frowned. Like me, she knew a lot of artists. There certainly *were* people who did all sorts of different things in different mediums, but in our experience people tended to find a focus and hone in on it. Yeah, it was great to take classes in other stuff and see what you liked, but usually something *called* to you. You didn't end up doing more than two things, and usually the two things were related if you did. Photography and design, for instance.

We both sat there and puzzled this out for a few minutes before Felicia heaved a sigh. "Well," she said, "don't do anything I wouldn't do, I guess," which was really funny, considering.

"Yeah," I said. "I'll get right on that."

"Take a long bath and just try to be a little less surly than you usually are," she advised me. "I think Anton was wanting to do some business with Ward at some point in the future."

"Oh no," I groaned.

"You don't have to put out or anything like that,"

she said. "Just don't... you know." She gave me a little smile.

Don't try to shock him or scare him off, is what she was saying. Well, shit. There went my escape plan.

She pinned me with pleading eyes until I finally gave in. "Fine!" I said. "I'll try to be an adult."

"Thank you, Sadie. And try to have fun. I worry about you. This job seems to be stressing you out."

What? That was totally not true. I was, if anything, bored, and I opened my mouth to tell her so, but just then a heavy *thump* came from above us and Felicia looked up.

"Oh," she said. "It sounds like Anton might have gotten out of his restraints. Can you see yourse—?"

"Yes!" I snapped. Of course they were in the middle of some weird sex thing. Of *course.* "I will see myself out, please don't bother yourself on my account."

"Well, who else will?" Felicia asked, giving me a grin.

Ouch, I thought. Felicia and I have known each other for years. We're best friends. We can say shit like that to each other. But sometimes, I wonder if we really *should.*

It was time for me to go in any case. Felicia crossed the room and hugged me and I tried not to think about how naked she was under her robe, and then she *skipped* out of the kitchen and up the stairs. I sighed, drained the last of my coffee, and let myself out of the house.

Outside, the cold slap of damp wind smacked me full in the face. It was February, and I'd been over a year on the job with Felicia as my boss. Pulling a cigarette from my coat pocket, I stuck it in my mouth, lit it, and took a long drag, willing the nicotine to cut through the hangover fog. This had to be my eight thousandth cigarette since starting this job as Felicia's personal assistant, and I was beginning to feel it. The cold rattled my bones and the smoke burned my lungs.

Maybe Felicia was right. Maybe I *was* stressed out. Maybe I should just try to enjoy my afternoon posing for a rich crazy guy, smiling and laughing and pretending I wasn't a surly failed artist spending her time organizing the lives of the rich and famous.

And maybe I should scoop my eyes out with a melon baller. I sucked my cigarette down as fast as I could and threw it on the ground before stomping off toward the subway station to go home and get ready. If I was going to keep up a facade, I might as well put some effort into it.

3

At precisely four o'clock I arrived at Malcolm Ward's mansion as ready as I would ever be: primped, powdered, and wishing I were high. The house sat on a corner uptown where all the better people lived. It was a tall, red brick building with a polygonal tower and a peaked roof. The majority of the house stretched out behind the narrow facade, dotted with stained glass windows and iron railings and jutting gables, a classic example of the American Queen Anne style. It made me feel grubby and cheap, even though I'd put on a pair of expensive designer jeans and a thick sweater and taken an extra long bath at Felicia's behest.

Intellectually I knew my clothes were top-of-the-line, and Felicia and I had both had our hair done by one of the finer hairdressers in the city, but I'd been a starving artist for years, using cheap shampoo and getting all my clothes at *real* thrift stores, the ones that smell like mothballs, not the trendy ones in the cutesy artsy areas of Manhattan, and that sort of life is hard to shake off. I'd never, ever felt weird and out of place when I was poor. I wore my poverty like a badge of honor, flaunting it in front of the people in suits with "real" jobs who infested the city like roaches. There had been kind of an honor in it, even though most of the time it sucked. Now that I was expected to wear nice clothes and be polite, I felt poor and grubby without even having the nominal honor of actually being poor and grubby. Standing in front of Malcolm Ward's magnificent house, I felt it even more acutely than ever.

It put me in a foul mood.

I rang the doorbell. Once. Twice. Then I started compulsively pushing it, trying to force my bad mood out through my fingertip. I fell into sort of a trance. *Push, push, push...*

Abruptly the door opened, startling me, and I stepped back.

Malcolm Ward stood there, looking... well, magnificent. Also exhausted. Huge dark circles were smudged under his beautiful eyes, and his hair stuck out at odd angles, as though he had been running his hands through it. He also wore a plain white t-shirt and pajama bottoms. His feet were bare, and he held a huge black monster of a camera in his hand.

Now I felt *over*dressed.

"Uh," I said. "Weren't you expecting me?" Had I steeled myself for nothing?

"Oh yes, of course, come in, come in." He paused, letting his gaze sweep over me. I must have been getting used to it because this time I only felt a small, illicit shiver at the intimate touch of his gaze. "Good, good," he murmured. "Come in." And he stepped aside.

I slipped through the door and entered...

...a hoarder house.

Okay, maybe not that bad, but my god. I'd never seen so much *stuff* in one place that wasn't on television with a professional psychologist staring into the abyss as the owner of said stuff waxed rhapsodic about the cat-hair collection they were going to felt into dolls some day when they got around to it.

Every surface was crowded with curios and knick-knacks, some of them extremely valuable and some of them utterly worthless. Just the table in the foyer was a wealth of treasure and junk. Right next to what I recognized as an extremely valuable sculpture—probably done by a student of Rodin—was an antique tin Pepsi advertisement, proclaiming the drink to be refreshing and healthful, streaked with rust. Next to that was an old pocket watch, studded either with diamonds or rhinestones, though it was impossible to tell, and the chain holding it disappeared into a collection of moth-eaten Madame Alexander dolls.

My brain tried to shut down at the sheer volume of input. The walls were covered in framed photographs, prints, mirrors and paintings, organized seemingly only by their size and whether or not they would fit into current available space. Beneath the riot of color, the wall was white, and when I forced myself to look down, I saw the floor—between Persian-style rugs—was a simple blond wood. The house had a color scheme ideal for refinement and sophistication, but instead it was utterly buried under a ragtag collection of *things.*

He is *crazy,* I thought to myself. Only a crazy person would think this was acceptable. This was not the house of an artist, but the house of someone who grabbed everything they could think of that might have value and held onto it for some deep, psychological reason. No wonder he hadn't cared about the vase. He probably just grabbed it off a random table before running out the door in the morning.

"Um," I said.

Malcolm Ward was oblivious to my sudden tension. "This way, this way." He gestured to me to follow him. Taking a deep breath, I did so. He led me to the stairs, just down the short entryway, and we started climbing up to the upper floors. I caught a glimpse of the living room through a pair of French doors and it looked just as cluttered as the foyer. What had I gotten myself into?

The walls of the stairwell were also lined with photographs and paintings, but as we passed the second floor, they tapered off in intensity, until we finally reached the top floor. Here the walls were bare. Clean, white. Sane.

I licked my lips as he led me out of the claustrophobic stairwell and into the room beyond.

My mouth twisted as I took it in.

It was a huge room. Just enormous. It wasn't quite the length of the house, but it was close. And it had been set up as a photography studio.

Okay.

To my surprise, I found I relaxed a bit now that I was in a studio. I've never really had one of my own, but a creative space is powerful, and I was reassured simply by the trappings of someone sincere and interested in his work. With a sigh, I shed my coat and purse and moved aside while Malcolm strode to his lights and began to fiddle with them.

After about five minutes, I realized he had no idea what the hell he was doing.

What was going on here?

"Do you need some help?" I asked him without thinking. It came out sharp and kind of snide, and immediately I remembered Felicia's admonition to be less of a surly jackass. *Oh well, already screwed the pooch on that one, I guess.*

"Oh yes, if you could. I've never worked with these before."

I sighed and walked toward him. "Then what are you doing with them? I thought you were an amateur photographer."

"Amateur artist," he said. "And I figured that if I was going to do photography I might as well have a studio."

"A studio you've never used?"

He shrugged at me as I arrived by his side. He smelled the same as he did last night, but it was a riper scent now, as though he had been sweating slightly. The smell, rather than repulsing me, did weird things to my thoughts. I couldn't help but wonder what his sweat would taste like, if it would bead on his brow and run down his face as he strained and worked, doing... *something.*

Swallowing hard, I reached up to adjust the light for him. "This isn't that hard," I said after a moment. "Are you just pretending to never have used this to get me to come over here?"

"No, of course not. It was installed just this morning."

I paused, processing this. "Excuse me?" I said at last. "You had this studio installed... *this morning?*"

"Yes. I did."

Taking a deep breath, I tried to control my irritation. "So you *aren't* an amateur photographer?"

He laughed, a rich, deep sound, as he leaned around me to see what I was doing with the various knobs on the back of the light. The heat of his body rolled into mine. "Of course I am. I'm a very *new* amateur."

Don't think about how close he is, I commanded myself. "So you draw, then?"

"Not yet."

"Paint? Sculpt?"

"Nope. Not yet."

"So last night, when you told me you were an amateur artist, you were lying." My voice was flat and angry. I hate being lied to.

I heard him breathe in sharply, and he moved back slightly. "No, I didn't lie," he said. "The moment I saw you from across the room, I decided I wanted to be an artist so I could capture you in whatever way I could. I have decided to become a brilliant and tortured artist, inspired by you."

I am not falling for this. I am not.

"Really," I said flatly. "You just decided to be brilliant and tortured?"

"Yes. I am going to be a madman in touch with the pulse of the universe through my art, and you are my inspiration."

My lips thinned down into a line. "Yeah, well, I guess it's easy to be a starving artist when you have billions of dollars."

"Only one point four billion," he said. "There are far more cells in the human body than I have dollars. It's all relative if you think about it."

Only a rich shithead would say something like that.

Anger rose in me, and I whirled around, meaning to confront him. But the sight of him stopped me in my tracks.

He was looking down at me, his expression open and curious, as if he really *didn't* understand why what he had just said had infuriated me. In the bright light of the studio, his beauty shone, probably far better than my paltry looks ever would. His clear skin, tinged with the hint of a tan, glowed with health and vigor, and the sandy locks of his hair spilled over his forehead in golden waves. The brown of his eyes startled me, deep and intense, with hidden depths, like well-polished cherry wood, and his mouth, full and soft, quirked at my dumb, wide-eyed staring.

I couldn't help the sudden picking up of the pace of my heart in my chest. He was near, too near to me, but even though this room had to be over a thousand square feet, I couldn't move an inch. I *wouldn't* give an inch. I absolutely could not let this guy know how much he affected me.

The shadow of his beard, now almost two-day's growth, stubbled his cheeks, and I found myself aching to run my own face over his skin, to feel the rough evidence of his masculinity on my smooth, feminine jaw. It was an impulse I was almost entirely unaccustomed to. Deep, raw. Primal. An animal attraction I hadn't felt since the heady days of doing E at raves in college. And I was one hundred percent sober right now, feeling everything, feeling it *all,* and it was entirely in response to Malcolm Ward's proximity.

It scared me.

That alone gave me the strength to step away. Otherwise I might have leaned in and kissed him right then and there.

God, what a tragedy that would have been.

Ward seemed to realize that I was uncomfortable, and he stepped back as well. The lights were warm lights rather than traditional hot lights, but I was still feeling too heated. The brightness gave me a headache, and I retreated, stepping away from the set up.

"That's a really lame line," I told him. "Wanting to become an artist for me, I mean."

He tilted his head. "It is the truth," he said simply.

I didn't know what to say to that. I crossed my arms in front of me and cast about for something to talk about other than my inspiring beauty, which was a lie. Clearly a lie. I had a mirror. I knew quite well it was a lie. Why then couldn't I get my heart to stop racing?

"You saw me do it?" I asked him finally, my breath light and fast. "Set up the lights, I mean?"

He nodded at me, and the spell of him began to fade. "I think I can handle the rest of it." He waved a distracted hand at an old-fashioned dressing screen about twenty feet across the room. "I know we said no nudity unless discussed first, but would you remove your clothes? You'll find a length of cloth to wrap yourself in over there."

I opened my mouth to protest, but something stopped me. I knew just as well as anyone that the nude form is superior to the clothed form. I hadn't spent a bazillion years in art school sculpting and drawing and painting naked people just to protest my own nudity.

Besides, the thought of being naked around him, but not *truly* nude... it thrilled me, in small, shivery, secret ways. Yeah, we're all naked under our clothes, but sometimes you want to make that *really* explicit.

My mouth dry, I moved to the screen and slipped behind it.

On the floor, neatly folded, was a square of satiny fabric in a shade of white so bright it hurt my eyes. I wondered if he had chosen white as an afterthought, or because he thought it would look good on me. Lots of people looked washed-out in white. I wasn't one of them. I just hoped he knew *something* about lighting and color, or I was going to end up looking like a ghoul anyway.

Nervously, I began to shed my clothes. First came the high, dark brown leather boots—low heels—the swish of the zipper loud in the quiet of the penthouse studio. Then came my socks. Yes, I wear socks under my boots. Homemade wool-knit socks. My feet are narrow, and it was cold outside. Don't judge me. My manicured toes met the chill of the floorboards with a shiver. Now came the hard part.

Crossing my arms in front of me, I lifted my sweater over my torso. The buttery-soft alpaca slipped over my bare skin in an intimate caress, and when I dragged it over my head my hair crackled with static electricity. Smoothing my hair down with my hands, I lowered my fingers to the front-closing clasp on my bra. Clumsily I undid it and my breasts—such as they were—bounced free. Pert and tiny. My nipples hardened automatically at the change in temperature, and knowing that only a thin partition of wood separated my naked tits from Malcolm Ward's gaze just made them tighter. Between my legs I felt a tiny rush of heat, a sweet little gush of warmth and wetness.

Was I... was I actually getting *turned on* by this?

I was. I *was* getting turned on. I must be a secret exhibitionist!

Now I can no longer tease Felicia about her public sexcapades in good conscience, I thought to myself. Good thing I don't *have* a conscience.

Bowing my head, I put my hands on the waistband of my jeans. My hair slid over my shoulders, sending a shudder through me, and when I unbuttoned my jeans my fingers were trembling. With a shove, I pushed the denim down over my hips, letting it fall past my thighs to my knees, and I stepped out of my pants, the cool air pebbling the skin of my body. Now only my underwear remained, cheap, practical black cotton panties I'd bought on sale. Old habits die hard. I hooked my thumbs into the waistband and prepared to pull them down.

My hands wouldn't budge.

I bit my lip.

"Can I, uh, keep my underwear on?" I asked through the screen, cursing my cowardice as I did so. Couldn't even take it off for a photo shoot? What kind of artist am I?

"Sure." Ward's voice floated around the screen, deep and rich. "Whatever you're comfortable with."

Hating myself, I picked up the white satin and wrapped it around my body.

The fabric was long—very long, and wide, like a bridal train. I wondered where he'd managed to get it, but then I pushed the thought out of my mind. What did it matter? He was rich. He could get anything he damn well wanted. Taking a deep breath to brace myself, I slipped out from behind the screen, the fabric trailing over the floor behind me.

Ward was peering at his camera, adjusting some setting or other, and didn't notice me for a moment. I would have been content to watch him frown for an hour, but my reactions were starting to severely unsettle me, so I cleared my throat instead. He looked up. His cherry wood eyes widened.

"Wow," he said.

I gave him my best *bitch, please* eye roll. I may have been susceptible to his charms, but I liked to think I wasn't *that* susceptible.

His mouth turned up. "I meant that you look different in white," he said.

"Different from what?" I asked him. "We've known each other less than twenty-four hours. You haven't seen me in *anything.*"

"Black," he said immediately. "And if I had to guess, you really like to wear black."

"Of course I like to wear black. It goes with everything."

He smiled, as if he knew something about me that I didn't, and I scowled back at him. "Let's just get started," I snapped.

"Sure," he said, and gestured for me to step onto the black backdrop, in front of the blinding lights.

Tossing my head back, I did so, dragging the stupid satin cloth behind me, keeping it wrapped around my chest so that it would cover the important bits. When I reached the center of the dark rectangle on the floor, I turned and flung my hair over my shoulder, giving him my dirtiest look.

Ward snapped a picture.

My mouth dropped open. "What the hell?" I demanded. "Aren't you going to warn me when you take a picture?"

"Well, you'll be on your guard now," he said affably, inspecting the photo he'd just taken on his camera. "That was my only chance to capture the most raw you."

For some reason, that made me even angrier. "Who said you could take pictures of the raw me?" I said. "That's personal!"

He blinked. "Isn't that what art is?" he asked. "Personal?"

"Personal *for you.*"

"You *are* personal for me. I find you fascinating."

The fists clenching the satin around my body tightened, and as it did so his sharp cherry wood eyes honed in on it, and he lifted the camera again.

"Wait!" I said.

He halted and tilted his head at me. "Yes?"

"Just why do you find me fascinating? I know it's not because of my looks or whatever." I mean, I *hoped* it was for my looks. I wouldn't mind being Felicia. I wouldn't mind being beautiful to someone.

He lowered the camera and appeared to think about this for a long moment, and the longer it stretched out the more nervous I got.

"I suppose because you are alive," he said at last.

He really had a way of confusing me. "Everyone's alive. Except dead people."

But he shook his head. "No. Not so. In that entire room of people last night, you were the only person who stood out to me against the crowd. You were *alive.*" He lifted the camera again and stepped in, closer and closer, crouching so that his camera was level with my breasts and honed in on my hands clutching the white fabric to my chest. I prayed he wouldn't notice how rapid my breathing became with his increasing proximity.

I licked my lips as he took a picture of my pale-knuckled hands. "That still doesn't make any sense," I told him.

He backed up, and looked at me. And for a strange moment, I felt as though he was the only person who had ever really *looked* at me before. Looked, and saw.

"Then perhaps I recognized you," he said. "From a past life. Perhaps we are bound together by the red thread of fate, as the Japanese say." He paused. "A red thread. Red ribbon. You would look beautiful bound in red."

His words sent shivers through me. "Would I? And would you be the one doing the binding?"

Those dark cherry wood eyes glinted at me. "Would you like me to?"

I didn't know what to say. He was a man who could make me speechless. I *always* know what to say, how to send people off balance, and yet I seemed to have met my match in Malcolm Ward. I opened my mouth, my whole body vibrating with something dark and sweet, as though I were a string on an instrument and he had plucked me, made me sing.

He snapped a picture of my parted lips and wide eyes, my hesitation and desire, a woman standing on a cliff side on the fifth floor of a Manhattan mansion.

"Perhaps," I said at last. "If you wanted." Another rush of heat bloomed between my legs at my frank admission, as I thought of all the ways I wanted him to tie me up.

For the first time, I saw a crack in his serenely nutso exterior. His Adam's apple bobbed as he gulped. "I might," he said. "Will you turn around?"

Mouth dry, I did so. The soft sound of our

breathing and the click and whirr of the camera were the only sounds in the room. The noise of the city outside barely registered with me. I felt his presence, hot and hovering, just behind me, like a caress on my skin. The muscles of my back tightened and wound up, and my spine arched, thrusting my breasts out. The clicking of the camera came faster, and I began to move, tossing my hair, letting my head fall back on a limp neck, my arms growing heavy as I lost control of them beneath a wave of drunken desire. I posed artlessly for him, my thoughts running wild with the fantasy of skin on skin, breath to breath, his fingers on me, in me, his tongue tasting my body as I devoured him, bit him, dug in my nails and pulled him inside.

My need must have shown on my face, and though there was a camera between us, I knew he saw it. From the corner of my eye, I watched his shoulders grow tense and tight as I threw everything I had into seducing him.

His breath was coming hard and fast by the time he knelt beside me, aiming the lens of his camera upward, and I lifted an arm and turned my face from his, letting the fabric slip from my grip to reveal one pert breast with a nipple as hard as a pebble.

He hissed between his teeth as he snapped the picture. The sound made my knees go weak, and I sank to the floor, letting my limbs go limp as I lay down, swathed carelessly in white satin against black, my hair fanning out around me, my breasts freed at last.

"Yes," he said, and his voice was harsh with want. "Yes, like that."

I tossed my head, writhing in the throes of some

imagined ecstasy, and through it the camera clicked on, capturing me with complete honesty. Malcolm stood again and straddled my hips so he could get a good view of me from above, and I thrashed beneath him, like a pinned butterfly.

I wished I'd taken my panties off, but now that he was above me I really had no way of removing them discreetly, so I threw caution, and my satiny shroud, to the wind. His sharp inhalation as I bared myself almost completely to him was all I needed. Reaching down, I worked my panties over my hips, grateful that the black cotton would stand out against the white. Malcolm took a thousand and one pictures as I slid them down my legs, twisting and turning so he could get the maximum number of angles. Sliding one foot out, I cocked my hip and slowly stretched the cotton out, pulling at it as though it were inextricably hooked on my other foot. When at last the elastic snapped over my toes and rebounded into my hand I was almost moaning. One of my fingers had found its way into my mouth and I bit down on it as I tossed the panties away.

Malcolm sank to his knees, still straddling my legs. The camera clicked, a rapid staccato beat as I arched my back, completely bared to him. "My god," he whispered, rough and low, and then my hands found his thighs, burning hot through the thin flannel pajama bottoms.

The barrier of the camera broke, and his hand found my stomach, rough and wide, skating down the skin of my belly to the soft mound of my pussy, still trapped between my thighs. Without parting my legs, he slipped a rough fingertip between the lips of my pussy and found my creamy slit and aching clitoris.

His touch was electrifying, sending sparks dancing across my skin, and I thought at any moment they might catch, fan into flames and consume me, but as his hand picked up a slow, rough rhythm, fucking me with the pad of his finger, I failed to combust. Instead I gasped as he dragged his fingertip against my clit, drawing a moan from my mouth as my legs tensed and my toes curled. My hands ran over my skin, up into my hair where they curled and pulled, then down over my breasts, pinching and pulling them into taut peaks. Above the sound of my gasps, I heard the camera clicking madly, but I didn't even care.

Let him take pictures, I thought fiercely. I wanted him to see me in all my abandoned glory. If I was alive like no one else, then I wanted everyone to know it. Then he dipped his finger inside me and I forgot all about the whirring camera as the world condensed to my quivering cunt and his strong, insistent finger. Deeper and deeper he went, then curled his finger inside me.

"Ah!" The sound ripped from my lips, a noise of pure surprise and shock, as though I had never been touched before. My hands clawed their way up my throat, spreading over my face as I tried to stifle my cries at the slow, inexorable fuck he was giving me with only his hand.

Something cold touched my wrist, and I opened my eyes—when had I closed them?—to see the camera resting against my arm. He was holding it out to me.

I took it.

His hands freed, he moved down my body, his other hand alighting on my thigh, sending fiery shivers through my body, racing up my leg to curl in the small of my back. "Open for me," he said, his voice dark and hard. "Let me taste you."

My thighs parted for him almost of their own volition, the cool air of the studio hitting my heated flesh like a splash of ice water. I hissed between my teeth, and then the heat of his mouth descended on my pussy and all discomfort was obliterated. My fingers tightened on the hard plastic camera in my hands and it gave a creak of protest as his tongue flicked over my clitoris, lapped and licked down the inside of my labia, dipped inside my tight channel. Glancing down, I saw that the screen on the camera was still on, and I could see him through it, licking my pussy, his eyes half-closed in pleasure as his hands slowly massaged my thighs. He looked lost in desire, and strangely vulnerable.

He was beautiful.

I took a picture.

Immediately his eyes flickered up to mine, and he smiled at me, that devilish grin contrasting with the tiny frozen moment on the camera screen where he sleepily licked my clit with his long, delicious tongue. Then his grin faded as he opened his sensuous lips wide and sucked my entire pussy into his mouth, labia and all. The pull of his lips sent my head spinning. My legs curled, my heels finding his back and digging in as my hips bucked off the floor and into his face. He seemed to be encouraged by this reaction, and he chuckled, my pussy still in his mouth. The vibrations sent my eyes rolling back in my head and I twisted, my thighs clamping down on his head to hold him in place. I didn't ever want him to move.

His hands, trapped between his head and my legs, slipped out, circling around my thighs and then down to my ass. There they spread out, massaging, squeezing, and I moaned as he dug his fingers in and then pulled his head away from my pussy with a loud *smack*, the suction releasing in one great pop that echoed around the empty studio. Then he returned and sucked my clit back into his mouth before pulling away, again and again. The soft, wet sounds of his mouth on my pussy clicked and clacked against the walls, until the whole room was full of the echoes of his mouth lavishing attention on my intimate places.

In the pit of my belly, I felt my climax begin to coil, like a snake about to strike, but abruptly he pulled his head away and dropped me. Rearing back on his knees, he knelt between my thighs, and through the haze of my thwarted orgasm I saw his erection—huge, my god—straining against the fabric of his pants. He must have been wearing no underwear, because it bounced freely with his movement. Precum stained the tip dark.

Then he reached out and took the camera from my hands.

I blinked at him stupidly.

Carelessly he reached down and threw the white satin over me, half-covering my body, and, apprehension building, I reached down to cover myself entirely as he suddenly snapped off a series of photos.

"Don't hide from me," he said, his voice hoarse with need. "You are amazing."

I licked my lips. "I don't do porn."

He lowered the camera and reached down between my legs again, his hot, rough fingers finding my pussy and stroking into my slick channel, harsh and without control, which just made me wetter and hotter. "No," he said as my hips thrust up into his hand and he shot another photograph, "you aren't doing porn. You will see."

"Don't take pictures of me—*ah*—like this!"

"You inspire me," was all he said. He slipped his finger out and shoved his thumb inside me, sliding his creamy index finger down the crack of my ass where it curled over my puckered entrance, pushing and retreating, pushing and retreating. My body quivered around his hand, my back arching. The white satin tangled around me, twisting me up. I managed to trap myself in it like a butterfly tangled in a spider web. Relentlessly his fingers pushed their way inside me, stroking and stirring, and above me the camera clicked and whirred, capturing every moment.

I should have been ashamed. I had certainly been raised to feel that way. But I didn't. My climax, previously denied, began to build again, mounting harder this time, faster, higher. He played me like an instrument, and I let him. The satin slid against my skin, looping and tightening, my breath coming hot and fast. The cool air on my body, the dazzling lights, the darkness of the backdrop burning against my eyes as my back arched like a bow pulled taut—all of it exposed me to him, to the unforgiving lens of his camera.

Yet I trusted him to make it beautiful, to transcend it.

You were alive.

Maybe he *was* crazy. But if I was alive, I wanted to feel like it.

His harsh breathing cut through my haze, scraping over my ears as he moved over me, placing a foot by my shoulder and staring directly down at my face.

Closer and closer the camera came, and I forced myself to be still as he stroked me, so the shots wouldn't come out blurry. Below the waist, my hips bucked, thrusting into him as he fucked me with his hand. I tried to touch myself, but my arms were caught in the satin, and I could only close my eyes and give myself over to him.

My pussy clenched, drenching his hand, and my climax was coming, just on the edge.

"I'm—" I started to say, but the clatter of something heavy hitting the floor startled me and I turned my head just in time to see the camera skitter away over the dark black cloth covering the floorboards as Malcolm Ward suddenly crouched down and slipped an arm under me. I became weightless as he lifted me, clutching me hard to him, and I, tangled and twisted as I was, could only lay limp in his embrace as his mouth found my throat. Then his fingers gave me a little push, and I was tumbling over the edge of my climax, pleasure rushing up to meet me.

Great shudders raced through my body and I curled up, my legs clamping around his arm as I came. The waves of my orgasm threatened to sweep me away, suck me into an undertow I could not escape from. More than anything I wished it were his hips I were clinging to instead of his arm, and as his hand drew my orgasm out of me, his mouth traced gentle, soft patterns over the fragile skin of my throat, a sharp contrast to the violence of his fingers in my ass and pussy. I writhed as he brought his index finger and thumb together inside me, only the thinnest of inner walls separating them. I was stretched wide, aching, and when at last the ripples subsided I collapsed in his grasp, all the tension of my body flowing away like water down a hill.

Our ragged gasps mingled together in the studio, his breath coiling in the hollow of my throat, and mine bouncing off the walls. His forehead was sheened in sweat and I remembered my own curiosity as to what it would taste like. Turning my head, I let my tongue slip along his brow, tasting him.

Salty, sweet. Dark. *Good.*

Then my body jolted as he jerked away from me. I inhaled sharply at the expression on his face.

He looked... confused. As though he had no idea what had just happened, even though his fingers were still buried inside my body. The smell of sweat and my juices hung in the previously cool, stale air, and his wide, dark eyes searched my face as if he were looking for some clue that might be hidden there, something that would tell him what to do next.

Personally, I'd thought we were going to fuck. But that look on his face told me that things were not quite as simple as that.

"Oh," he said suddenly, and then, as quickly as he could without injuring me, he set me down and pulled his fingers from my cunt and ass. The swift loss sent a tremor of remembered pleasure through my body and I jerked in my twisted satin bonds. I was caught where I lay, but he retreated from me, leaving me to work my way out on my own. He stood at the edge of the black backdrop and watched, as though he had had no part in my predicament. Sitting up, I struggled out of the tangled white satin, and then stood up. The sweat on my skin was drying and cooling rapidly, and I started to shiver.

I stood, naked, in the middle of his studio, and he

stared at me as though he had never seen me before.

Well, I thought to myself, *that's what you get for trying to fuck a crazy guy.*

I tossed my tangled hair back and met his stare head on, daring him to say something. But he just took another step back.

"I'll call you tomorrow," he said. "Will you see yourself out?"

My jaw clenched, but he backed away again, and I was suddenly reminded of my mother's old cat, who, after a lifetime spent in our house could never tolerate people and never wanted to be touched or spoken to. An abused cat. That's what he was reminding me of.

Wow. Sexy.

What the fuck was wrong with me?

"Yeah," I said. "I'll see myself out. No problem."

"Okay then," he replied, and with that he turned and walked out of the studio, his footsteps thundering on the stairs until he stepped off on one of the floors below. His camera lay on the floor and I thought, briefly, of going over and stealing the SD card, but some artistic camaraderie stopped me. I hadn't stopped him from taking those pictures. They could still be wonderful. And he certainly didn't need money from porno pics.

I left it where it lay, got dressed and gathered my things, then descended the stairs, my knees still weak from the delicious orgasm he'd given me. When I finally walked down the steps to the sidewalk in front of the house, I paused and looked up.

A curtain on the third floor twitched and then was still.

I walked to the subway station, one thought echoing in my head:

What the fuck *just happened?*

4

"So did you fuck him?" Felicia asked me the next morning when I showed up at the door of her studio, an unlighted cigarette dangling from my lips and a six pack of Pabst swinging from my fingers. I pinched the cigarette out of my mouth and glared at her.

"Depends on what you mean by fuck," I said.

"Sounds like you have a story to tell." She opened the door wide and I followed her inside.

The place was familiar to me. It had been Felicia's apartment before she had married Anton, but now she kept it purely for her sculpture. A huge wad of clay sat in the middle of the floor on a large tarp, ringed by tables covered in tools large and small of her own devising. The only other piece of furniture in the apartment was an old mattress sitting on the floor, the bed she used to sleep on before she found a better one with the world's most eligible billionaire.

Felicia returned to her project. She wore jeans and a sweatshirt, but padded around the studio barefoot, even though it was freezing cold. Gray clay coated her feet and arms in patches, evidence that she had been working on something real. Creating.

God, I envied her.

"So tell me everything," she said, resuming her sculpting. I watched her for a moment as she picked up a table leg and began to pound on the wad of clay. Wet smacks echoed against the walls. I lit my cigarette and inhaled the smoke into my lungs. One of my many vices. I just can't seem to give them up.

"Well," I said, "I showed up. His house is a mess. Like, a real mess. It's kind of like a hoarder house. It's full of *stuff.*"

Felicia frowned. "What kind of stuff?"

I thought for a moment. "Like if you crossed Sotheby's with a flea market."

She stopped whacking at her clay. "Seriously?"

"Would I shit you?"

"Yes."

Okay. That was true. But still. "Well, I'm not shitting you. And then he took me up to the top floor of his house where he had a photography studio installed *that morning,* and then he asked me to take my clothes off and wrap myself up in white satin so he could take pictures of me."

"You look good in white," Felicia said, which was a very artist thing to say.

"Yeah, I know. But then he kind of fingered me and then went down on me and when I was done he freaked out and left!"

Felicia's eyes narrowed at me. "It went from pictures to finger fucking just like that?" she asked. She was clearly not buying it. My best friend, disbelieving my innocence.

I sucked my cigarette down and blew a stream of smoke at her. "You know how things just happen," I said. Granted, I had sort of *decided* that those things would happen and then done my level best to ensure that they did, but come on. Finger fucking *just happens* all the time. Sometimes it just needs a little nudge.

She studied me for a moment. "Uh-huh," she said at last, then shook her head and sighed. "You always go for the crazy ones, don't you?"

I scowled. "Malcolm Ward is *not* crazy. Weird and probably damaged, maybe, but crazy, no. And I don't always go for the crazy ones, thanks."

"You don't remember Simon?" she asked me. "Simon who thought you were cheating on him with his brother who lived in Tokyo and burned all your underwear in revenge?"

I shrugged. "Fine. Maybe Simon."

"And Jorge? The one who refused to look at mirrors and wouldn't enter through front doors?"

"That was just a quirk of character," I said. "That wasn't really crazy."

She crossed her arms. "And what was Misha?"

"A drunk."

Felicia rolled her eyes at me. "You have a thing for damaged guys, you nutbar. And you just said yourself that he's damaged."

"I said *probably* damaged." I couldn't help but feel stung, insulted, and a bit annoyed. Before Anton, Felicia's previous boyfriends had all been dumb as rocks. The last one she'd had before she got married had called himself Steele. *Steele,* for Christ's sake. Where did she get off judging *me?*

"Yeah, but you're so good at picking out the damaged ones that that probability is awfully high.

Besides, he acts crazy in public, right?"

I shrugged. "I don't know, you're the one who knows him."

"I don't know him, I know *of* him. And yes, he does act crazy in public. If he's *not* actually crazy, then it's an act." She pursed her lips. "Which, ironically, would be totally crazy."

I barely suppressed an epic eye roll. "Trust me, he's not crazy, and if he's damaged at least he's really hot." I sucked the last of my cigarette down and stubbed it out in the ceramic ashtray by the bed. Felicia doesn't smoke, so it's mostly there for my benefit. I saw that the stubs I'd left in there the last time I'd come over to her studio were still languishing at the bottom. What a sad existence. I sighed. "And he gives really good head, and that's not the sort of thing you want to just fling to the wind at the first sign of trouble."

Her mouth pursed again, and I could see she was struggling to formulate a counterargument, but I knew she probably didn't have one. Her own husband was pretty fucked up, too, but, from what I could tell, he was amazing in the sack. You can't just throw that shit away lightly. Of course he was also madly in love with her and the feelings were reciprocated, so I suppose he had that going for him, too. All I had from Malcolm Ward was a bunch of weird interactions and one great orgasm.

It had been a really, really *good* orgasm, though.

Why is life so hard? I thought to myself.

"You're into him," Felicia said at last.

I wasn't quite prepared to admit that, so I made a joke. "Yeah, I was in his mouth yesterday afternoon," I said.

Felicia made a face, but my crude attempt at changing the subject was nevertheless effective. "So that's it?" she said. "Did he take any pictures?"

I blinked. "Oh! Yeah, he did. A ton of them, in fact." Some of which I was feeling quite embarrassed by at this point, but I couldn't do anything about that now. "He's never done anything artistic as far as I can tell, but yesterday he said he wanted to become a... a brilliant madman, connecting to the pulse of the universe through his art and that I was his 'inspiration.'"

She arched an eyebrow at that. "Oh, really? He just decided he wanted to be a brilliant artist?"

"That's what I said."

She returned to her clay, giving it a few good whacks with the table leg before pausing. "I guess that's one way to go about it. I mean, don't we all decide we want to be brilliant artists at some point?"

"Yeah. After *making* art, not before."

Whack. Whack. "So? Maybe he's got a talent for it. Have you seen the pictures yet?"

I shook my head. "Nope. He said he'd call me today."

"Before or after he gave you head?"

"After."

"Well, he still wants to see you after giving head. At least you didn't scare him away by smelling bad or something."

I lit another cigarette. "Watch out," I told her. "I've decided to be an arsonist and I'm going to burn down your studio."

"You've already tried that a couple times," Felicia said. "You don't have the knack for it."

Dammit. She was right. I cracked a beer and

sipped it while she tried to beat her clay to death. I was just contemplating drinking the whole six pack by myself to erase my memories of the past twenty-four hours when my phone rang. I jumped and nearly dropped my beer.

Felicia clicked her tongue. "You're *really* into him."

I rolled my eyes and checked the number. Yup, that would be Malcolm. Said so right there on the screen.

I hesitated.

"Maybe you'll get anal this time," Felicia said.

"Shut *up,"* I told her, and hit *answer.*

"Yeah?" I said. Totally nonchalant. I'm hardcore like that.

"I was wondering if you would like to come over and assist me in going over these photographs," Malcolm said without any preamble. His voice was distracted and distant, and it rankled me.

"I don't know," I told him. "Are you going to stick your tongue in my twat and then run away again?"

"Sadie!" Felicia hissed, scandalized.

What? I mouthed back at her. He deserved to be called out. You can't just go around treating people like things. You gotta maybe buy them dinner first or something, or at the very least don't literally *run away* afterward. It was part of the social contract. That sort of thing could give a girl a complex.

On the other end of the line, Malcolm was silent, clearly impressed by my big brass ovaries. I was willing to bet no woman had ever spoken to him that way. I'd left him speechless with my wit.

"I'm not sure," he said at last. "Did you enjoy it?"

...Great. Now I was the one who was speechless. I tried hard not to look at Felicia. "Yes," I said. "I did, thanks."

A gust of air as he let out a sigh. "Good," he said. "I was worried. Please, come over and we can look at these photos. You can give me the critique of a professional."

And I had nothing to say to that, either, except, "Okay."

"See you soon." And he hung up without saying goodbye, like people on television do. I stared at my phone for a long moment before stuffing it back into my purse.

"Well?" Felicia was leaning on her lump of clay, staring at me as though she knew something I didn't. A little smile played on her lips.

"I'm going to his house to go over the photos he took," I told her. "He wants my professional opinion."

"And is he going to stick his tongue in your twat again?"

I'm so proud I didn't blush at that. "We left that open-ended," I said. I gulped a few more mouthfuls of beer and got up. "See you on the flip side, ladies."

"Don't trip and fall on his cock by accident!" she shouted after me as I closed the door.

Don't worry, I thought. *It won't be by accident.*

I rang Malcolm Ward's doorbell about ten times before trying the knob and finding the house open. Reasoning that I'd been invited over, I let myself inside and shut the door behind me.

Immediately the claustrophobic atmosphere descended on me again. So much stuff, everywhere.

There weren't actually piles of shit on the floor, but there were so many end tables and foyer tables from the beginning of the last century piled high with junk that there might as well have been. I allowed myself to stop and inspect the incredibly valuable sculpture he had just *sitting* inside his unlocked door where anyone could waltz in and take it, but the press of *things* on all sides and the musty smell of antiques soon drove me to the stairs.

I took them two at a time. "Mr. Ward?" I called at each landing until, faintly, I heard him from the fourth floor.

"Come up!" he yelled down.

I sprinted up the steps to the fourth floor and breathed a sigh of relief when I walked out into another large room like the one at the top of the house. This one was completely empty save for a luxurious bed at the back end and a desk at the front, looking out onto the street. Large windows let light stream in from the cloudy day outside, and Malcolm Ward was sitting at the desk, staring intently at the computer he had set up there.

My God. I was in his bedroom.

It's cool, I thought. I'd been in plenty of bedrooms before, most of them not even attached to either me or my partner. I'd just play it like I was totally fine. Because I was.

Totally fine.

Straightening my spine, I strode across the floor toward Malcolm, the low heels of my boots clacking on the wood. I couldn't quite make out what was on the computer screen since it was backlit against the windows. I squinted at it as I drew closer. Blurry lines slowly resolved until I was halfway to him, and then I suddenly realized what they were.

He was looking at pictures of me on his computer.

...Well, of course he was.

My footsteps slowed as I found myself overcome by embarrassment, seeing my face plastered across the screen. Then he began to zoom out, and I realized this was one of the pictures he'd taken as I'd slipped my panties off. My naked body came into view and I ground to a halt, halfway to the desk. Ward sat in his chair, hunched over and staring intently at the monitor. He didn't even acknowledge my presence.

I found it a bit insulting that he'd rather look at pictures of me when he had the real me standing right behind him, so I cleared my throat. It was too loud in the quiet of his room, but he turned. Surprise first crossed his face. Then pleasure. A wide grin broke over his face.

"Sadie," he said warmly. "Come over here. I'm afraid photography may not be our medium, but I believe there are some good shots hidden in here."

"Yeah?" I said. "No shit photography's not my medium. I could have told you that. I'm as photogenic as a dead pigeon." His welcome gave me the guts to continue walking toward him until I stood just over his shoulder, staring at the picture of me dragging my panties down my legs.

To my surprise, it wasn't a bad photograph. Despite the fact that I was on the ground, my head tossing and turning this way and that, Malcolm had managed to somehow capture an angle that didn't make me look fat or distended in some way. I was still the trashy tramp with small tits and a big ass covered in tattoos that I'd always been, but somehow I *looked* like someone who was a little more than that. I was still a long way from beautiful, but as Malcolm began to scroll through the pictures he'd taken, I started to see myself in a slightly different light. The planes and angles of my face became less harsh, more... striking. Bold.

Perhaps Malcolm did have some latent artistic ability after all.

I let my gaze slide down so I could study him from the corner of my eye. He wasn't wearing the same clothes I'd last seen him in; instead of pajamas he now wore a fine cashmere sweater and well-tailored slacks, though his feet were stockinged. A pair of fine shoes languished a few feet from the desk, as though he'd brought them over, meaning to put them on but had forgotten to do so. He'd also shaved, so that was good. It meant he'd probably taken a shower.

He still seemed a bit off, though. He had a strange, hunted look on his face, as though he hadn't slept, dogged by some unrelenting compulsion. Glancing back at the images on the screen and his riveted attention to them, I could believe it.

"Some of these are pretty good," I told him. "I mean, considering your subject matter and all."

Next to me, he shook his head. "That's kind of you," he said. "But it's not here."

I blinked. "What's not here?"

"My masterpiece."

I felt my mouth twist. "You don't think so? You asked me over to look at your photos as a professional. I think they're pretty good. You have talent. And I'm admitting that grudgingly considering you didn't decide to become an artist until yesterday."

"Two days ago," he corrected me, "and that was just an excuse. I asked you over to do this again."

I could see it all in my mind as he moved the mouse down to the lower bar of his photo editor, clicked on a box, and up popped the picture of him between my legs, eyes half-closed with ecstasy as he laved my clit with his tongue.

Just the sight of it made me aching and empty for his cock, even as my face flushed with humiliation. And yet the picture I'd taken was beautiful, in a purely artistic sense. I'd captured my subject perfectly: the only thing truly in focus was Malcolm's face. The face of a cat lapping at a bowl of cream.

I still wasn't entirely prepared when he turned his chair and gripped my hips gently to pull me to him.

"Whoah!" I said, my hands flying out to grab his shoulders. "I... uh..." My brain shorted out as my fingers met his body. He was well-muscled. *Very* well-muscled. And hot. He burned through his sweater and undershirt. Burned for me.

I'd worn a skirt. A heavy wool skirt. No tights. He stared up at me with his beautiful, intense eyes as his large warm hands smoothed over my hips to my ass, squeezing gently. His lips, level with my breasts, were thwarted only by the thick coat I wore.

He didn't seem to care. "You've been on my mind since I saw you," he said, his voice thick and husky. "But I haven't captured you yet."

It took me a moment to realize that he meant artistically. He hadn't captured me *artistically*. Of course by that point he'd stood up, maneuvered me to the chair, and sat me down in it.

"Uh..." I said again as he towered over me. I'm really brilliant in a tight spot. He unbuttoned my coat, but didn't remove it, instead simply letting it fall open.

"There," he said. "Wouldn't want you being

uncomfortable."

"For what?" I managed to say. If I'd been smart or had more blood in my brain, I would have said, *Too late.*

But I wasn't uncomfortable, except in the excited, breathless way everyone is uncomfortable as they take a new lover, someone whose habits they don't know, whose likes and dislikes are not yet second nature to their lips and tongue and hands. This discomfort didn't seem to afflict Malcolm, of course. He gazed down at me, his warm, beautiful eyes still riveted to my face, then reached into his pocket and withdrew something limp and red. A long length of red satin ribbon.

"I used to be into bondage," he said, his voice strangely detached. "Once upon a time. Let's see if I still have the touch." And he reached for me.

I shot to my feet like a bolt of lightning. Behind me, the chair clattered as it rolled away, shoved across the floor by the strength of my momentum.

For a long, tense moment, we stared at each other, the sounds of traffic outside unnaturally loud, as if the tension between us actually made the air thicker.

He didn't look hurt, merely surprised. But curious.

So I said, "I don't trust you." Which was the truth. Beneath the heavy arousal zipped the zest of fear, deep and primal, that I had not felt for years.

His eyes softened, and suddenly he was reachable again, no longer distant. Human. "You are right," he said. "I understand." He opened his hand, and the ribbon fluttered to the ground as he stepped forward, bringing the distance between us to nothing.

I could have backed up then. But I didn't.

He bent down, his face drawing closer and closer

to mine. Dizziness overwhelmed me, made the world spin and tilt as he came closer. His scent filled my head, and I thrilled at his nearness, every inch of my body awake and alive to his proximity. Then his full, sensuous lips met mine, and I melted, like wax before a flame.

Malcolm Ward could *kiss.*

He wasn't demanding, not at first. At first he seemed content to gently massage my lips with his, sweet and soft, teasing me down from the height of fear. Slowly the echoes of the past receded, replaced with first a slow smoldering, and then fast burning embers as he continued his slow play of mouth on mouth, lips on lips. His nose brushed against mine, our breath mingling between us. There was nothing outside of our kiss, even as it brought me to the brink of frustration.

Gimme some tongue, *damn,* I thought.

As though he read my mind Malcolm paused and smiled against my mouth before flickering his tongue over my lips. I opened for him readily, aching from my tongue to my curling toes.

He invaded me gently but inexorably, stroking his tongue over mine in a slow, strong caress that had me reeling, my body listing toward his. I felt the heat coming from him, but we had yet to touch anywhere but our lips, and I longed for more. A moan escaped my chest, and then his hands alighted on my face.

My cheeks burned where his flesh met mine, white hot points of contact that shook me down to my bones, and I reached up, gripping his arms lest I fall. I was swaying, unsteady, and he was a steel pillar, holding me up, keeping me from collapsing completely. Our bodies met, my breasts brushing against his chest, his thighs meeting mine, the bulge of his cock bridging the gap between us, nudging my belly and sending streamers of fire out over my limbs. I wanted to reach down and touch it, take it in my hands, and with any other man I would have.

Malcolm was different. I didn't know how, I just knew he was. I twisted my hips instead, letting my stomach rub over his erection and feeling the contact ripple through him as he shuddered, ever so slightly, like a great wind gusting against an ancient tree, or a skyscraper bowing to a hurricane. The pressure of his hands on my face increased as I circled my hips against him, feeling the delicious bulge grow harder and larger as his arousal caught and fanned into flame, but then, abruptly, he broke away, first planting a kiss to my earlobe, then dragging his open mouth down my throat, over my chest, until he was kneeling before me, his face buried in my stomach.

He inhaled deeply, and I got the sense that he was reveling in my smell. It made me wish that I'd spent more time primping this morning, but that wish was soon forgotten as his hands skated down my body from my face, traveling over my throat, grazing the outside swell of my breasts, smoothing over my stomach until they met my hips. Slipping his hands around me, he splayed them over my generous ass again, and a flood of moisture between my legs responded to his possessive touch.

My breath came in short, hot bursts as he let his hands wander down the backs of my thighs. Inching forward on the wood floor, he nudged my feet apart with his knees, until he knelt between my legs as his hands found the hem of my skirt and began to lift it up.

I braced myself on his shoulders, my knees suddenly weak and watery. He was face to pussy with me, and I knew he was going to do it again. He'd said as much. That he had respected my wishes and let me stay unbound excited me, and made me almost wish I'd let him tie me up.

Almost.

His hands spread over my thighs, lifting my heavy skirt away, and I reached down and grabbed the hem, lifting it up with one hand while I held onto him with the other. I couldn't get enough air. My body quivered and quaked as he stared at my pussy, still clothed in my panties. Leaving his fingertips on the inside of my thigh, he moved his hand up and up, until he met the edge of the elastic leg bands. I wished I'd worn something sexier. Then one long finger moved to the damp crotch of my panties and rubbed.

I whimpered and faltered, my knees giving way, but he steadied me with his other hand. His eyes rose to mine, and we stared at each other as, slowly, deliberately, he moved the cotton aside, exposing my aching pussy to the cool air.

I could barely keep my eyes open. Desire washed over me, threatening to knock me off my feet, and when he stroked his finger over my slit I groaned. My thighs were still close enough together that there was little room, and my crowded flesh was hypersensitive. My hips rocked toward him and he finally looked away. I let my eyes slide closed as he moved his head forward and gave my pussy a long, luxurious lick.

Oh. Oh, he felt so *good.*

Slowly, achingly, he circled my clit with his tongue, keeping it firm and direct in the obscuring folds, and I quivered and cried out. I needed a finger inside me, something in me, but he only teased the little nub at the apex of my pussy lips, his tongue pointing hard, then flattening softer, circling, circling. He stroked his fingers over my labia, letting the slickness of our mingling juices tease me softly as his tongue hardened its approach. At the base of my spine, in the backs of my thighs, my climax began to mount.

"God, don't stop," I begged him, and I felt him smile against me. His fingertip ghosted over my entrance, and I had the distinct impression he was laughing at me, telling me he had just what I wanted, but that he wouldn't give it to me yet.

My orgasm built slowly. My legs ached as I struggled to stay up, my hand digging into his shoulder, my toes curling for purchase inside my boots. The fingers holding my skirt up and out of his way were damp with sweat, and I was nearly on my tiptoes, feeling my release just out of reach.

A frustrated sob escaped me, and then Malcolm flicked his tongue against my clit, driving it into his teeth, and my quaking, aching legs nearly gave out as a warm, delicious orgasm spread out from my pussy across my entire body.

My skin dissolved into shivers, my knees buckled, and I cried out as I came around his tongue, my inner passage twisting and squeezing nothingness in a sweet release. I collapsed as wave after wave lapped gently over me, and he dragged it out with his mouth, until I knew I could take no more and begged him to stop.

When he did, he drew away from me and I collapsed gracelessly to the floor, my legs askew, my brow sweaty, my mouth gaping open as I tried to catch my breath. My bare, slick pussy pressed into the wood floor. Malcolm stared at me, almost tenderly, and licked his fingers and lips clean.

"Your taste is delectable," he said. "I could lick you all day."

I had to give an exhausted laugh at that. "Please don't," I said. "Give me a little time to recover first."

He smiled at that as he lowered himself to the ground, reaching out and pulling me into his lap. I let him, because I was feeling pretty boneless, though the reminder that he was a man who wanted to fuck me rather than just a pussy-eating machine came crashing into me when I felt the rock-hard swell of his cock against my ass. I tried not to let it impinge on my afterglow, but already it was making me think of other things I wanted to do with him—and to him. We could have a jolly good time in that bed across the room...

His hand stroked my hair and I leaned against his shoulder, fantasizing for a moment that we were intimate lovers rather than almost total strangers. It felt nice to be held. I couldn't remember the last time I'd let someone hold me.

Then a low growling sound scraped across my ears, and I frowned.

"Did... did your stomach just rumble?" I asked, pulling back and frowning at him. I mean, some growling is sexy, but that was kind of... not.

To his credit, he looked faintly embarrassed. "Yes," he admitted. "I'm afraid I've been forgetting to eat."

I stared at him in disbelief. "Seriously?" I said. It was barely lunchtime. "How long have you been forgetting to eat?"

He shrugged. "Since those hors d'ouvres at the auction?" he said, and the way he said it made me think that he was only guessing.

I gave him a scowl. "Really? I mean... really?"

He tilted his head. "What's so shocking about that?" he asked me. "I've been working on my art since then."

"Artists eat, too," I told him.

"What about starving artists?"

"That's a bug, not a feature of being an artist." I blew a sweaty strand of hair out of my face. "Okay, you need to eat something. Before we do anything else, you have to eat."

"I just did."

I gave him a hard look, but his face was entirely innocent. He was fucking with me, right? He had to be. "Man cannot live by pussy alone," I said, hauling myself gracelessly out of his lap and standing up. Reaching under my skirt I readjusted my panties, getting my own slick juices all over my fingers as I did so. I took my hand out and held it up, glancing around for a tissue or something, but then Malcolm stood up as well, reached out, and took my wrist in his hand, drawing my fingers to his mouth.

With a slow, sensuous suck he cleaned my fingers for me.

I stared into his dark cherry wood eyes, my cheeks burning, before I found the strength to pull away. The second growl from his stomach might have helped me make that decision.

"Food first," I said. "Art and sex later."

He reached down and adjusted his cock in his pants, but I'm pretty sure his hunger was cutting through his arousal, because it was already shrinking from its previously large size. "Very well," he said. "If you insist."

5

I waited on the sidewalk for Malcolm to come downstairs, trying to collect myself. The icy wind and gray sky were going a long way towards helping me get centered and alert. Mostly I was reeling from our sexual encounter and trying to maintain my customary ironic distance. It was rather difficult, however, since my legs still shook with the aftermath of his ministrations.

What was going on with me? I wondered. I'd been really into guys before, but this didn't feel quite the same. The way I fell into his embrace, welcoming the pleasure he gave me... it truly did feel as though we'd known each other before. Bound by the red thread of fate? Was that what he'd said the other day? We'd known each other in another life?

The idea freaked me right the fuck out, and by the time he exited the door of his mansion, impeccably dressed, I was well on my way toward my much loved ironic distance.

But when he reached me, he pulled my hand into

the crook of his arm and began to lead me down the sidewalk, just like a Victorian gentleman, and my distance was halved. At least.

"So where do you want to go to lunch?" I asked him. I kept my eyes straight ahead, but I could see him smile from the corner of my field of vision.

"I'm not sure," he said. "I am a very easy date. I have only negative preferences."

"Negative preferences?"

"Meaning I only know what I do not want."

Oh. One of those people. "Okay. Well, we're in New York, there's really nothing in the world we can't find here."

He nodded. "What would you prefer?"

I pursed my lips and took a fearless inventory of my wants and desires. "What about... Vietnamese? This is the perfect day for pho."

He nodded and I almost smiled, but then he said, "It is, but I'm not in the mood for broth."

"Hmm. How about Lebanese?"

"I enjoy Lebanese, but it is more of a summer food. I always think of summer when I am eating food laced with lemon."

Great. "Chinese? Greek? Italian?"

"Maybe."

"That's not helpful. You're the one who hasn't eaten for two days, you tell me what you think your stomach can handle."

He appeared to think about this for quite a while, and I glanced around as we exited his neighborhood and set out toward the nearest subway station. For the first time, I wondered why he hadn't just called a car, but I thought it would be rude to ask. I didn't care about private cars or limos or anything like that, but I thought it was a little weird that a billionaire with all that money and prestige at his fingertips would instead choose to walk to the subway station.

Then again, a billionaire forgetting to eat and living in a house crowded with the most useless nick-knacks imaginable was not what I had imagined either. My Batman was in the middle of his soul-searching phase, it seemed. Or, since he was in his late thirties, perhaps he had simply never exited said phase. It happened to the best of them.

"I know a little Indian place," he said at last. "They make the most wonderful lamb shahi korma. I could eat it all day."

"Like pussy?" The words were past my lips before I could stop myself and I clapped my hand over my mouth, mortified.

But he just laughed. "Only yours, Sadie. Only yours."

My pussy was on par with lamb shahi korma. That was good to know. I guess.

We walked the rest of the way to the subway in companionable silence, and when I used my metrocard for both of us he didn't object. Somehow, I liked that. He was walking around with the riffraff, just as if he were people himself. When we boarded the train heading downtown, I flopped into my seat and let out a sigh of relief.

"Tired?" he asked as he settled down beside me. His knee brushed against mine, sending little shivers of heat through me, but I didn't move away. I let my leg stay there, touching his. A bit of illicit contact, right out in the open. I forged into the breach of his conversation starter with a shrug.

"I don't know," I said. "It's nice to go out to

lunch, I think. I haven't gone out to a lunch that wasn't a business lunch or a hotdog on the street corner in... Jesus, I don't know how long. It's been a long time. I don't have a lot of a social life now."

He raised his eyebrows. "Now?" he asked. "I read that you and Felicia have been friends for a very long time. Is being her personal assistant really so difficult?"

I waved a hand. "Oh man, you don't even know the half of it. She's gotta do all this dumb shit to keep up appearances in society or whatever and I have to organize it all. She's huge into charity, so I'm always running around trying to get charity events up and running without letting all the rich folks know exactly what they're giving to."

He laughed at that. "Oh?" he said.

I gave him a sly smile. "Felicia fancies herself a revolutionary. She likes to give her money to anarchist groups and such. When she married Anton, he set up an allowance for her 'pet projects,' as he liked to call them, and whatever she raises for charity for a more acceptable organization she dumps an equal amount into something else. Or a large number of something elses. She's a bit scattered in her ideology, but she does good work. I can't really fault her for it. It's just exhausting running around trying to make everything all hoity-toity for the rich folks when you grew up poor in Jersey."

"Oh, you did?"

His voice was merely curious, not judgmental, but I immediately went on guard. I'd been saying too much, distracted by his knee against mine. I didn't like talking about my childhood. All that shit was over and done with, as I liked to say, and I'd spent years convincing Felicia of the same thing. She'd been hung up on her parents and fixing their lives, and it had been holding her back. Marrying Anton, though he was a rich man like her father, had been the best thing to happen to her, frankly. Me, I'd already moved on. That was in the past, and they say that place is a whole other country, and I'd probably get dysentery there.

"Yeah," I said, making it clear that I didn't want to talk about it. To his credit, Malcolm took the hint and backed off. "So what about you?" I said, trying to change the subject.

"What about me?" he asked.

Yeah, that would probably be a good thing to specify... "Don't you have a personal assistant?" I asked him. "Hopping around from place to place, booking appearances and accepting invitations to charity functions and whatnot?"

Malcolm shook his head. "I have a secretary at my office," he said, "but I rarely go in any more. He holds down the fort while I'm away."

The way he said it left me with the impression that he didn't work much at all. Which might explain his behavior. Perhaps he was bored and looking to spice up his life with a little eccentricity and a little sex in front of a camera? For some reason, the idea annoyed me. I'm not sure why it did. After a bad breakup I'd once seriously contemplated feigning amnesia so I wouldn't have to go through the inevitable postmortem period with all our mutual friends. Surely that was worse? "So he knows all your business stuff?"

Malcolm nodded. "He does. He's very dedicated to his job, and we go out for dinner twice a week where he tells me everything that's been going on. Most of the meetings can be handled by people under me, and I compensate them for the risks they take. Really, the life of a CEO can get repetitive, and most problems are the same problem in different clothing. Most of the time the heads of other companies just want me to go play golf so they can convince me to do some business deal or other." A rueful smile crossed his lips, and I realized I had turned completely toward him as he spoke. I was leaning forward, hanging on his words. I had to force myself to move back as I made a curious noise, trying to not make my interest in him so screamingly obvious. I'm not sure why. After all, his interest in me was apparent, and if I weren't so attracted to him it might have been rather creepy.

"I chose the wrong thing to do," he said. "I hate golf. I'm not sure you can hate golf and be a CEO. It's just not possible.

"Do you hate it because you're bad at it, or because it's boring and wasteful?" I asked him.

A grin broke across his face. "The latter," he said. "I'm very good at it. I'm very good at most things."

I raised my eyebrows. "And modest, too."

He shrugged. "It is just fact."

Oh really? "And what are you not good at?"

He pursed his lips. "Art. Yet," he said.

I supposed that was true. "You do have talent," I had to admit to him. "There was something in those photos that was very... magnetic."

"It's you," he said, catching me off guard. "You are the magnetic part of those pictures."

I looked away. "I didn't look half as terrible as I usually do in photos," I conceded grudgingly. "But that was maybe the lighting. And I actually took the time to do my make up yesterday."

"And today?" he said as the subway car screeched to a halt. People got off, and people got on. An old hobo staggered through the doors. One of the ones that likes to sing. I hate those guys, because I never have enough cash to give to all of them, and it makes me feel like shit. I know, I know, living in the city, I should be over this by now, but I could have been one of those guys. Anyone could. It's just an accident of birth. Absently I patted my pockets as I tried to formulate an answer to his question.

"I probably dolled myself up a bit," I admitted with a sigh. Just as I'd thought, I didn't have any cash on me. I'd spent the last of it on beer and cigarettes. If I'd had one of those beers still with me, I could have given it to him, but that probably wasn't the wisest decision. I'd feel better, but the next thing you know there's a homeless dude frozen stiff under a bridge.

The hobo clanged a beat-up cane against the subway car pole. "Attention," he said. "Attention please." The car started up and he stumbled, only managing to catch himself at the last moment. He cleared his throat as he straightened up and I looked away. I hated to see people like this. I wish I had Felicia's idealism when it came to the world, but no amount of money was going to change that guy's life. Money could never make him sober, or induce his kids to talk to him again, or whatever terrible, sad story he had hidden away inside.

He gave a little speech in a gruff voice, and then launched into Goodbye, My Coney Island Baby. I wanted to sink into the floor. He held his hat out as he walked up and down the car, and he passed me quickly, seeing that I had nothing. His voice was quite fine, but it was so sad to see his talent wasted on a subway car full of commuters that it mostly made me depressed, and I averted my eyes.

Next to me, Malcolm stood up as the hobo launched into the "never gonna see you" part.

Malcolm flung his arms wide and took a deep breath. "Never gonna see you any more," he sang in harmony, a deep bass voice booming from his chest as he leaned into the man, clearly indicating that he should lead. The man's eyes lit up and together they finished out the first verse in perfect harmony to a smattering of applause. Then Malcolm reached into his inside pocket, pulled out his wallet, and handed the man a wad of bills. Then he sat down again.

I stared at Malcolm. I wouldn't have been more surprised if he'd ripped off his skin and revealed himself to be a robot underneath. In fact, I would have been significantly less surprised by his behavior than I had been up to this point.

"I didn't know you could sing," I said stupidly.

He held a hand up and tilted it back and forth, indicating that of his panoply of talents, singing merely fell into the fair to middling range. I watched the hobo counting his haul, his eyes wide as saucers. "How much money did you give him?" I asked in a low voice.

"A little over a thousand," he replied.

I backed away and stared at him. "Are you serious?" I said at last.

"Why shouldn't I?" he said. "What good is it doing me?"

I had no idea. Probably buying me lunch, but that

was selfish. "And the singing?"

He shrugged, a little one-shouldered affair, self-deprecating. "Allah will not show mercy to the unmerciful," he told me.

Of all the things I had expected him to say, that certainly wasn't it, but when I opened my mouth and tried to comment on it, we arrived at our destination. The train screeched to a stop and he stood up again, holding his hand out. "Let's go eat," he said.

Without thinking, I put my hand in his and I felt the zing of attraction spark between us. Then he was pulling me to my feet and we were out among the press of people, jostling through the corrals of the underground until we reached the surface, all together, and streamed out into the city.

ꙮ

"So are you Muslim?" I asked him finally as the waiter wandered off to the kitchen with our order. The Indian restaurant he'd taken me to was a little out-of-the-way place that I'd never heard of before, and the proprietor seemed to know Malcolm, though he only said, "Welcome back," before ushering us to our table—the best in the house, though that was a dubious honor.

We sat together in the booth, as though we were boyfriend and girlfriend. Where our knees had touched on the subway train, here Malcolm pressed his entire thigh against mine, and I had to remind myself not to swoon. The food also smelled amazing, and Malcolm insisted on ordering for us. I let him. His thigh may or may not have had something to do with the allowance of that liberty. And, well, I know what I like and what I don't, and he hadn't ordered anything that would send up alarm bells for me. Such as too many chickpeas. I like chickpeas, but one of my friends used to live on chickpeas, and they made him gassier than a heifer.

Malcolm looked at me with surprise. "Am I Muslim?" he said. "Why would you ask that?"

I tried to suppress the eye roll that welled up within me, but like a force of nature, it could not be denied. I rolled my eyes. "Because you just spouted some line at me about Allah's mercy."

"Oh, that," he said, as if people quoted the surahs or the hadiths or whatever that had been all the time in casual conversation. "I just think of that line whenever I see someone who needs help."

"Really?" I said. "Why that particular phrase?"

He appeared to think about this for a moment, and then shrugged. "I'm not sure," he said. "I think it resonated with me during the time of my life that I heard it."

"What time was that, if you don't mind my asking?"

"I don't mind your asking," he said. Then he hesitated. "But I think I might mind telling. Please excuse me. That was was an excellent question and I had to shoot it down like that."

I held up my hands. "Don't feel bad on my account," I said. "I'm just trying to get to know you better. Things you say and things you don't say are all part of that."

He smiled. "That's a very interesting way of looking at it. Very eastern, or possibly Kabalistic."

I had to admit to myself, Malcolm Ward got weirder and more interesting the more he talked, which was the opposite of most of the people I had run into. Usually the mysterious people you meet are only mysterious up until the moment they admit to growing a shroom farm in their closet or confess they are bipolar or something else that explains their behavior. So far Malcolm had listed off Shinto and Muslim thought to me. And also reincarnation. "You know a lot about religions," I said. "Did you study them in school or something?"

"I know very little *about* religions, but I know *of* a lot of them." He smiled. "It's a hobby of mine, studying religions."

I noted he didn't answer the question about school. "That's a strange hobby for a really rich guy to have," I said. "All the rich guys I know are all about making business deals or picking up hookers or doing blow or golfing until their hands fall off."

"I know," he said. "I don't find the society of people I belong to to be particularly suited for my temperament." His mouth twisted, somewhat ruefully. "But I can't very well move downward to socialize. I don't really fit in anywhere right now."

"Fitting in is overrated," I said. "Especially if you're going to be an artist. You need to cultivate that individuality."

"You think so?" he asked. "But if what I say doesn't mean anything to anyone but me, what point is saying it?"

Holy shit, I thought. This conversation was getting far more existential than I was used to. I'd had plenty of conversations about *the nature of art, maaaaaaaaan,* but they had usually been while I and my friends were high as hell, and they didn't make sense afterward. "Personal satisfaction?" I hazarded.

"Is that why you do it?" he asked me.

I sat back in the booth, not sure how to answer that. Part of art was a fundamental LOOK, LOOK AT ME desire, but essentially you wanted people to look at you because you thought you had something unique and interesting to say. I wasn't sure if I had ever managed to do that. My sales certainly didn't indicate that I resonated with many people. Usually I soothed myself by hoping I had merely transcended human consciousness and touched the realm of the divine or some other such garbage, but I knew it was because I wasn't communicating clearly. Or I was alone.

Not like Felicia. Felicia's art was stunning. Raw and exposed, she peeled back the niceties of society and revealed the emotional muscle and bone and sinew beneath. Her art was nothing like mine. And besides, I hadn't really put paint to canvas in the past month. Or two. Or was it three...?

Horrified, I thought back, trying to remember the last time I'd done any sort of artwork, and I couldn't remember. I gave a bitter little laugh. "I don't know why I do it. Or did it. I don't do art so much any more. I'm usually pretty tired after work." That sounded ungrateful. "I mean, my job is a great job and all and I love working for Lis, but I'm so drained by the time that I get home that I don't have much to say."

The waiter brought our naan and rice, the prelude to our meal, but when he retreated Malcolm put his hand on my knee. Warm ripples of sensation spread out over my skin, and I swallowed, hard. I'd been trying not to think about how close he was, about how every cell in my body seemed magically attuned to his presence. His hand wiped all that pretense away and I caught my breath. "Isn't that something to say in and of itself?" he asked me. "Isn't weariness an emotion?"

I shrugged, feeling silly. "Yeah, but everyone feels that way."

"Then that should resonate with your audience."

I hadn't quite thought about it that way. Yes, saying the same thing over again wasn't *new,* but that didn't mean I couldn't try to say it in a new way.

Of course, how I was going to do that with paint and bits of flotsam found in Central Park was the question. I liked my mediums. I probably just didn't know how to use them.

"I don't know," I said. "That seems like a long time ago for some reason.

The waiter returned with our meals—the lamb shahi korma for Malcolm, and the saag paneer for me—then retreated, and Malcolm, to my disappointment, removed his hand and began to apportion the dishes. "May I see some of your art some time?" he asked me.

"Yeah, I guess. It's all at my apartment, stored in the spare room in the back. And some of it is in galleries around the city."

"Any nearby?"

I thought. "I don't think so. Not here anyway. Maybe closer to your house. Anton has a piece of mine, I know that."

"I would like very much to see some of it, to witness how a professional does her work." He tore off a bit of naan and used it to sop up some of the sauce before wrapping it around a chunk of lamb and delicately popping it into his mouth. His whole body relaxed when it hit his tongue. "Aaaah," he said. "There is nothing like knowing the peace of a well-seasoned meal."

The expression on his face was one of pure bliss, and I found myself strangely jealous that it should be a hunk of dead farmyard animal that had made him so happy. Our sexual encounters so far had been entirely one-sided, although I suppose Malcolm got quite a bit of pleasure from eating me out, if his straining erections afterward were anything to go by. I felt rather annoyed that I hadn't yet reciprocated, but it made sense. In his studio, in his room, I was the object of study, of worship by the camera lens. But out here in the world, we were two equals. Well, not equals, but we were at least on neutral ground. I slipped my hand under the tablecloth and placed it on the inside of his thigh.

His flesh burned through the fine fabric of his slacks, and the muscles tensed and jumped at my touch. It gave me a wicked, illicit thrill to touch him this way, unseen by anyone else. Serenely I sopped up sauce with my bread and chewed it without comment, but under the table I let my fingers wander over his thighs, dipping between them and then back up, as though I were climbing mountains and fording valleys with my hand. Above the table, his eyes showed no emotion other than bliss. His lids were half closed, and he ate with gusto, commenting here and there about various spices he could taste in the sauces.

Then I slipped my hand up to his groin and his breath hitched in the middle of saying the word *turmeric*, and I couldn't repress the wicked smile that sliced across my face.

"Sadie," he said, "what are you doing?

I let my hand go still. "Just returning some favors I owe you."

He scowled at that and I wondered if I had misread the situation. His hand on my leg, his thigh pressed against mine... I mean, we'd already been pretty close... didn't he want this?

"You don't owe me any favors," he said. "If you do not want me in the same way, I'd really rather you didn't."

His voice had gone stiff, as stiff as his cock was growing under my palm. I'd messed up somehow.

"That's not what I meant," I said. "You just seemed so happy eating that food, like it was some kind of rare pleasure... I kind of wanted to be the one to put that look on your face." Ugh, it sounded so hokey when it came out of my mouth. Not at all playful the way it sounded in my head.

But he relaxed a bit, and a smile curled the corner of his mouth. "Is that so?" he asked. "Have you ever done anything like this in public?"

I had to think about that. I didn't think private parties counted, and everyone had been doing things and no one noticed because we'd always all been drunk beyond belief... "No," I said.

His hinted smile grew into a real smile at that. "Then let me guide you at it."

I licked my lips. "You've done it?"

"I know what I like," he replied evasively. Propping his elbows on the table, he hid my arm from the view of the rest of the restaurant. "Please, continue."

For some reason, doing it at his direction made it even hotter. I did as he told me, letting my fingers wander up and down, around his crotch and between his legs, feeling the heat growing there. What sort of underwear was he wearing? Boxers? Briefs? The devil wears nada? I wanted to find out, but there was no way for me to draw his cock out into the open without making it completely obvious what I was doing.

"Keep eating," Malcolm reminded me. "Otherwise someone will suspect something is wrong. There's no reason to go wasting a good korma just because you're giving a hand job."

My cheeks flared and I ducked my head, reaching for the bread. I ran into a problem here. How was I supposed to tear the bread with only one hand?

I should have known Malcolm would have the answer for that.

"Turn toward me, just a bit," he said. His voice was remarkably steady, and I wanted to push his boundaries a bit, so did as he bade, and ran my fingers up to his cock again, where I let them stay.

His thick erection burgeoned in his pants, a hard, aching swell against the fabric, and I cupped my hand over it, giving it a little rub. Malcolm let out the tiniest grunt, but just the sound of it made me wet and hot and eager. I glanced around, making sure no one was watching us. The lunchtime crowd had definitely started to fill the place up, and though we were in a corner booth, one would only have to glance over at us, take note of my hand in his lap, and deduce what we were doing.

It was so dangerous. Illegal. How long had it been since I'd done something illegal?

Granted, I was with one of the richest men in the city and riches tend to make legal troubles go away, so even if we were outed there would probably be no repercussions. Except perhaps in the papers or the gossip mills.

His cock felt good against my palm.

I licked my lips as Malcolm tore off a piece of bread for me, but when I extended a hand to take it, he held it just out of my reach.

"Food for favors," he said. "If you do exactly what I say, you'll have the best meal of your life."

I pressed my lips together and let my hand go still. "Okay," I said.

He smiled. "Good. Hike up your skirt."

My breath caught. He was turning the tables on me. I rather thought I might like it. Reaching down, I lifted the hem of my skirt, just as he had done about an hour before, in his bedroom, the precursor to giving me the sweetest head I'd ever received. I shivered at the memory, the echo of pleasure sending hot spears of desire through my body, my pussy growing wet and slick with the thought. As I lifted the skirt past my thighs, Malcolm dipped the piece of bread in sauce and wrapped up a cube of cheese in it. "Open your mouth," he instructed.

I did.

He popped the morsel inside, placing it on my tongue like a priest giving sacrament, and I closed my lips on his fingers, giving them a good, long suck. Blood darkened his cheeks and his pupils dilated at the sensation. "Very nice," he murmured. "Now push your panties aside and put your fingers on your clit."

Almost as if I were in a trance, my fingers went to the apex of my thighs and slid the crotch of my panties over my vulva. I was wet and aching, the flesh of my pussy burning hot and soaked with my juices. I wanted very much for him to touch me there again, but doing it to myself under his supervision was somehow just as good, if different.

"Don't forget to keep your hand moving on my cock," he said. I swallowed. I'd already forgotten, so enraptured was I by the thought of him fingering me by proxy in public. I gave his cock another gentle rub, and his intake of breath and fluttering eyelids told me I'd hit on something he liked. He fed me another morsel of food, and I sucked at his fingertips again. The spices mixed with the taste of his skin, making him sweet, savory, a delight in and of himself.

"Using only your clit, bring yourself to orgasm," he said. I scratched my nails over his cock, feeling the contours of the bulbous head and the veiny shaft through the fabric, but I did as he ordered. I spread my lower lips with my hand, and, using only one finger, I began to gently circle my clit. It was so small, but it still stood at attention, as erect as any penis and just as needy for release.

I flicked it, circled it, faster and faster, struggling to keep my activities a secret above the table while I tried to simultaneously keep a strong, steady pace on Malcolm's cock while he fed me. Slow, fast, eat, suck.

I watched his eyes flicker as I brought him closer to release, his hips nudging up into my hand in tiny thrusts. He started leaving his fingers in my mouth, just for a moment, and then a moment more, and when a bit of savory sauce escaped, he dabbed it away with a napkin. "No worries," he told me, and his voice was deep and husky, thrilling me to the core. When at last my orgasm came, I had to bury my face in his shoulder—large, warm, solid—as I gritted my teeth and rode it out. My whole body clenched and released, and underneath my hand I felt his cock jump as he came, too. A bit messier, to be sure, but probably no less satisfying.

When I took my hands away, I found the meal had been finished, and I was just getting my first sip of wine when the waiter brought our check. Malcolm paid, and together we exited the booth, he donning his long coat first, and I couldn't help but be a little satisfied that I'd given him some pleasure in return. And he hadn't run away this time. I'd have to count this as a victory.

As we meandered back toward the subway in silence—not exactly comfortable, but not tense or awkward either—I realized he had been right. It had been the best meal of my life.

Now if only I could remember what any of it had tasted like.

We stopped in front of Malcolm's mansion. We still hadn't said a word to each other since the restaurant, and now I was starting to feel a bit awkward. It's not every day that you feel yourself up at your companion's insistence on the first date. It's not every day that your date comes in his pants. It's not every day you do both of those things out in the open, like a couple of subway perverts. I'd once asked Felicia if Anton's semen contained some kind of mind-altering that made her just go along with whatever he wanted to do and forget why she agreed to do so, but now I was beginning to wonder just what kind of hold Malcolm Ward had over *me*.

I mean, hell, I wasn't even his wife. And his cum hadn't even touched me yet. I had no excuse. None at all.

"I'm not running away again," Malcolm said suddenly.

I started. I hadn't even gotten that far in my thinking. "Are you saying you're not running away and then running away and saying you didn't because you said you weren't going to and therefore what you are about to do is not running away?" I asked him.

For the first time, I think I'd left *him* speechless. Although it had less to do with my shocking libido or scandalous thoughts than my improperly organized brain. "What?" he said, confused.

I shook my head. "Nothing. Never mind. Okay, so you're not running away. What does that mean?"

He looked up at his ridiculously huge house. Why would a single man need such a huge house? I had to wonder. I mean, aside from storing boxes full of eight-track tapes and incomplete collections of the Encyclopedia Britannica. What is a house if not a storage unit, I ask you?

"I think it means I would like to continue to explore our artistic relationship," he said at last. "I believe a union between us could be quite fruitful."

Now I had to stare at him. "You're kidding, right?"

He looked down at me. He really was very tall. His beautiful dark eyes narrowed as his brows drew together in worry. For a moment, he looked almost... betrayed. "No. I'm not kidding. What makes you think that?"

I raised my eyebrows. "You're really talking about our *artistic* union being fruitful?"

His mouth dropped open. "Oh!" he said. "Oh, yes, I can see where you might be getting the wrong impression. But yes, I meant that. I would like to explore... other mediums."

"And I still inspire you?" I asked.

To my utter shock he reached out and ran his thumb down the side of my face. "Yes," he said huskily. "Very much so. Please come back here tomorrow at two in the afternoon."

A queer feeling curled in my stomach at the touch of his finger against my cheek. "I, um, I have to work tomorrow..." It sounded like the lamest excuse ever, but his touch, though it inspired anticipation in me, also gave me a strange little quiver of longing. Longing, and regret. I had no idea what to do with it, so I backed away and he dropped his hand. I felt the loss like a blow.

"Will Felicia not give you the day off if you ask?"

I had to think about that. "I don't know," I said. "I don't think I've ever asked her for one."

"Then I'd say you're due. Be here. Tomorrow. Two." And he turned and walked up the stairs and into his house.

What a weird fucking guy, I thought. Definitely not crazy, though. Not by a long shot.

I turned and went home.

6

I awoke to the phone ringing in my ear. Groggily I rolled over, grabbed my phone, and answered. "'lo?" I muttered.

"So you had to get your lover boy to ask me to give you the day off?" Felicia's voice buzzed in my ear and I winced.

"What?" I said. She sounded angry. I couldn't imagine why. "I have no idea what you're talking about."

She huffed into the phone. "I'm talking about Malcolm Ward calling me up and saying you needed the day off today so he could paint you."

This was news to me. I mean, we'd sort of left it at *maybe* yesterday. That he'd taken matters into his own hands rankled. "I didn't tell him he could do that," I said, indignant. "I told him I'd ask you for the day off. Or just the afternoon, if you need me in the morning. Do you need me this morning?"

"Do I ever need you?" Felicia asked.

"Yes. All those times you got on the front pages of

the tabloids with your indiscretions? Remember when you first got married and I covered for you? Remember all those times you forgot you had to go to one of those fancy dress parties and I just so happened to have it on my calendar and you showed up fashionably late without clay under your fingernails?"

There was silence on the other end of the line for a moment. "Yes, well, fine. I know I need you. But I don't need you today. It's a Monday. Nothing ever happens on Mondays."

Even I had to admit this was true. "I suppose," I said. "So he wants to paint me, huh?"

"I thought you said he took photographs."

"He says he hasn't found his medium yet."

"Oh jeez. What a twat."

For some reason, I felt defensive. "I don't think so. He has some talent. The photos he took definitely show promise. You know, if they weren't of me. Maybe if he had a really beautiful woman to photograph he'd do better."

"He could have a really beautiful woman to photograph. He's rich. He wants you."

"Oh. Thanks," I said, crankily.

"You know I didn't mean it like that. Anyway, he called and asked for you to have the day off. I said yes."

I lay in my bed and blinked at the ceiling. My clock was just about to tick over to my alarm, which was... strange. "Wait, he called you at six in the morning?"

"Late last night," she corrected me. "I'm gathering he's rather eager to see you again. You fucked him yet?"

I bit my lip. My dreams had been full of Malcolm,

of things that we hadn't even done to each other in the waking world. I had no idea what kind of relationship we had, but it was certainly sexually charged, even though I hadn't even touched his bare cock. Or his bare skin. Or... well, much of anything, really. I'd never been with a guy as reserved as Malcolm. He seemed to only want to touch me, and was largely uninterested in reciprocation. I'd once thought, after one too many blowjobs with one of my exes who never told me when he was about to come—it's called common courtesy, my god—that it would be lovely to have a man worship my body and never ask for anything in return. But I was finding out that I was pretty randy to worship Malcolm myself. He did have a wonderfully hard body—what I had felt of it under his clothes—and sex seemed to draw him out of his shell. He would have been fun to play with. It would be really fun to see what made him tick.

"No," I said at last. "I haven't fucked him yet. But I plan to."

"Good," Felicia said. "I don't think you've gotten laid since you started working for me, and that's too damn long."

"I have!" I said, though I couldn't quite remember when. "It's just that you get laid enough for the both of us."

"I don't think it works like that," Felicia said. "You don't get to average sex out across multiple people."

"I know." Boy, did I know. Maybe my unbelievable attraction to Malcolm was because of how long it had been since I'd just gone out and had fun with a guy. I was a ball of repressed sexual energy, clearly, and Malcolm had picked up on it. Perhaps that was why he thought I was so magnetic.

"Well, whatever, go over to his studio, get painted, get fucked."

I made a face, though I knew she couldn't see it. "Damn, that sounds like you're mad at me."

"I'm not mad," she said. "I'm just cautious about this guy. What kind of man calls up your employer to ask to give you the day off?"

"A rich man used to getting his way?" I guessed.

"I suppose."

"You sound like you don't like him."

There was silence at the other end of the line for a long moment. "I don't think he's good for you," Felicia said. "You said he's damaged. You always try to save the damaged ones and it never works out."

I sighed. "I know." I remembered the way he stood up and belted out a classic barbershop tune and dumped his wallet out to help a hobo he'd never met before and probably would never see again. And then told me Allah said he should, even though he wasn't Muslim. Absently, I rubbed one of my tattoos, feeling the marred skin beneath. He was weird... and probably damaged... but... "But he's... different. I think."

"You think?"

"I know. I know he's different."

Felicia sighed on the other end of the line. "I know I can't talk you out of it," she said finally, "so try not to fall into the trap of trying to fix him. Please?"

"I won't," I promised.

"Okay. Have fun today. Go get a massage or something beforehand. You deserve it."

I smiled. Felicia was always trying to take care of me, when I was the one who always took care of her.

It was sweet. "I will. See you tomorrow."

"See you tomorrow."

ꙮ

I arrived at Malcolm's mansion ready for anything. A good massage will do that for you. Gazing up at it, I heaved a sigh and steeled myself to once again enter the hoarder's den.

Except when I tried the door and it opened easily into the foyer, I was greeted with the sight of boxes. Stacks and stacks of boxes. Circling around, I peered into the long stretch of the house behind the entrance and saw still more boxes, and a group of men making more boxes, putting stuff into them. What the hell? I thought.

I didn't even call out this time, just started up the stairway. Reasoning that Malcolm wanted to paint me in his studio rather than his bedroom, I went all the way to the top floor.

A wave of heated air hit me as I stepped into the room to see Malcolm setting up a large drop cloth.

"Are you moving?" I asked him.

He looked up at me. His eyes were still haunted, smudged with dark circles. "No. Why?"

My mouth twisted. "You know there are a bunch of guys packing up your stuff and putting it in boxes downstairs, right?"

"Oh, that." He shrugged. "Yes, I know. I have decided to get rid of my things."

I blinked. "Just like that? You, uh, have a lot of stuff."

"Yes, I know. I've decided that it doesn't make me happy. I'm going to give it away."

I just never knew what to expect with Malcolm Ward. "You're giving all your things away? What about the really valuable stuff?" My mind went immediately to the sculpture that had been sitting in his foyer, the one by the student of Rodin. I would have liked to have touched that sculpture.

"What about it?" he asked. "I couldn't care less about how valuable something is to other people." He smiled. "Do you know what the most valuable thing in the world is, Sadie?"

Oh, I thought, *please don't get all mushy on me*. "You're not going to say love, are you?"

He shook his head. "Go ahead. Guess."

I looked around this huge room, and thought about the boxes moving downstairs. "Peace?" I hazarded.

"Nope," he told me. "The most valuable thing in the world is the head of a dead cat."

I suddenly felt small and cold. Tendrils of the past tickled at my brain. "What the hell?" I blurted. "Why would you say something like that?"

Malcolm looked up from his work in surprise. "It's only a koan, Sadie. A mental exercise posed by the Zen master Sozan."

I didn't care *who* said it. "Don't say shit like that. It's creepy. *Fuck*."

Immediately he looked contrite. "I'm so sorry. I've offended you. It was just a stray thought. I've taken to saying what's on my mind lately, and I didn't stop to think how it sounded. I'll never mention anything like that again."

I took a deep breath, and firmly pushed my feelings down. If I didn't feel them, they didn't exist. "No. No. Why did he say the head of a dead cat is the most valuable thing in the world?"

He tilted his head. "Because no one can name its price," he replied. Then he frowned. "But now that I say it out loud to you, I'm starting to wonder if he wasn't wrong."

I could sort of see it as a sick joke, but it was one that had completely turned me off from the jittery excitement that had dogged me all morning. If I were someone else, I might have responded differently, laughed or something. It was true, in its own way. But still.

Malcolm stood up. "Sadie," he said. "Are you all right? You look very pale."

Dead cats make me pale, I wanted to tell him, but I didn't. Plenty of things would make me pale, and I wasn't about to share them with anyone. You never knew who could use a weakness against you. Sharing triggers was a surefire way to get got. I shrugged, as if to say it was no big deal. "I'm fine. Why is it so warm in here?" I asked, trying to change the subject.

"Ah, that." He smiled. "I read that one of the best ways to keep a model happy is to make it warm enough in your studio. I'm going to paint you today."

"Yeah, Lis told me." I looked around. "So where's your canvas and easel and stuff?" All I saw was a large white cloth in the middle of the room, and a collection of pots of paint and brushes on a small, low table next to it.

"I had planned on *you* being my canvas."

My eyes shot back to him, but he was deadly serious. "What do you mean?"

"I mean I want to paint your naked body," he said.

Okay, that got me nervous and jittery again, in the delicious way that made me warm and shivery all over. "I don't believe we discussed nudity today," I said.

"Then you do not consent?"

It was such a weird way to say it, but his face was open and honest, as though he meant nothing by it. He truly wanted me to be his canvas, naked beneath his brush. The thought excited me. I swallowed.

"I consent," I said. "I would love to be your canvas."

An almost imperceptible relaxing of his shoulders. He had been worried I'd turn him down. "If I go too far," he said, "you must tell me. I will stop whenever you say stop."

A zing of anticipation zipped up my spine. "Okay," I said. "I will tell you if you go too far." But I had no intention of telling him to stop.

There was no screen for me to change behind today, so I held his gaze and shed my coat, tossing it carelessly to the floor. I wore a cardigan underneath it, and I unwrapped it and tossed it down as well. My ribbed t-shirt joined them, and I stood before him in my bra, jeans, and boots.

The cherry wood of his eyes was almost eclipsed by the expanding of his pupils, and the skin of his face became lightly flushed as he watched me disrobe. I felt powerful, keeping his attention to me. He wore simple clothes today, only an old t-shirt and jeans, but they showed off his physique quite nicely. Well-muscled, but not overly so. Long waisted. A swimmer's physique. I licked my lips and bent to take my boots off.

"Let me help you," he said.

My breath caught, but I didn't tell him no. Instead I stood back up and waited. After a moment of drinking me in, he closed the gap between us, his bare feet slapping against the floor as though he were deliberately making a large amount of noise, as if he were flushing out prey from the shadows of the woods.

He knelt at my feet, bringing to mind the last time we were in this position, and he had licked me until I came. His hands ran up and down my thigh, and I felt the heat of his fingers through the denim of my jeans. I was already unsteady on my feet, and he made me more with each gentle stroke of his palms, as though he were soothing a skittish horse. I almost liked that comparison, actually. Strong and wild, he tamed me, but only with my consent. He found the zipper on one boot and slowly slid it down. The warmth of the leather fell away, and he wrapped one arm around my leg, his hand cupping my ass, as he nudged me onto the other foot, sliding my boot off. It clattered to the floor, and I winced, realizing I was wearing a thick pair of socks that one of my friends had knitted for me. It was too cold to wear anything else, I'd thought, and I hadn't thought ahead.

Embarrassed, I laughed. "Sorry about the socks. I know they're not—"

"Shh," he said. It was curt, and it cut my babbling off immediately. I felt the tips of his fingers playing with the sole of my foot through the fine-knit wool, and I inhaled sharply. Slipping his thumb into the cuff, he slid it off my foot and threw it away. His fingertips returned to my sole, and traced a soft pattern. I started to pant. Then he set my foot down and treated my other leg to the same attention, though this time his fingers brushed past my pussy on the way to my thigh. Again he peeled my boot away, and again he ran his fingers over my feet. No man had ever paid such attention to the less important parts of my body before. It was as though he liked all of me, and not just the bits that gave him pleasure.

All of me gave him pleasure, I realized.

The thought shocked me, and it suddenly came to me through the haze of desire slowly building in me, that he wanted all of me. He didn't know me, but he wanted to know me. Every bit of me.

The realization frightened me, but it aroused me at the same time.

Then he set my other foot down, this time on his crotch, and I felt the bulge of his erection through his jeans.

"You don't know what you do to me," he said, looking up at my face. His voice dragged over my skin, as though all my nerves were raw and exposed. I swallowed and licked my lips and felt his cock jump in response to the action of my tongue.

His hands alighted on my waistband, and then he was unbuttoning my jeans, zipping them down, then reaching up and hooking his fingers into both my pants and panties. He slid the fabric over my hips, dragging his fingernails over my exposed ass as he took them off, and when he had to lift my foot from his cock he made a small sigh of sadness and loss.

My mouth went dry.

"Take off your bra," he said. "I want to study my canvas."

Shivers raced over my skin. Reaching behind me, I unhooked my bra and let it slide down my arms to fall to the floor. Malcolm stood and began to circle me.

I remained still, my head held high, wanting nothing more than to leap across the space between us, hook my legs around his waist, and ride him until I came over and over again. What was he doing to me?

Driving me just as crazy as he is, I thought. Maybe he was a bit mad. But it was a good sort of mad. The madness of artistry, the madness of genius. He finally stopped in front of me and reached out, his hands cupping my small breasts, lifting them up and running his thumbs over my nipples. My core quivered and I moaned softly at his touch.

"Sensitive there, are you?" he said.

I nodded.

"Good." He slid his warm hands up my chest to my shoulders, and then let his fingers drift down, down, down the back of my arm to my hands. Gently, he tangled his fingers with mine and led me over to the cloth in the center of the floor.

"Kneel," he commanded me, and I did so. The warmth of his palms sliding over my body guided me into the position he wanted, and I reveled in his every touch as he pushed my face down to the floor, stretched my arms out in front of me, arched my back so my ass stuck in the air. He lifted my heavy mass of hair and slid it over one shoulder, then traced his hands over my spine.

"You have many tattoos," he said after a moment. "I love them. You are a work of art."

No man had told me I was art before. I closed my eyes, praying he would paint me and then fuck me. I couldn't take the teasing much longer.

My exposed pussy quivered in the air, though the warmth of the room kept the caresses of the drafts from being uncomfortable. I ached for him. I ached for anything. I wished, suddenly, that I wasn't the passive canvas, that I could touch him as much as he touched me.

He knelt down beside me. "Your back is beautiful," he said. "You are exquisitely structured." The scrape of the table legs on the floor echoed around the studio as he dragged his materials over to himself. I heard the unscrewing of a cap and the rustle of his movements as he dipped a brush into the paint. Then he touched brush to skin, and I sighed in pleasure.

Slowly, torturously, he dragged the tip of his brush over my back, winding down my spine in spirals, wandering where it would. I had no idea what he was doing. My forehead touched the floor and I could only see his knees from the cave of my body, but whatever he was doing felt amazing. Swift, then slow, strong, then soft, he painted my skin. Occasionally he would dip the brush into the paint again, and I quivered, wondering where he would paint me next. I was never disappointed. First he painted the back of my thigh, then the curve of my waist. Then, finally, his brush found my breast. It curled under and over, circling my nipple, until I nearly moaned in frustration.

"Would you like me to touch your nipple?" he said. He sounded amused. "Nod if yes."

I nodded.

I watched as he reached down to the hard little point of my breast. Then my breath caught as he pushed his pointer into his thumb, and then flicked me.

Pleasure laced with pain shot out across me, darting straight from my nipple to my heart, and I cried out.

"Too much?" he asked. "Nod if yes."

I remained perfectly still, and I heard his breathing pick up the pace.

"Good," he said. He ran the brush over the now throbbing nub, soothing it. I was so wet between my legs it was a miracle I wasn't just dripping down my thighs. He flicked me again, then soothed me, flicked and soothed, flicked and soothed, over and over, until I was crying out and twitching with each burst of pleasurable pain.

At last he stopped, then ran his fingertips over my back and side. He traced the swell of my ass and reached around, brushing his fingers against my quivering cunt, feeling the soaking wetness there.

"Ah, Sadie," he breathed. "You truly are alive." He shifted, moving around to my back. God, why wouldn't he let me touch him? I needed to touch him. I wanted his cock in my hands, in my mouth. I'd never wanted anyone like I'd wanted Malcolm Ward, and the wanting was all the more potent because he didn't seem to want me to have him.

"Hmm," he said suddenly. "I need a new brush. But I have forgotten a place where I could store my used brushes. I truly am an amateur."

His voice had a wicked undertone, and my pulse quickened. Was he going to do what I thought he was going to do?

Hot breath gusted between the cheeks of my ass, caressing the tight puckered entrance there. Then he slid his tongue over my asshole, soft, sensuous, layering it with moisture, so that when he finally pressed the rounded tip of the brush handle past the tight ring of muscle, it went easily, and I moaned and quaked around it.

"Do you like it?" he asked me. "Nod if yes."

I nodded.

"Good."

I heard him select another brush, and then he began to swirl it over the mounds of my ass, dragging paint here and there, tickling and teasing me until he rinsed it out and then inserted it alongside the first one. Then another, and another. Slowly he stretched me out, and I quivered with desire to be used so. My pussy was melting. I needed him inside me, but I knew he wouldn't give me what I wanted yet.

He selected another brush. "I like this part of you," he said.

There was a pause and I almost opened my mouth to ask him what he meant, but then he swiped the bristles of the brush over my burning slit and I squeaked as they flicked against my clitoris.

"This part is very alive," he said. "It almost has a mind of its own." He flicked my clitoris with the brush again and I groaned at the intensity of the sensation. The pleasure coiled and curled in my belly, and I felt myself beginning the long, slow climb up to the top of the mountain, and when I finally let go I would plunge into pleasure. My mouth watered, my body strained, even as I struggled to stay still. The brushes in my ass filled me up. and I ached to feel the same in my tight core.

"I'd like to watch you come," Malcolm said. "Would you like that? Nod if yes."

I didn't want to nod. "Yes!" I cried.

He reached around and flicked my nipple again, and I bucked and shrieked. So much more intense, so much more satisfying, now that he was touching me where I most needed him. He began to flutter the bristles of the brush over my slit, gathering the slick juices there, as though he were loading the brush with paint, and when he dragged it over my clit as if he were layering paint onto a canvas I couldn't help but cry out and writhe under his tender attention.

With every cry, he sent a lance of pain over my nipple, and with every jolt of that incredible sensation I bucked and wailed as he flicked my clit faster and faster, until I couldn't tell the pain from the pleasure and it was one and the same. "Malcolm!" I cried out as I coiled tight and then burst apart, shattering into a million pieces. Each piece fell to the floor, and I collapsed against the cloth when it was over, my quivering pussy still aching and wet, begging for his cock to enter me.

Slowly he slid the brushes from my ass, and I felt the emptiness that followed their loss keenly. Panting, I felt sweat rolling down my brow and sheening my back, and when he ran his hand over the skin there, I shuddered with pleasure.

"Good, good," he murmured. His own voice was throaty with desire. Would he finally give me what I wanted?

His hands guided me until I was curled up into a fetal position on the floor, and then he turned me over and spread me out. Sweat cooled in the air, and I tried not to stare shamelessly at the bulge in his jeans. His full lips were parted, and again he dipped a brush into paint. Putting it to my skin, he swirled up around the outside of my breast, shimmying and spiraling up and up, over the inside of my upper arm. "I wonder if I could make a tattoo you would love," he said, almost to himself.

I almost smiled at that, but the words brought a

tiny bit of anxiety to the fore. I had designed all my tattoos myself. It would have to be a stunning design for me to really want to put it to my skin.

Then he trailed the paint over the tattoo on the inside of my arm, a leaping koi fish done in the Japanese style. I felt the bristles move over the numb spot there, and I gritted my teeth.

Malcolm paused.

I couldn't help myself. I looked up, and I saw that the solid color of the paint had obscured my tattoo, revealing what lay beneath.

A long, angry scar.

"Stop!"

The word burst out of my mouth, and Malcolm froze, startled. He glanced down at my face, and whatever he saw there told him I was serious. He withdrew the brush and backed away.

I sat up.

"Sadie?" he said. "Are you—?"

"I'm going," I said. "I just remembered. I have to go somewhere. I'm sorry. I have to go." My hand was already on the paint, wiping it away, until my leaping fish emerged again and I smeared the paint on the drop cloth beneath me.

"Sadie..."

I was on my feet. I didn't care if my clothes were ruined. I hurried over to them and pulled them on, my bra, my shirt, my cardigan. My jacket, my jeans. My boots. Each layer soothed me, hid me, and when I was done, I grabbed my purse, my breathing so fast I thought I might faint. "Sorry," I said. "I have to go." And without looking back, I jogged across the floor and took the steps down the stairs two-at-a-time. I sounded like a herd of buffalo, but I didn't stop until

I was outside, breathing in the icy air.

I paused on the sidewalk and looked up. I couldn't see Malcolm looking down at me, but I knew he was. What I had just done was exactly what he had done to me after our first session. Run away. I was a coward.

I started for the subway station, but my breath wouldn't slow down. I was hyperventilating. I knew I should stop, bend over, but the only way to stop was to breathe less or use up that extra oxygen. My feet picked up the pace, until I was barely skimming the ground with my toes, dodging and weaving through other people. Yells followed me whenever I bumped into someone, but I couldn't stop.

Great. Now I really am *the one running away.* But I couldn't make myself slow down. I couldn't make myself turn around. I just kept on running.

Time passed. I don't know how long. I just wanted to *escape,* but I couldn't run away from the things inside. I thought I'd run the whole way home even though it wouldn't have done any good, and I would have done it if a sleek black car hadn't pulled up next to me and kept pace. I glanced over, and saw Malcolm through the open window in the back seat. I slowed down.

"What do you want?" I said.

"Sadie, please, get in the car."

"No thanks. I'm out for a jog."

"I crossed a line. I didn't know it was there."

I looked away. "It's fine. You didn't know. And now you said sorry. So it's all hunk dory now. Is that why you just ran me down in your car?"

"I hardly think I ran you down. And yes, that's partly why."

I slowed to a stop, waiting for him to finish the

thought, but he didn't. Fine. I'd bite. "And why else did you want to talk to me so badly you couldn't call me on the phone?"

"You wouldn't have answered, and I want to take you to Dubrovnik," he told me.

I'd never even heard of Dubrovnik. I stared at him.

He smiled. "Let's get out of Manhattan. Let's go. I'm sick of this place. I want to take you out. I heard its warm in Dubrovnik this year."

"I don't even know where Dubrovnik is."

"I want to take you there. You are an artist. You will love it."

I'd told Felicia I'd see her tomorrow.

But this was Malcolm Ward, offering to take me somewhere else. If I went home, I knew I'd spend the rest of the day drinking wine and washing away the paint, running my thumbs over my tattoos, shivering and shuddering and afraid to go to sleep.

If I went with Malcolm, I'd end up on another planet. At least, that's what I was assuming Dubrovnik was. It was warm? I'd kill for the warm. I was cold, inside and out.

"Fine," I said, got in the car, and away we drove.

7

Dubrovnik, it turns out, is in Croatia. I did not know this. I didn't even really know where Croatia was. I only stopped long enough at my apartment to grab my passport before running back down the stairs and throwing myself into the car. Malcolm smiled to see me frantically buckling up and throwing my hair out of my face. My little blue book, unstamped but for a trip to Barbados I'd taken with Felicia last fall, sat in my hand, its slick cover slightly slippery with the nervous sweat that I didn't want to acknowledge was seeping from my palm.

"You didn't pick up clothes," Malcolm said. "Good."

"You told me not to," I said. I would do anything he asked of me, frankly, as long as he didn't ask me about the scars beneath my tattoos. I was happy to go wherever he wanted. I was happy to run away from the feelings he had stirred in me. Very mature, I know, but sometimes you have to run away so you can live to run away another day.

"I did," he mused as the car pulled away from the curb and jetted into the city streets. "I just didn't quite expect you to obey."

I scowled at him. "I'm not obeying, I'm taking your suggestion. Although I don't know what I'm going to wear in Dubrovnik."

"You will wear what I dress you in," he replied. "I require it for my art."

I suspected that he actually did not require it for his art, but I wasn't really going to argue with him. I didn't want to ruin the illusion that we were lovers jetting off to a romantic getaway, leaving behind the hustle and bustle of the city to lose ourselves in each other's arms.

Then Malcolm did his part to continue the illusion by reaching over, unbuckling my seatbelt, and pulling me into his lap. He spread my thighs over his hips and buried his hands in my hair, drawing my lips down to his.

I sighed, letting the warmth of our attraction chase away the cold that had settled in my gut. His lips and hands traveled over my body, here and there until I was gasping and sighing at his touch, my pussy rubbing against the bulge of his cock in his jeans. I still hadn't given him an orgasm, except for one messy hand job beneath a restaurant table, and I wanted to give something back to him. The car seemed like as good a place as any, squeezing it in before we clambered onto a plane. I didn't know if we were taking a commercial flight or a private flight. I didn't know *anything.*

I didn't want to know anything. I wanted to forget. I wanted to lose myself in the moment with him. Glancing over my shoulder, I checked to make sure the privacy window was up between the back seat and the driver's seat. It was. I slid out of Malcolm's lap and wedged myself into the space between the driver's seat and his hips. He gazed down at me, his dark eyes growing wider and darker with desire.

I smoothed my hands over his thighs. I wanted him naked. I wanted to see him. Reaching out, I began to work the button of his pants, my mouth watering in anticipation.

His hands closed around my wrists.

"Stop," he said.

Seriously? He was asking me to stop? I almost flashed him a sly glance and kept going, but remembering how he stopped immediately for me gave me pause. I raised my eyes to his, trying to gauge how serious he was.

A muscle leaped in his jaw as he stared down at me, but his hands were firm on my wrists. Warm and large. I wanted to curl up in the palm of his hand and let him warm me through and through.

"Why?" I asked. "Don't you want me to?"

He used my wrists to draw me up and set me on the seat beside him. "I don't know," he said after a moment.

Stung, I scooted away from him, the leather of the back seat making it easy. I wished it weren't so easy. Again the distance, again the strangeness from him. Malcolm Ward intrigued and frustrated me. I wanted nothing more than to peel away his layers and figure out what made him tick, but for every layer removed, it seemed he scraped away ten of my own. I was too pliable towards him, all because I wanted him to get in my pants. And yet I hadn't even achieved that yet. And maybe I never would because he didn't even know if he wanted to do so.

His tongue on my clit, tenderly probing my quivering inner core, and the huge, aching cock that resulted from those activities weren't enough to tell him he wanted to fuck me. What was?

Perhaps I could be forgiven for what I said next. Perhaps not. But I tell you this: it came from a very honest place.

"What the fuck is wrong with you?" I demanded. "Why can't I suck your cock? I suck great cock. What the hell?"

His brows rose at my crude words. I didn't care. I wanted to shock him. "Sadie..." he said. I saw him searching for the right words, and I crossed my arms, waiting. I suddenly didn't want it to be easy for him. I'd been easy for him for the past two days. I wanted him to be easy for me for a change. Or at the very least throw a wrench in his works.

Stop playing with me, I wanted to say. *Stop running hot and cold, you enormous fuckstick tease.*

Even I knew that saying something like that was probably beyond the pale, so I bit my lips together and waited for him to tell me why he didn't want to fuck me.

"I don't know," he said again. He drew back, his shoulders straightening, his face smoothing. He seemed puzzled, and then a strange look passed over his face. It was almost... sad. "You do things to me, Sadie," he said at last. "I don't know if I'm comfortable with them."

I knew what he meant, but I said it anyway. "I don't do anything to you," I replied. "That's the point. When am I going to get to make *you* happy?"

His brow smoothed, and a small smile tugged at

his lips. "You do make me happy," he said, and then the smile faded, replaced by shock. "You *do* make me happy."

"Well don't sound so surprised by it," I said crankily. "You're going to give me a complex." I tossed my hair and looked out the window, meaning to stare out at the cold February day in a huff to let him know I was really totally mad at him, okay?

His hand on one of mine, warm and uninvited, shattered that resolution. Before I could stop myself, I was gazing at him from the corner of my eye.

"Sadie," he said. "I want to fuck you. I want to fold you up and fuck you until you scream. But I won't yet. I don't want to ruin it."

His words made me dizzy. "Ruin what?"

"My masterpiece," he said. "You will see what I have in mind when we get to Dubrovnik. It will be perfect. And I will give you everything you want when we get there. Until then..."

He trailed off and drew my hand down into his lap, mere inches from his straining erection, but he kept his hands between my fingers and his cock. Gently, insistently, he stroked the back of my hand with his thumb, reminding me of how he had plunged into my core with that very thumb during our photo session. "Until then what?" I asked finally.

"Until then, I want to keep you coming."

I wavered. *Just accept it,* I thought. *When are you going to find another guy who just wants to give and give?*

"Fine," I said. "I grudgingly accept."

His eyes met mine. "I don't want you to accept," he said. "I want you to submit."

I swallowed. Submitting. The idea was strange, foreign to me. I didn't lie down and die for anyone. I didn't lie down and take it.

And yet there was a trembling note of need in his voice. Vulnerability. He *needed* me to submit. I didn't need to be his puppet, his plaything, his far-off muse come to earth to inspire him. He *needed*. it. I *wanted* it.

"All right," I said.

He ran his fingers over my cheek, sending shivers down my spine. "You will be the most brilliant thing I have ever done," he said as we pulled up to the airport. "You will see."

He had a private jet, of course. And the moment we took off, he had me standing in the middle of the floor, taking my ruined, paint-stained clothes off. Smears of color covered my skin, making me look like I'd rolled in a Jackson Pollack painting. Malcolm sat in one of the leather-bound swiveling chairs, watching me. "You are startling," he said when I finally stood before him, completely nude except for his own markings.

"Thank you," I said.

"Don't speak."

I licked my lips.

"Lie down on the floor," he commanded.

I glanced down dubiously at the fine carpet. Wouldn't the paint ruin it? But hey, I wasn't a freaking billionaire, what did I care? I did as he bade, stretching out, my arms above my head, my toes pointed towards him.

"Open your legs," he said. Then he reached down and opened a bag I hadn't seen there, withdrawing a familiar-looking tin. A box full of charcoal sticks.

"Where'd you get that?" I said.

"What did I say about speaking?" he asked me.

I clammed up.

"Spread your legs," he commanded again.

God. I'd never known how much I liked to hear a man talk dirty to me. My breathing picked up as I let my thighs fall open, exposing my inner flesh to his gaze.

"Yes," he murmured. "Like that." And he left his chair and knelt down between my legs as he opened the tin of charcoal.

I wanted to ask what he was going to do. I didn't think he'd be so amateur as to stick charcoal inside me, but you never knew with some people.

He didn't though. Instead, he took one stick of charcoal out and held it lightly, poised to draw on my skin. Tilting his head to one side, he took me in.

"You aren't finished yet," he said, more to himself than to me. "But how will I know when enough is enough?"

I could have told him that sometimes you never do, but then he lowered the charcoal to my belly and began to write. Not draw. Write.

The tip of the stick tickled me, and it was all I could do to stifle my giggles as he dragged it over my stomach, dipping it inside my navel, letting it wander and swirl around my hip. Swift cursive letters flowed into each other as he scrawled something across my flesh, branding me with who knew what. Then his other hand alighted on my pussy and without preamble he pushed his way inside. I was slick and wet and ready, but it still surprised me, and I gasped.

"Don't move," he said. "You will make the letters all wobbly."

Curling his finger inside me, he ran the pad over the sweet, aching spot at the top of my tight passage that I knew could make me come. Technically. I technically knew that. I'd never had an orgasm from that before. I wanted to see if he knew how to do it.

"'I have gone out,'" he said suddenly, his voice rich and dark as he rubbed his finger in circles over my g-spot, making my toes curl and my back arch. "'A possessed witch, haunting the black air, braver at night.'"

Something began to build deep in my belly. A heaviness that I had never felt before. It was almost uncomfortable, a dark, lurking experience, waiting to be released, and I couldn't stop it. The circling of his finger inside me was relentless. I quivered and quaked around it, knowing that he could give me things I'd never known.

The charcoal continued down my thigh. "'Dreaming evil,'" he murmured slowly, and I realized he was writing the words on me. I could barely concentrate on his voice. The thunder of blood in my ears was almost too much for me to bear. It was a poem I had never heard before, but it sent the hairs on the back of my neck on end even as my body twisted and thrashed, out of my control. The terrifying feeling in my belly mounted, growing larger and larger. I didn't know how much more I could take.

"Malcolm," I pleaded, my voice shuddering in my chest. My arms had come down, of their own volition, and crossed over my breasts. I cupped them in my hands, rubbing my palms absently over my nipples as my lower lip found its way between my teeth.

His hand stilled and I cried out, bereft. "No speaking," he commanded. His dark cherry wood eyes had fixated on the flesh of my inner thigh and the tip of his charcoal stick poised there. I bit down hard on my lip and waited, trembling, for his indulgence. The hum of the plane was all around us, under my back, in my bones. At some point we had broken above the clouds and sunlight poured in through the windows, spilling across the cream and gold and mahogany interior. Warm light touched my shoulder, and I realized that I had finally escaped the cold. I was surprised my skin wasn't incandescent with the fire Malcolm stoked in me.

At last he began to write again, and his finger picked up its magical rhythm. "'I have gone out," he repeated, his eyes wandering over my nude body, marked and branded as his own, "'a possessed witch, haunting the black air, braver at night. Dreaming evil, I have done my hitch over the plain houses...'" My release began to coil within me again, hard and tight, and I struggled to hold my body still, the way he had asked me to. The charcoal left off suddenly, then alighted on my elbow where it lay against my ribcage as I cupped my breasts in the palms of my hands. "'Light by light,'" he whispered, and another finger slipped inside me, "'lonely thing... twelve-fingered...'" A third inside, and then he picked up the pace, slamming his fingertips into the soft yielding mound inside me, and I tried not to cry with the unbearable delight of it.

He crawled over my body, let the charcoal reach my forehead. "'Out of mind,'" he murmured. Then he dropped the charcoal stick on the carpet by my head and moved his newly freed hand down to my pelvis. There he laid a heavy palm across me and began to work my tight cunt as vigorously as if he were feeling the same mounting pleasure and needed it just as badly as I did. Faster and faster he went, and my body left me behind in the dust. My brain became blank as every muscle within me tightened and coiled around his fingers, a dark wave swelling up inside me, threatening to take me over, wash over me and drag me out to sea.

"Come, Sadie," he whispered fiercely then. "Come for me."

I broke.

The black wave of pleasure crashed into me, bowling me over, sweeping me under. I became lost inside it as it filled me up. I shrieked, terrified, transformed, just a blaze of light and heat on the floor of his private jet. The staff may have heard me. I couldn't say. Everything melted away and I writhed and thrashed, my body jumping and leaping on the carpet as though I had been struck by lightning.

It felt as though I had.

The sensation drew out, longer and longer as he pounded his fingers inside me, holding me down by my hips until at last I began to cry from the intensity, the incredible, wonderful, mind-altering force of it.

At last he stopped plumbing me, and I sank down to the carpet, my body slick with sweat. I gasped staring at the ceiling of the plane while the hum of the engines filled my head.

Malcolm let his fingers slip from my tight passage and moved up, covering my body with his own. Hiking my legs around his waist, he cradled me against him as I panted, exhausted and fulfilled. His lips brushed over my ear.

"'I have gone out,'" he said, voice low and rough with arousal, "'a possessed witch, haunting the black air, braver at night. Dreaming evil, I have donned my hitch over the plain houses, light by light: lonely thing, twelve-fingered, out of mind...'"

Pulling back, his eyes drifted up to my own, and he held me with his gaze. "'A woman like that is not a woman, quite,'" he murmured. "'I have been her kind.'"

I bit my lip and tried to catch my breath. "What... what was that?"

"Anne Sexton," he said. He watched me, his eyes burning with desire. "After I bought you at the auction, I thought I might become a poet as well." He smiled as though this were a far sillier notion than becoming a tortured artist. "I was very drunk at the time. Poets are notoriously drunk, you see, and I thought it would be perfect. I have never written poetry before, though, so I went looking for a poem or two to describe you. I found that one."

Releasing the hold of his hand on my shoulder, he moved it down again, between our bodies and then ran his fingers over my slit, sending another shudder of bone-shattering pleasure rocking through me.

"A twelve-fingered witch?" I said, grasping at rationality.

"A singular woman, unbound by society," he corrected me. "You exist outside of all things."

For some reason, tears stung my eyes. I felt that way sometimes. Often. I felt that way *often.* How did he know?

"Or perhaps," he said, his smile growing, "I just felt as though you had laid a spell on me."

I rolled my eyes and he laughed. The bulge of his

cock, covered in rough denim, rocked against my slick entrance as he did so, and I realized that perhaps he understood me better than I'd ever thought. He'd struck at the heart of me with his poem, revealed sides of me I hadn't known existed with his art. Cradled against him, I felt strangely small and vulnerable.

Lowering his head, he captured my lips in a slow, sensuous kiss, his tongue reminding me that it loved to give me pleasure as well. I returned the kiss, hard and insistent, as though I wanted to fight him, and it made him laugh. One hand tangled in my hair as he slipped his other arm beneath me and scooped me up, rocking back onto his heels and holding me around him. Too spent by the orgasm he had given me, I collapsed against him, my arms moving around his shoulders, limp and weak.

For a long while, he kissed me, and I let him, too tired to do anything but let him. He could have done anything he wanted with me—dressed me up in a clown wig and a tutu for all I cared—and I couldn't have put up a fight. In my brain, the realization that I had put myself completely at his mercy without ever feeling the bite of a rope against my skin was, intellectually, a bit jarring, but I felt no emotions about it at all. So what? If he did crazy things like *that* to me, I really had no objection.

After a bit he pulled away. "You seem tired," he said, smiling. "Perhaps you would like to take a nap before we get to Croatia?"

"Oh," I said, "I hate sleeping on planes. It's always so uncomfortable." Well, except for that one time to Barbados with Felicia. First class. My god. The *seats*. I'd been a class traitor and I hadn't been able to care, what with the champagne and the seats that sort of became beds. It had been crazy. Also? Fucking steak for dinner. That had been a good time.

But Malcolm was smiling, his dark brown eyes crinkling at the edges. "Oh?" he said. "But you have never slept on *my* plane before." Gently he set me down and stood up, helping me to my shaking feet. His clothes were streaked with paint and charcoal, and so was I.

We're rubbing off on each other, I thought, and giggled.

Placing a warm arm around my shoulders, he guided me to the back of the plane, where a wood paneled wall stood. An unobtrusive door was set into it, and he opened it to reveal...

...a bedroom.

Oh *my*.

"This is *decadent,"* I said.

"Not even the best part," he told me. "See that?" He pointed to a door set into the back of the bedroom. "Through there is a shower. Hot water. Massage head. Would you like to try it?"

I looked down at myself, covered in paint and charcoal. "Don't you want to take a picture of your masterpiece?" I asked.

I felt the surprise radiate from him. "This?" he said. "This isn't my masterpiece. A thumbnail sketch, at best."

Jesus, I thought. The masterpiece might very well give me a heart attack if this had been a thumbnail sketch. I took a deep breath and moved away from him. He let his hand fall from my shoulder. "Yeah," I said. "Then a shower would be great."

"Wonderful," he said. "I'll leave you to it, if you don't mind. You have given me some lovely ideas and

I'd like to write them down before we land."

I nodded, and he reached out, capturing my hand. Pressing a kiss to the back, he bowed to me before backing out of the bedroom, a smile on his face.

As soon as the door clicked closed I wanted to collapse, but I was afraid of getting his jet any more dirty than I'd already made it, even though he clearly didn't care about its interior. Stumbling to the door in the back, I let myself into the bathroom.

And it *was* a bathroom. Utterly decadent. I felt like a jerk just standing in it, but I wasn't about to let a good hot shower go to waste. I turned the water on and stepped inside.

For a long while I stood in the hot spray, watching the water run black and brilliant as the pigments on my skin washed down the drain, until finally it ran clear. Only then did I use the luxurious soap and wash myself. By the time I was done the water was running cold, and I shivered as I stepped out and wrapped myself in a large, fluffy towel that had been sitting on a heated towel rack. I took the opportunity to relieve myself before stepping into the bedroom.

Someone—Malcolm perhaps, but probably a private and discreet in-flight steward—had drawn the shades down on the windows, making it lovely and dim inside the bedroom. The bed stood against one side of the plane, up against the windows, and for a weird moment the thought of sleeping next to a line of windows thirty thousand feet in the air gave me a little thrill of fear, and I realized that if I slept here, I wouldn't have my gun with me.

It'd been years since I'd slept without my gun by my bedside. I always had it. I never stayed over at men's houses. I had to have my gun.

I hadn't thought this through very well...

On the other hand, I didn't think Malcolm was the sort to assault me while I was asleep, seeing as how I was quite willing while I was awake. And it wasn't like someone could just break into a plane, thanks to the aforementioned thirty thousand feet of air between me and the ground. I should be safe.

I didn't really expect to sleep, though. I felt naked. Far more naked than actually being naked felt, which I didn't care about.

I bit my lip, then decided that since I had no idea what was in store for me, I'd better at least try to get some shut eye. Shedding the towel to the floor, because I'm classy like that, I slid under the soft white down comforter and thousand thread-count sheets. The bed was surprisingly warm, and I wrapped myself up in it.

I must have been more tired than I thought, because the moment my head hit the pillow, I passed out.

It was the best sleep I'd ever had.

ꕥ

I *really* had been more tired than I'd thought, because I slept until we landed in Croatia early in the morning the next day. I'd forgotten that we were passing into a whole new time zone. When I opened my eyes, I was reaching for my bedside table as I always did before I realized it was Tuesday, and I was nowhere near New York City.

The thought shocked me and I sat up.

"Oh, you're awake."

I turned my head to see Malcolm sitting in a

buttery leather chair at the other side of the plane, drawing in a sketchbook. Had he been drawing me while I slept? The thought should have creeped me out a bit, but instead I just felt a burning curiosity to see his sketch. I kept my tongue, though. I hated it when people asked to see my rough work. Or loved it. I could never tell. But I didn't want to know if he was good or bad at it. It would ruin the illusion he had built up around himself, a brilliant man capable of anything.

I wanted to believe in that. I'd been disappointed in too many men before. I wanted to live the fantasy just a few days longer.

While I'd slept, Malcolm had changed into a beautiful pair of slacks, another incredible sweater, and a jacket that was far too fashionable for a man of his age. But he made it look good. He worked it. I realized I was still naked. Behind him, one of the window shades had been pulled up, presumably to give him some light to work by, and I saw the runway outside. Mountains hulked beyond it.

"I need to get dressed," I said.

"Your clothes will be here soon," he replied. "I will be very upset if they are not." He continued sketching in his book. He looked like he actually knew what he was doing. For a moment I watched him, the light from outside illuminating his beautiful face, all planes and angles and hidden strength. The sun on his hair gleamed golden, and I longed to run my fingers through it, but before I could gather up the energy to act on the impulse, the door opened and a young woman entered, carrying an armful of clothes.

Immediately I felt shabby. Impeccably dressed and with long, golden hair curled up on her head in an elaborate coiffure, she was gorgeous. Wide blue eyes took me in, assessing, and then laid her burden down on the chair. "Thank you for your patronage," she told Malcolm, her beautiful accent rounded, with sharp ends bracketing each word. Smiling at me, she exited.

"Please," Malcolm said, "get dressed." He closed his sketchbook and leaned back in his chair, steepling his fingers in front of his mouth and fixing his eyes on me. It took me a moment to realize he wasn't going to leave. Instead, he was going to watch me.

I swallowed and stood up, letting the comforter and the warmth of the bed fall away. I shivered a bit in the cooler ambient air, but I threw my shoulders back and padded over to the chair where the pile of clothes threatened to tip over. Reaching out, I began to flip through them.

Every single one was beautiful. Lovely, well-made. And *not fussy*. Thank god. I just hate fussy clothes. Pulling out a dark shirt and holding it up, I realized it was warm cashmere. For a long moment I ran my fingers over it, enjoying the fine texture.

"There's under things in the bag," Malcolm said, his voice startling me. Looking down, I found a discreet bag, colored silver, at my feet, full of tissue paper. Bending over, I peeled back the paper and found a small collection of lacy bras and flimsy panties in bright, startling colors.

Urgh. Colors. I selected the least offensive—a dark indigo-purple—and pulled the panties on before sliding my arms through the straps of the bra and hooking it in back. I tried not to think about Malcolm and his intense eyes watching me get dressed, though I felt a heat light up my cheeks anyway.

But the bra made my tits look amazing. And the indigo complemented my skin, dammit.

I slid the sweater on, then pulled out a white wool skirt from the pile, slipping that on as well. My boots, low-heeled and black, had survived the paintpocalypse, and I slipped those on as well before selecting a gray scarf from the pile and then shrugging into a soft black leather coat covered in pockets. I'm not a fashion girl, but I have to say: I looked *good.*

Malcolm stood, a smile on his face. Without a word, he led me out of the bedroom and to the front of the plane, where he donned his own coat, and then we exited, walking down a stairwell to the runway, like the rich and famous do. I knew Malcolm was technically rich and famous, but it seemed weird to see him surrounded by wealth. His sparse room at the top of his mansion suited him far better than sumptuousness.

We entered a private car, and I watched out the window as we drove from the airport to Dubrovnik.

8

Mediterranean countryside. That was what greeted me. And a crowded Mediterranean city. I hadn't expected these things, I suppose, when I had realized where we were going. Croatia was forever wedded in my mind to Bosnia and Serbia. Mountains and cold, and a war that had happened when I was very young—those were the things I had called up in my mind.

But this place was lovely, by the Adriatic Sea. It was like Rome, or how I imagined Rome to be—I've never been—and it took my breath away.

A castle sat guarding the Old Town of Dubrovnik against the threats of the sea. Red-roofed buildings and ancient stone churches and crowded the streets peeked up at us from the walled city as we rode down toward the sea. Our driver, far more adventurous than any New York cabbie, wove and bobbed between other weaving and bobbing vehicles, until we got down to the wall and I discovered that the old part of town—where we were going, I assumed—was pedestrian only.

Wow, I thought. I didn't have a lot of coherence at that point. I felt like I had stepped into a completely new world, one that I had never even imagined existed. Our driver stopped and we exited the car, Malcolm holding the door for me, murmuring something about how our luggage would be brought behind us, but I wasn't really paying attention. A chill and the smell of the sea wrapped around me, and I huddled up next to Malcolm as he snugged his arm around my shoulders and held me close, gently leading me where he wanted to go.

We passed through the old stone wall and down stone steps to land in a square mostly devoid of people, but filled with gray stone and architectural details and puddles of rain reflecting the patches of blue sky overhead.

"I'm sorry," Malcolm said. "I'd heard it was warmer here this year."

I tried not to look like a tourist as we began a leisurely stroll through the streets. Narrow alleyways peeped at me from between buildings, terraces jutted around corners in the little paths off the main thoroughfare, long stone stairways of a hundred steps flashed here and there. People passed us, dressed beautifully for the cool weather, and fine clothes shone prominently in shop windows.

I was utterly taken. Malcolm had been right. The place appealed to my artistic sense, a city out of time. Another country, where magic might happen.

After a few minutes of walking, Malcolm turned and led me down a narrow alleyway. The old stone buildings reared up around us, stately and imposing, blocking out the sky. A wooden door, ornately carved, was set into the wall with a lovely arch over it. Malcolm pulled a key from his pocket and opened it, gesturing for me to enter.

We climbed the narrow stairs inside, switching back on themselves over and over again, until we reached a door at the top. Malcolm put another key in this door and unlocked it before pushing it open and bowing to me with a flourish.

"Our accommodations, my lady."

I couldn't help but inhale sharply as the rooms beyond were revealed to me. The entire top of the floor of this house was Malcolm's. Blonde wood floor, clean white walls, sparsely populated with furniture... it was how I had imagined his house would look, or how it would look after he was done purging his actual house of *stuff*. It was beautiful, elegantly appointed, and yet somehow also homey. Photographs and works of art hung on the walls here, too, though they clustered and didn't sprawl over every available space. A wall of windows, barely concealed by flowing sheer white curtains, opened out onto a terrace. I crossed the floor and peered out.

"Oh, *wow,*" I had to say.

The red roofs of Dubrovnik's old town swept down and away from us, and I could catch a glimpse of the gray winter sea beyond the castle walls. In the summer, this place would be stunning. As it was, I wanted to make myself a cup of hot tea, wrap myself in a blanket, and just stare out at the sea from the comfort of the warm penthouse, curled up on the white overstuffed couch facing the windows. Maybe read a good book. Maybe write one.

Maybe draw a bit.

"This is exactly what I needed," I said to Malcolm.

"Yes, I thought you might," he replied. "I am glad I brought you here."

I turned and studied him. He seemed very pleased with himself, a beautiful smile gracing his full lips, his sandy hair falling in messy locks against his forehead and curling over his ears and the collar of his jacket. He was still a mystery to me... but a mystery that I was content with for now.

"Did you plan this?" I asked. It was stupid, but he seemed to have known just what was in my heart, even when I didn't know it myself. I was being stifled by the city, by my responsibilities. He'd *seen* that.

My heart gave a little flutter. *Stop that nonsense,* I told it, but it didn't listen to my brain. It never did. I turned back to the sea so Malcolm wouldn't detect the sudden, disquieting turmoil in my chest.

"I didn't quite plan it," he said, coming up behind me. His hands slid over my shoulders, his fingertips brushing against my neck and through my hair as he helped me out of my coat. "I've been wanting to... get away for a while. And I decided I wanted to take you with me. Yesterday. I thought it would be fun. Though I didn't think that we would be coming here so soon."

My leather jacket slid down my arms and he tossed it onto the couch. Turning, I smoothed my palms over his chest, under his own coat, sliding my hands up and over his shoulders, slipping the fabric from his body. He felt good and warm. I had the sudden impulse to lean forward and press my forehead into his chest and just let him cradle me in his arms. "And why did we come here today? Why not next week?" I looked up at him.

His dark cherry wood eyes bored into mine. His

fingers found their way to my scalp, running through my hair.

"Because I didn't want to lose you," he said. "Whatever line I crossed, I wanted you to know I was sorry. I don't want to cross it again, until you tell me it's all right."

For a terrible moment I thought I might cry.

"Shut up," I told him. "Can we please just fuck now?"

His mouth broke into a grin. "You are so eager," he said. "And yes. We are going to fuck. I think it might be my masterpiece. Let me show you how."

I wanted to fuck *him,* not just fuck him as part of his art, but the way he said the word *fuck,* lingering on the *f* and drawing it out before cutting it off abruptly had gone straight down my spine to my pussy.

I had it bad for Malcolm Ward. I didn't like it, but, well, can you blame me?

Linking his fingers with mine, Malcolm led me away from the windows, through the kitchen and dining area, and then around the corner where a piano sat in a room lined with bookcases and full of books. Then we turned and circled to the back of the flat, into a narrow hallway. At the end of it I saw a large, open room with a bed in it. The master bedroom. Two other doors in the hall were open, letting light from the small windows fall inside, and we entered one.

It had been turned into a studio. A sculpting studio.

It looked remarkably like Felicia's studio, except there were no tables of tools, only a large lump of red clay in the middle of a plastic tarp in the middle of the floor with two buckets of water beside it. Wet towels mostly covered the clay, and the air in the room was almost uncomfortably warm. I stood just inside the door, wondering how badly my clothes would be ruined this time. It would be a shame; they were so new and so lovely...

But then Malcolm turned and reached out, his fingers gathering the hem of my sweater, and gently he pulled it over my head, revealing my new bra. Reaching around, he unhooked the back of the bra, and slid it down my arms, leaving me topless as he moved his hands to my waist and fiddled with the hook and zipper enclosure on my wool skirt. I realized that he had watched me dress in the plane so that he would know how to undress me.

He was good. I was glad he was good.

The wool skirt slipped to the floor, and he knelt down in front of me again, removing my boots before hooking his thumbs into my panties and sliding them down my legs, until I stood naked before him, vulnerable and trembling, needy and filled with desire. I wanted him to touch me so badly. I wanted to touch him so badly.

He stood.

"Undress me, Sadie," he commanded.

Yes, I thought. God, yes.

I wasn't as methodical as he was. My hands shook as I assisted him out of the soft cashmere sweater he wore, trembled as I helped him shuck the fine cotton undershirt. I reached his trousers and undid them, my fingers brushing against the growing bulge that I'd never touched directly. It excited me like nothing else ever had. I wanted him inside me, pumping and fucking, until we both couldn't stand.

I moved his trousers over his hips, taking the

opportunity to finally run my hands over his ass, letting my fingers take an illicit squeeze before moving on. He wore boxers beneath his pants, and his erection was now full and hard, straining against the fabric. I swallowed, wanting to take it into my mouth, just to taste him. I wondered what he would taste like. Would his precum be sweet or salty? Would he leap and harden further in my mouth? Would he grab my hair, or let me lead him?

I untied his fine leather shoes and helped him slip his feet from them before gently peeling his socks off. He had startlingly beautiful feet, I realized. Well formed, not hairy. Warm. Well taken care of. I let my fingers wander over his toes for just a moment before assisting him out of his other shoe and sock. Then I slipped his trousers from his legs and he stepped out of them, standing before me only in his underwear, his cock beneath his boxers hard and ready for me.

I licked my lips and reached up, grabbing the waistband of his boxers and dragging them down his hips.

His cock leaped out at me, proud and tall, long and thick, and I almost moaned at the sight, imagining it inside me. He was well-groomed down there, and I found myself smiling. The dark, clean smell of his skin hit me, and I leaned forward and buried my face in the soft flesh of his testicles, inhaling deeply. He smelled good, like soap and cock. I opened my mouth and took one ball past my lips, sucking on it gently, and above me he cried out, his strong, muscled legs trembling.

I reveled in my power, nipping and licking his balls, feeling the weight of them on my tongue, but avoiding his cock, even as it strained toward me, aching for my touch. He'd kept me away from him for quite long enough, I thought, he could stand a few moments of teasing. Payback is a delicious bitch goddess from hell, and she gives great head.

His fingers wound through my hair, but he didn't try to guide me, only cradled my skull in his hands, as though he wanted to reassure himself that I was real. I smoothed my palms over his straining thighs, and then, finally, I sat up and licked the clear, gleaming jewel of precum from the head of his cock.

"Oh," he said. "Sadie." And there was such wonder in his voice that I was afraid to look up into his face. What intensity of emotion would I see there? I wondered. And was I ready to confront it? Ready to accept it?

I'm a coward. Instead, I opened my mouth wide, slid my tongue under the head of his cock, and forced myself to swallow all of him.

God, he was huge. I felt the soft head of his shaft pulsing at the back of my throat even as I fought not to gag on it. He was long, and wide, and when at last my nose came to rest against the base of his penis I was trembling with the effort of it. I could only hold it for a moment before retreating, but it was enough for Malcolm, it seemed. When I reached the base of his cock, he groaned, his fingers tightening in my hair, his legs faltering, and when I drew back he did so as well, popping his thick cock out of my mouth quickly as though I had already overwhelmed him.

Reaching down, he pulled me to my feet, his dark eyes burning, and then he put his arms around me and pulled me to him, skin to skin. His flesh burned against mine, his cock pressed into my belly, wet with saliva and so close to my aching entrance that I thought I would die if he didn't push his way inside me *right now*. I slid my hands over his hot body, feeling the quiver of his muscles and the sweet, tight tension inside him.

This was going to happen. Like, *really* going to happen.

His lips found my ear. "Let me fuck you," he whispered gruffly. "Let me come in you. Nod if you consent."

I couldn't have shaken my head for the world. Mouth dry, pussy wet, I nodded and closed my eyes.

Malcolm kissed my earlobe, and then let his tongue gently tickle the inner folds of my ear, his breath hot and harsh inside my head. My skin dissolved into shivers as he gave my belly a nudge with his cock, clearly wanting to be inside me now, but under my hands I felt him trembling, holding himself back. He wanted to fuck me badly, but he wanted to do it properly.

A hot kiss landed on the pulse point in my throat, where my jugular leaped with anticipation. Quickly, frantically, he placed burning kisses down my throat, drawing moans from my mouth as he reached up and cupped one breast in his hand before descending upon it and sucking my nipple into his hot, wet mouth. I cried out, holding on tight to him, as though I would fall apart at any moment and he was the only thing keeping me together. "Malcolm," I moaned as he nipped and nibbled at me.

He made an indistinct grunt of pure desire before dragging his fingers over the flesh of my back, massaging the muscles there and releasing the tension imprisoned in them. I cried out and quaked as his hands found my ass, squeezing and massaging, molding them together and pulling them apart. My quivering pussy lips opened and closed, and I ached deep inside, needing the pressure of his cock.

Then he broke away and twined his fingers with mine again, leading me over to the pile of clay beneath the wet towels that kept it pliable. Turning me to face him, he lifted me up onto the clay as easily as though I were a child, and I suddenly realized what he meant to do. He meant to fuck on the clay.

Clay as a medium is alive. Every push, every pull of it is recorded within the clay. A true record of the artist. And we were going to fuck on it. Whatever we did would be recorded forever on its surface.

The thought inflamed me and I opened my legs wide. Malcolm reached between them and ran his long finger over my slit, probing my wet, slick entrance. Then he reached around me and laid me back, gently letting me splay out across the clay. The warm air of the room caressed me, the warm damp towels beneath me were delightful, as though I were at a spa, about to be pushed and kneaded into bliss. And I was, I realized. Malcolm bent his sandy head to my pussy and gave me a lick and a kiss, as though saying hello to an old friend, then slid his hands over the backs of my thighs and lifted my legs into the air.

"Are you ready, Sadie?" he asked. "Nod if yes."

I nodded vigorously. I ached and quivered, needing him. It was almost surreal in that moment, knowing that I was going to get what I knew I had wanted from that first moment our eyes met across a crowded room. So corny. But true.

I closed my eyes and bit my lip as I felt him move between my legs. The soft, wet head of his cock slotted against my entrance, as though it were made for me, and then, slowly, he entered me.

It was bliss.

I cried out as he did it, my body curling and twisting, and I had to force myself to hold still, to relax and take the full girth and length of him. Three times he had to pause and pull back before gently pushing forward again, filling me up slowly, letting me become adjusted to his invasion. I wanted him to fuck me fast and hard, but I also didn't want this moment to end. I wanted him to enter me for the first time forever. I felt him inside me, and nothing else was real. In, out. In further, out. In, out, slow, steady, until at last I finally felt his pelvis run up against my soaked pussy lips and he was buried inside me.

For a long moment, we stayed that way, trembling with the sensation of each other. I was full to the brim, his thick, long cock brushing against something inside me I'd never felt before. It felt strange, but also delicious. I didn't want to move, because I knew if I moved we would fuck, and I knew that when we started, we would eventually stop.

But I wanted him inside me always. I wanted this feeling, this fullness. I needed it. I hadn't known I'd needed it until this moment.

At last I moaned and twisted, impaled on his body, my hands reaching up to my hair, tangling in it as I tried to comprehend the fullness of him.

"Ah, Sadie," he whispered. "I love to see you writhe and thrash. Let me make you scream."

"Yes," I begged back.

It was a surprise this time, when he flicked my nipple with his finger, but the pain and pleasure speared through me and I shrieked, my hips thrusting into him, and then he pulled out and pushed in, and we were fucking like animals.

His hips pounded into mine, small grunts escaping the back of his throat as he fucked me, and I was helpless under his assault. I moaned and writhed, my hands scrabbling for purchase on the clay, the towels slipping and sliding under me. I reached back and tried to dig in, feeling the clay give way under my grip as he plunged his cock deep inside me. Each time he bottomed out inside me the tip of his cock brushed over that sweet little spot that I hadn't even known existed and I shrieked. My head tossed as his fingers dug into my hips, my back arched. Beneath me the clay became more volatile, moving and slippery, like mud.

Then, reaching down, Malcolm began to rip away the towels, exposing the warm clay to the air, and I reached out and dug my fingers into it, feeling it cake beneath my fingernails as I held on for dear life while his thrusts became wild and uncontrolled.

"Fuck, Sadie," he grunted. "You feel too good."

I wanted to tell him there was no such thing, but I felt the same way. He was too good, frighteningly so. Humans weren't meant to feel this way, I thought, the part of me that hid under all my brashness, my crudities, my artistic flairs whispering its insecurities in my ear. Something this good can't last. Something this wonderful is not meant for you.

I bit my lip as Malcolm abruptly pulled out, and I felt the loss of him inside me so sharply I almost screamed No, but I didn't. He didn't want me speaking. I wanted to give him what he wanted. Everything he did to me was exactly what I needed, even though I hadn't known what it was.

Tugging on my hips, he pulled me from the block

of clay and removed the last of the towels before assisting me back onto it, on my hands and knees. His hands were large and warm on my skin, and as he took up his position behind me I braced myself. The clay moved under me. It resisted, but it moved.

Oh, I thought.

His cock found my pussy and slid inside again, an easy entrance this time. His hips picked up a quick, sharp pace, and I cried out, my limbs suddenly trembling with the effort of staying upright on the slick clay. Streaks of red earth traced paths over my skin when I slipped and fell, scraping my elbows and arms over the clay, but Malcolm didn't let up. Within minutes we had worn a groove into the sculpture with the force of our fucking and my arms and hands were caked with clay.

Sliding out again, he helped me down. My pussy pounded with my heartbeat and I felt the sweet beginnings of a powerful orgasm building in my belly. God, he was beautiful, I realized as I stood and watched him climb onto the clay himself, settling down on his back, his cock, slick with the juices of my cunt, jutting proudly in the air. He looked like one of those Greek statues, well balanced, perfectly proportioned, ready to leap into battle, throw a javelin, triumph over Persians or whatever, I didn't care and I could barely think as he extended one hand toward me, his beautiful dark eyes smiling, burning into my skin, his fingers awaiting my own.

I put my hand in his, and he helped me up onto the clay, bracing me as I swung a leg over his hips and stared down at him, stunning and mysterious, flawless and obscured. He was a work of art, too, I realized. Very much so. We were two very different kinds of art, mating and making a third. A sacred coupling, a symbolic procreation. My heart hurt for some reason, thinking of the clay beneath us as the product of our union. Had he thought through those implications, or was he only pursuing me in his own roundabout way, unsure how to deal with the things I inspired in him, putting a layer between us as he tried to connect with me?

His hands gripped my hips and guided me over his cock. Slowly I slid down onto his erection, panting and trembling as he filled me again. When at last we were flush with each other, he reached up and smoothed his hands over my ribs, trailing his fingertips up my spine. He lingered on the ink in my flesh, sending shivers out over my body, but he didn't seem to be startled by the scars I had hidden well with my designs, and he certainly didn't remark upon them. He was a gentleman like that.

Streaks of red clay traced across both of us now, and I felt tiny balls of it rolling between his skin and mine where he touched me. The smell of wet, sweet earth and fucking surrounded us.

I licked my lips, waiting for him to instruct me.

"Sadie," he said at last. "Ride me until you come."

He didn't have to tell me twice. Bracing myself on his shoulders, I angled my pussy over his cock and began to ride him. Under me, he arched and thrust in time, a perfect partner in our dance. His legs rose up, pushed down, and beneath us the clay began to give way, molding around us as we fucked.

His hands were everywhere on me as I rode him, squeezing my ass, cupping my breasts, scratching down my arms until abruptly he took over again, turning me under him, but by now the clay beneath us had been fucked away into a new form, and we twisted and braced against it, our hands scrabbling for purchase as I moaned and he plunged into me over and over, driving me relentlessly toward the release I needed. I didn't know what to do, my toes curling, my body winding up into a ball of pure need. His cock in my cunt pounded out a raw, primal rhythm, but his body as it arched over me, thrust into me, was poetic, classical. His muscles quivered under his skin and I ran my hands over them, feeling them bunch and pull, shift and slip. My core tightened, drew in, and I bore down on him, straining and reaching for my orgasm as the wet clay slipped and slid beneath my back. I groaned, pushing back, clinging, aching.

"Come, Sadie," Malcolm whispered to me. "Come and take me with you."

I cried out, my eyes flying open. I saw everything so clearly—his sweat-sheened face, his hard, pumping body, the play of light and shadow on the ceiling, the bright streaks of earthy red slathered over our skin like war paint. The sea wind rattled against the windows, his flesh slapped against mine, his breath grunted in his throat as he fucked me, and his eyes...

His eyes were dark and vulnerable and so achingly needy that I had to look away. When I did, he bent his head to my throat, opened his lips against the flesh there, and sucked my pulse into his mouth.

I came.

I felt as though my body sucked him inside, bearing down so hard I was afraid I would hurt him, but instead of pain he grunted in surprise and pleasure, and then his hips stuttered in their rhythm, bucking wild, and deep inside my core gushed hot spurts of his seed, pushing into me, his seal, his brand, his mark, his signature on me, making me his. I came silently as he pumped into me, my mouth an open sob of pleasure, and this time instead of breaking apart I felt as though he were putting me back together, his arms and legs curling around me as we orgasmed together, and together we slid down the mound of clay and he strove to wrap me up inside his body, even as my legs hugged his waist. His face was still buried in my throat, his breathing ragged and harsh on my skin, and I reveled in the feel of it dragging over my flesh.

At last he pulled away, but he only pulled back far enough to rest his forehead against mine. We still breathed in time with each other, our hearts in sync, and I closed my eyes, still trembling around his softening cock.

"Sadie..." His voice startled me in the quiet room, and I opened my eyes again to see him looking at me. Leaning in, he kissed me, lightly, then pulled away again. "Thank you," he said.

"Oh," I told him. "Don't mention it. Any time."

He threw his head back and laughed at that before pulling me close again and covering me in kisses, and I wrapped my arms tight around him and reveled in it.

ꕤ

We were a mess, covered in red clay and sweat and pussy juice and cum. Malcolm led me to the bathroom next to the studio room, and together we took a long, luxurious shower. He soaped me up, his hands smoothing over my skin as he gently cleaned me, and the water ran dark with clay as it sloughed from our skin. His fingers found my sore pussy lips and soothed them gently, stoking the fire inside me that burned for him until it was blazing once again.

I couldn't get enough of him. I hungered, dark and deep, for him to fill me up. I certainly didn't love him. I'd only known him for four days. But I *wanted* to love him. I *wanted* to fall in love with him. I hadn't fallen in love with anyone in years. And Malcolm... he was so promising. I almost believed he might love me back.

At the very least, however, he made my body sing, and I made him laugh. It was enough for now. When at last he turned the water off, his cock was hard as a diamond again, and he led me out of the bathroom, dried me in a towel as though I were a child, then scooped me up and carried me into the master bedroom. It was white walls and splashes of blue and dark wood floor, but I really couldn't be bothered to note it all as he tossed me down onto the down-filled comforter and slid my legs open, his eager mouth descending on my quivering pussy until I begged him to fuck me, which he did. The chill of the winter outside had crept in through the windows of the bedroom, and together we snuggled down and screwed, our muffled moans a soft duet beneath the covers.

I don't know how many times I came, or how many times he came, only that eventually I fell asleep, cradled against him, my thighs slick with our coupling. The last thing I thought of was how much I wanted to bang him on the terrace outside of the living room, and then I passed out.

~

Sex is a powerful drug. I slept hard and soundly

until the sky was darkening with the coming evening, and when I awoke I found myself reaching for my bedside table again. This time, however, I remembered where I was and turned over.

Malcolm was still wiped out. He slept like a baby, deep and serene, and when I realized I was watching him sleep I had to shake myself out of it. What was I, some mooning teenager? Slipping out of bed, I peeked in the closet and found a huge fluffy white robe. Wrapping it around myself, I padded back down the hallway to the main part of the house. I didn't look at our work of art. I wanted to imagine it a little while longer.

Stepping into the dining room, I winced as my stomach rumbled. I hadn't had anything to eat in... forever, it seemed. I moved to the refrigerator and opened it, but was disappointed to find only a few fine bottles of white wine.

Well, I thought, *it's probably after five, right?* I drew one out, located a corkscrew in the drawers, and opened it. The tang of alcohol tickled my nose and made my mouth water. I smiled as I pulled down a glass from one of the cabinets. I was pretty sure Europe was all about the wine, so when in Dubrovnik, do as... well, whatever. I was going to be in big trouble with just wine in my stomach, but I couldn't really bring myself to care. I poured a glass and moved to the windows, staring out at the quiet city and the iron-gray winter sea. I sipped wine, then gulped it. I've never been known for my moderation. I poured another glass and started on that one.

A ringing bell caught my attention. A phone.

Frowning, I turned around, scanning the room before I spied a pile of luggage—Jesus, was all that ours?—with Malcolm's jacket folded neatly across it. The sound was coming from it. Already tipsy as hell I tottered across the living room and spent precious seconds hunting through Malcolm's pockets before I located his phone just as the person on the other end of the line hung up.

Damn, I thought. But then the phone lit up again almost immediately, the ringtone loud in the quiet of the penthouse. In bold letters on the screen, the name Don Cardall shone out. It meant nothing to me.

I wavered and after a few rings the call went to voicemail. I had no problem with that, as I wasn't ever a fan of people answering my own phone--safely tucked away in my purse at the base of the tower of luggage, thank god--but when the home screen popped up I saw that Malcolm had seventy-eight missed calls.

Seventy. Eight.

Holy shit, I thought. This might be kind of important.

For a second I stood in the living room, trying to decide what to do. On the one hand, I wasn't Malcolm's personal secretary or anything like that, and we'd only known each other for a few days. I should, technically, go wake him up so he could field whatever emergency had popped up back home. On the other hand, I really wanted to stay here and just fuck the next few days away. Maybe drink some good liquor, eat some good food. Bone some more. Especially on that terrace... Perhaps I should just answer and see who was calling and what sort of fire Malcolm had to put out before bothering him. He looked exhausted. I didn't really want to disturb the first good sleep I was betting he'd had since we met. I didn't think he'd slept on the plane, and since he'd been forgetting to eat I didn't exactly trust him to take care of himself in my absence. I took another gulp of wine and pondered, and then the decision was made for me when the phone lit up again. Don Cardall once more. He was very persistent. I was willing to bet he was at least half of those missed calls.

Oh, I thought, *very well.* I hit answer.

"Malcolm Ward's phone," I said, very cool and sophisticated. "May I ask who's calling?"

"Fuck you, this is a fucking emergency!" Don Cardall spat at the other end of the line. "Where the *fuck* is Mr. Ward?"

9

One and a half glasses of wine on a very empty stomach did not make me the most delicate of people. "He's in a sex coma," I snapped, all my good sex vibes falling away and my typical crankiness reasserting itself. "Who is this?"

"No, you tell me who the hell *you* are and you put Mr. Ward on the phone right goddamn now."

Damn, this dude was rude to someone he'd never met. "I'm Sadie MacElroy," I said. Then, because I thought I could perhaps parlay it into some sort of social currency: "Mrs. Anton Waters' personal assistant."

At the other end of the line, Don was quiet for a moment, clearly reassessing the situation. *Yes!* I thought. Finally that stupid job came in handy for something other than boring shit like keeping food on the table and a roof over my head.

"I apologize, Miss MacElroy," Don finally said, his voice now stiff and formal, "but I am Mr. Ward's secretary. I hope you will understand that this is an emergency and put Mr. Ward on the line."

Ah. The secretary to whom Malcolm had given over the reins of the company. I could sympathize. I really could. It was always a frantic day when something big had gone down and you couldn't contact your boss. I know this because it happened frequently when Felicia and Anton decided to go on a sex retreat, although now that I came to think of it I was obviously not any better, seeing as how I had skipped work--and town--to screw some virtual stranger's brains out. And I didn't even have the excuse of being in a relationship with him.

Still. I didn't really want to wake Malcolm up. It was probably midnight in New York now. I'd been missing from my job for a whole day at this point. I probably had a million messages, too. Ugh.

I wavered for another moment, and then gave in. "All right, just a second," I said. "I'll go see if I can wake him up."

"Thank you," Don said. I hit the hold button and tottered back to the bedroom. That wine was really hitting me hard.

Malcolm lay on the bed in the same position I'd left him in. I hated to wake him up. But this was probably really important. I hoped he hadn't skipped out on some kind of life or death deal to bone me in Croatia. I mean, that's flattering and all, but I understand priorities, too. Reaching out, I put my hand on Malcolm's shoulder.

"Malcolm?" I whispered.

He slept on.

I gave him a little shake.

He continued to sleep. He was out.

"Malcolm," I said a little louder, but he might as

well have been a lump of clay for all the response I got from him. I shook him harder, then moved over to my side of the bed and began to jump up and down on it. "Wake up!" I commanded him.

He snorted, stirred, then turned over and slipped back down into dreamland.

Jesus. He was completely exhausted. I turned the phone back on.

"I'm sorry," I said. "He is completely passed out."

"Shake him!"

"I did. I even jumped on the bed and kind of yelled at him. He won't wake up."

In New York, I could hear Don pondering this as he felt the icy hand of termination creeping up on him. "Did you check to see if he's breathing?"

All right, forget the rudeness. No one treats me like an idiot. "Oh gosh, no," I said, "I'm just a dumb girl and I can't tell the difference between a living body and corpse. Asshole."

"Fine," he snapped. "You tell him I called the second he wakes up. This is an emergency, and he needs to be in New York as soon as possible. Wait, where is he, anyway?"

"You're his secretary," I said. "Didn't he tell you?"

I knew that would rankle him. "Tell me where he is!"

"Sheepfuckistan," I said, and hung up.

It was the wine. I swear.

Not knowing what else to do, I walked out of the bedroom and back to the living room, putting Malcolm's phone on top of his coat before pouring myself another glass of wine and glancing around. A TV sat against the wall. *Bingo*, I thought. I located the remote and settled down with my bottle of wine.

ꕥ

I was good and drunk by the time Malcolm stumbled out into the living room, wearing only a pair of silk pajama bottoms. His sex-messed hair and evening wood had me thinking dirty, drunken thoughts, and when he kissed me good evening I leaned into his lips and it felt like falling.

"I see you've located the wine," he said. He took the bottle from my hand—now only a third full—and wandered into the kitchen, grabbing a glass for himself. "I thought we'd go out to dinner. Do you like seafood?"

"I love seafood," I said. "*Ljubav.* Love. Love, love, love."

He took a sip of wine and raised his eyebrows at me. "You speak Croatian?" he asked.

"Hell no," I said, "I've just been watching Croatian music videos. You can figure out some words from pop songs, because pop songs are the same in every language. All about love and crying and hearts and stuff." I gestured drunkenly at the television as it flashed a gorgeous, fresh-faced Slavic girl at me, her perfect voice caressing the words as they flowed out of her mouth. I loved it. I love everything when I drink wine. I even loved Malcolm Ward, although I wasn't *in love* with him. I loved him deeply, though, because he was a fellow traveler on this road of life and all that shit. I'm a soppy drunk.

"You're drunk," Malcolm said.

"Yup," I replied. "There wasn't any food in the apartment."

"True." He seemed amused. "I'm going to make a

few calls and see who wants to give us a private dinner."

Calls, I thought. There was something about calls that I was supposed to remember, wasn't there? Calls, calls, calls...

Oh, shit, I realized. Malcolm's horrible asshole secretary! He needed to call him back. And I'd answered the phone...

Oh dear. I shouldn't have done that, should I? Well, I was about to be found out, because he was going to turn on his phone and then he'd see all those missed calls and the answered one would be in the record and I'd better confess right now—

But Malcolm wasn't going for his cell phone. He was instead lifting a handset off the wall and dialing out. Oh my god, a land line! This really *was* the Old Town. I giggled to myself as Malcolm spoke to the person on the other end of the line, in French. Surprisingly.

After less than a minute's conversation he hung up. "You speak French?" I said.

"Mais oui." He smiled. "But not as well as I speak German and Japanese. And I certainly don't speak Croatian. I never had the chance to learn. Luckily for me it seems everyone here is multilingual. Dominic knows French best, so I speak to him in French, and he, in turn, laughs at my French. But he will still make the most delectable meal you've ever tasted."

"He will?" I was dubious. I've had some damn good food in the last year or two. And New York is lousy with hole-in-the-wall restaurants that would make a gourmand weep for joy—if you know where to find them.

"Indeed. We should get dressed."

Getting dressed took a little longer than it normally does because I was too drunk to match my clothes up, especially because they were all new and I'd never seen any of them before. In the end, Malcolm dressed me, pouring my drunk ass into a corset and delicate stockings before wrapping me up in fine winter clothes and handing me my purse. His hands on me made me happy and warm, and by the soft kisses he planted on my skin I could tell he felt the same. Coming with him had been a good decision. I was sure of it.

When we finally wandered out into the streets, the city was different than it had been this morning. Lamplight filled the stone world, and the smell of the sea hung sharp and cold in the air. I reveled in it, letting it sober me up a bit as we walked the cobbled streets. Or stone-paved streets. They kept changing under my feet, and it wasn't long before I was completely turned around and lost. All I knew was that we were on a large, main thoroughfare. It had rained again while we slept, and the streets gleamed wetly, small puddles reflecting the street lamps, gilding the stone world in gold.

I was very warm from my stifling under things and the walk through the streets by the time Malcolm steered me off the road and into a little cafe. No chairs or tables stood in the street outside it, but inside a few lights burned, and when we stepped through the door I nearly fainted with hunger at the delicate smells of fine herbs and sweet shellfish. Traditional music played, tinny and old-world sounding on an ancient sound system. White tablecloths shone in the warm yellow light, and I immediately felt at home.

An older man, his face lined so deeply he looked like a raisin, came out of the kitchen and exclaimed something in French, his arms open wide. Malcolm returned the greeting and the two hugged and kissed like old friends.

Friends. That was what Malcolm was like. A friend to everyone. Straightforward. Open. Welcoming. And despite his strange talk and idiosyncrasies, he seemed to be exactly what he appeared to be. The realization startled me. I'd known so many men who hid things, who led double lives. But Malcolm was completely transparent. Everything there was to know about him was floating on the surface, written in plain words in a language I was learning to decipher.

Malcolm introduced me to Dominic, and the old man embraced and kissed me as well, his arms surprisingly strong for a raisin. Speaking in rapid French, he ushered us over to a table in the middle of the room decorated with fluttering candles. Malcolm helped me into my chair, and then seated himself.

And then my phone rang.

Real world calling.

The happy buzz of the wine receded somewhat before I realized that the ringtone was not Felicia's. I probably had a million texts from her, but she'd known I'd gone to see Malcolm on Monday because he'd asked her for the day off so he could paint me. If there was anyone in the world who would understand getting swept off her feet and off to some other place by a rich, magnetic man, it would be Felicia. So... someone else was calling me.

I didn't want to answer it. Whoever it was could wait. I kicked my purse under the table and shrugged out of my coat. The corset kept me sitting straight, and I suddenly realized how far my breasts were pushed out toward Malcolm. And he knew it. His eyes glittered at me, dancing mischievously in the candlelight.

Dominic rattled off more rapid French as he poured out small glasses of liqueur. Malcolm tossed his back immediately and I... well, I let mine sit after taking a whiff and feeling my stomach turn. I really needed something to eat first.

My phone rang again. I gritted my teeth, then gave Malcolm a bright smile. "Just a second," I said. "I have to turn that off."

He smiled back at me. "Very well."

I ducked under the table, the tightness of the corset making me wheeze as I grabbed my purse and ripped it open, fishing the offending piece of technology from its terrifying depths.

A number I'd never seen before flashed on the screen. New York area code.

I hesitated. What if it was an emergency? What if something had happened to Felicia and someone was trying to get a hold of me? What if something had happened to Felicia and Anton together? Felicia and Anton and Arthur, and the whole company...?

Well, okay, the more I thought about it the less likely it seemed that everyone I personally knew would have been consumed by the same disaster, except of course it had happened before. Many times. I hadn't seen the news lately...

"I have to take this," I said, suddenly feeling more sick than drunk.

Malcolm frowned at me. "Is everything all right?" he asked.

"Haha!" I said. "Probably! Is there a bathroom

here?"

Wordlessly, concern lighting his eyes, he pointed to the back of the restaurant, and I shuffled past him, my heels clacking loudly on the wood floor. I barely made it to the water closet before voicemail picked up. I answered the call. "Hello!" I chirped. "Sadie MacElroy speaking."

"Where the hell is Mr. Ward?" Don's angry voice surged across the Atlantic, pissed beyond belief. "I know he must be awake by now."

This. Fucking. Guy, I thought. Two could be righteously angry! "How'd you get my number?" I demanded.

"That's not important. I need to talk to Mr. Ward as soon as possible."

My buzz was thoroughly wrecked at this point and my stomach pitched and roiled, basted in acidic wine. I needed to eat something. Preferably a piece of bread. "I'll tell him you called," I said.

"Oh, will you? Think you can remember to do that this time?"

I hated this guy. "I remembered," I said. "I just didn't do it."

A sound of frustration came over the line, and I smiled. I mean, I'm not usually vindictive and unprofessional like that, but I was drunk, I really needed to eat something, and he was just a shithead.

He changed tactics. "I apologize, Miss MacElroy," he said after an audible sigh. "It has been a long and very trying few days. Mr. Ward *must* come back to New York. It is very important."

"You're not going to give me a hint about what's so goddamn important?" I said. I obviously didn't have any right to that information, but if it was a business deal or something I was certain it could wait until the end of our meal.

There was a silence. "Okay. Fine. He's wanted for questioning by the FBI."

I nearly dropped the phone in shock. "What?"

"Yeah. You'd better get his ass back to New York, or he's going to be arrested."

I licked my lips. "I have no reason to trust what you're saying. You've been nothing but a shitlord to me since the world *hello*. You better tell me right now what you need him for or you're just going to have to call him yourself."

"Does he have his phone on him?"

"No." I wasn't sure, but I wasn't going to give him any quarter.

"And I have no reason to trust what *you* are saying. You're just a gold-digger."

Now I was so shocked I couldn't even speak. Was that why he was such a terrible person to me? Don seemed to take my silence as an admission of guilt. When he spoke next I heard his smile.

"He's not crazy, you know," he said. "It's all an act. You can't get his money by duping him."

I felt cold. "I know he's not crazy, you ass. I'm not after his money, either."

"Sure you aren't," he said, his voice brimming with smugness, as though he knew all my motivations. I'd have had no problems marrying someone for their money as long as we were perfectly honest about our relationship... but this wasn't like that.

"Good luck getting a hold of him when I accidentally drop his cell phone in the toilet," I said and hung up before I became the target of any more invective.

Sobered, I stood in the bathroom and stared at myself in the mirror. I hadn't put on any make up and my hair was loose, but the clothes I wore were beautifully made and they mostly hid my tattoos. I didn't look like someone who would sleep with a guy for the money... did I? And I certainly wasn't the sort of person who would take advantage of a crazy person for monetary gain.

That dickhole knows nothing about you, I thought fiercely. Leaning over the sink, I splashed some cold water on my face and, feeling a bit more clear-headed than before, I turned and strode back to the table where Malcolm was speaking with Dominic.

"Sorry about that," I said, settling back down in my chair.

"Who was it?" Malcolm asked.

I shook my head. "No one important." *Just your secretary, telling me you're wanted for questioning by the FBI. Oh yeah, about that...*

He held my gaze for a little longer than I would have liked, but after a moment he turned back to Dominic and spoke again in rapid French. Dominic smiled and laughed, left and then returned almost immediately bearing a loaf of crusty bread, olive oil and vinegar, and a smattering of herbs on a plate. With a flourish, he poured out the oil and vinegar onto the plate, somehow managing to create a pool of oil with a perfectly-formed black-vinegar heart in the middle. Malcolm shook his head, but it was indulgent.

"Dominic claims we are destined lovers," he said as the old man bustled off, presumably to get the rest of our meal ready.

"You said that we might be the day after we met," I said. "Don't you remember?"

His eyes softened. "I do, but I said it was the red thread of fate, which ties together those who are destined to meet, not necessarily become lovers. So the red thread of fate connects us, perhaps, and even if it were to designate us as destined lovers that is not necessarily a good thing. Often lovers in Eastern mythology are tragic figures." His eyes twinkled, as though he thought being a tragic figure would be quite a lark. "Dominic doesn't mean it that way, but he's a remarkably optimistic man."

I tilted my head, "And you aren't?"

He seemed surprised that I had misread him so badly. "Me? Oh, no. I'm far more fatalistic. The Buddha himself tells us that suffering is inevitable. It must be true."

He was getting mystic on me again, and I was no longer in the mood for his whimsies. "I know you're not crazy," I blurted suddenly.

Silence fell across the table.

Me and my stupid drunk mouth.

His eyes hardened and he leaned back in his chair, and I suddenly realized that there was another side to him. The side I'd seen when he commanded me to submit to him. The side of him that had made him a formidable businessman and a billionaire at a relatively young age. Mastery. Dominance. Implacability.

I gave an involuntary shiver and forced myself to not look away.

He steepled his fingers in front of his mouth, every inch the CEO. "And how would you know that, Sadie?" he asked. "Does it have anything to do with the scars hidden beneath the ink on your skin?"

I stiffened, inhaling sharply. The strictures of the

corset restrained my ribs, and I became lightheaded. "That's none of your business," I said. "But yes. Yes it does. Now don't change the subject."

He blinked, and his shoulders relaxed slightly. He hadn't expected me to admit anything. "What subject?" he said.

"The subject where I tell you I know you aren't crazy, so why do you act the way you do?"

He tilted his head. "And what way is that?"

I narrowed my eyes. "You know exactly what I mean. Skipping the country with a woman you barely know and buying her thousands of dollars worth of clothes." God, tens of thousands, probably. The thought made me slightly sick to my stomach. Eschewing decorum, I nibbled on a piece of bread to settle my stomach before continuing. "Declaring yourself to be a tortured artistic genius. Singing with homeless men on the subway and then giving away a thousand dollars just because. Spouting off religious aphorisms in every day conversation. You know. *That* sort of thing."

He was silent for a moment, and we stared at each other as Dominic emerged from the kitchen with our first course, a delicate display of fresh mussels with a drizzle of cream sauce. The bread had settled my stomach and it smelled heavenly, but I didn't want to be the first to look away. Dominic, clearly sensing something had gone awry with his fated lovers, faded back into the kitchen.

Finally Malcolm picked up his fork and deftly pried a mussel from its shell. "Who was that on the phone, Sadie?" he asked me. He didn't exactly sound like a disapproving father from a sixties sitcom, but it was close.

"Why?" I demanded. "What does it matter?"

"Because the moment you came out of the bathroom after speaking to them, you acted differently. Whoever it was told you something about me, or warned you against getting involved with me, or something else to that effect, and I would like to know what it was, and who told you such things."

I pressed my lips into a line. He didn't have a *right* to know. But then again, I didn't have a right to interrogate his personal secretary.

And I really liked Malcolm Ward. He was weird, but he wasn't trying to be. He was just a guy who had removed his social filter and decided to do whatever the fuck came into his head. The only reason he wasn't singing on the subway as a homeless person himself was because he was so goddamn rich. Why he'd decided to do that was the question.

Surely it didn't have something to do with the fact that he was being investigated by the *FBI,* could it?

It was all the wine, I swear. And I guess some of it was my own bad judgment, but mostly it was the wine.

"Your secretary called me," I confessed at last. "Don Cardall, or whatever."

That surprised him. His eyebrows nearly shot into his hairline. "Don called you? How did he know your number?"

Now I had to look away, worrying my lower lip with my teeth. "He sort of called you on your cell phone about a thousand times while you were asleep and I answered, thinking it might be important."

I sneaked a glance at him from the corner of my eye, and was relieved to see he looked more puzzled than anything. I'd expected him to be angry. I pressed on. "I asked him what he wanted, and he said he needed to talk to you. I tried to wake you up, but you were passed out. Like, drugged passed out."

"Mm," he said. "I do sleep fairly heavily. And I haven't been sleeping much in the past few weeks."

Few weeks? So not just since he'd met me. *Interesting.* "Anyway, he was really rude to me, so I was rude back, and by the time you woke up I'd had too much wine and watched too much Croatian television to remember that he wanted you to call him back. So he got *my* number from somewhere and called me to yell at me for not informing you that he'd called." I thought for a moment. "And now that I say it out loud, it's all very high school. I also told him I'd accidentally drop your phone in the toilet if he wasn't nicer to me."

"He was rude to you?" Malcolm asked.

"God, yes. Swearing and everything. And he called me a gold-digger." That last part came out without my consent. Wine. Seriously. *I'll never drink wine again,* I vowed. I was absolute shit at keeping things under wraps when drunk. In the hopes of delaying any further embarrassment or confessions, I set about attacking my mussels, which is hard to do when expensive wine has given you the fine motor skills of a penguin on crack.

"Ah, yes, he's under a lot of pressure," Malcolm said. He seemed to relax and leaned forward again, deftly plucking another mussel from its shell before extending it across the table and feeding it to me. I accepted it gratefully. Honestly, who in their right mind serves mussels to a lady wearing designer clothes?

The answer was, *Someone who knows his mussels are so*

goddamn good you'd sacrifice a finger to have another one. The morsel melted in my mouth, sharp and sweet and salty, a perfectly cooked piece of shellfish. I couldn't help but moan with pleasure. For a moment, Don was forgotten as Malcolm helped me eat my portion of the appetizer, and it was only when I was done and leaning back, feeling more content that I had any right to be that I brought the subject back up again. "Anyway. Don was really rude. You should fire him."

"Oh, I can't fire him," Malcolm said. "He's just feeling a bit stressed out at the moment." He appeared to think about this as he chewed and swallowed the last mussel. "I don't blame him, really. I defied his expectations by leaving the country with you."

I blinked. "You did? I mean, I asked him why he didn't know where you were, and he said—"

"Did you tell him?"

"What, where we were? No."

Malcolm relaxed further. "Good. Go on."

Dominic came and removed our plates before returning with another course, this time shellfish bisque. I waited until he had retreated before continuing. "Well, he said that you hadn't told him, but that it was really important that you come back to New York."

Malcolm spooned soup into his mouth. "Did he say why?"

I looked down at my soup, embarrassed. "Yeah. I asked him, and he said you were wanted for questioning by the FBI, and that you needed to come back to New York before you got arrested."

To my surprise, Malcolm nodded. "Yes, that does put a bit of a kink in his plans."

I lifted my gaze and studied him in astonishment. "Wait a second," I said. "You actually *are* wanted by the FBI for questioning?"

He nodded. "No doubt my sudden flight forced their hand. I bet it will be all over the news soon."

That Don *hadn't* been lying to me was almost as astonishing as the fact that Malcolm seemed completely unperturbed by his status as motherfucking *wanted by the FBI.*

I mean, let's be real here. That is some serious shit.

"What did you do?" I demanded. My brain began to replay scenes from *Silence of the Lambs* and suddenly I realized that Malcolm was just *so* Hannibal Lecter, why hadn't I seen it, I was going to end up served with fava beans, oh *god*—

"Oh, I haven't done anything," Malcolm said, cutting off my paranoid fantasies. "Don is framing me for massive embezzlement of my company."

I stared at him some more. "What?" I said.

Malcolm smiled. "He doesn't know I know, nor that I have proof that it is he who is doing the embezzlement. The FBI's been watching me for some time, and he's been their mole."

"What?" I said again.

"Isn't it delicious?" he asked. "It's the most interesting thing to happen to me in years." Then his eyes focused on me, and he smiled again. "Except for you."

I have to admit, I was not assimilating this information very well. "So wait," I said. "You're being watched by the FBI, because they suspect you of embezzlement and fraud, and your secretary is ratting you out to them, except he's actually the one embezzling and defrauding the company, and you know this and have proof?"

He nodded. He took another serene sip of soup.

I put my hands to my forehead. "Are you... do you act crazy in public just to screw with the FBI? To place doubt in people's minds about your sanity?"

"Oh no," Malcolm said. "Not at all. Don was simply one of the closest people to me in my life. He was like a brother to me. After I found out he was betraying me, I just... didn't care any more. It didn't seem to matter much what I did. And I wasn't having any fun being the staid and stately CEO, so I decided to... not be." He shrugged. "I've had far more fun these past few months than I ever had in my entire life, Sadie. It's definitely been worth it to go crazy. Crazy suits me."

None of this was making sense to me. "But... but if you have proof that it's been Don doing the embezzling, then why don't you just show it to the FBI? That would make the problem go away."

An expression of pure shock passed over his features. He was beautiful shocked. "I couldn't do that," he said, and he sounded scandalized. "I told you. Don was like a brother to me. You don't just turn your brother over to the feds."

"But... but he's the one turning *you* over!" I almost shouted.

He nodded as though he had no idea to what I was objecting. "But I couldn't do the same to my brother. We were very close. Very close, a long time ago..." He trailed off and a faraway look passed over his eyes, like a cloud over the moon.

The betrayal cut him deeply. Far more deeply than just a friend or a business rival screwing you over. This was personal. On Malcolm's side, at least.

My heart went out to him. “So that’s it?” I asked, my voice softening. For want of something to do, I picked up my spoon and scooped up a spoonful of bisque and held it in front of me, letting it cool.”You were just going to let your best friend, the best friend you say is like a brother to you, steal money from your company and then frame you for it and send you off to federal prison?”

Malcolm shrugged. “No, I never have any intentions of going to prison,” he assured me. “That will not happen.”

I frowned, so confused at this point I didn’t know which way was up and which way was down. “Then what did you plan to do instead? You know, before the FBI decided to arrest and charge you for a crime you didn’t commit?”

Malcolm smiled at me, and it was a sad thing. “Oh, that was easy,” he said. “I’d planned to kill myself.”

10

I dropped my spoon. Bisque splattered everywhere, but I was far too shocked to care or even acknowledge it.

"Excuse me," I said. "Could you please repeat that? I don't think I got it."

"I planned to kill myself," he said. He even helpfully enunciated the words, as though I were hard of hearing. I was anything but. His words boomed through me and echoed around inside my head.

Kill myself, kill myself, kill myself...

"Oh dear," Malcolm said, looking at my outfit as though he were some shocked society maven. "You've spilled a bit of soup on your clothing."

"What the fuck?" I said. "What the *fuck*?"

He blinked and took a demure sip of soup. "What do you mean?" he asked.

My fingers itched with the sudden urge to reach across the table and strangle him. "You fucking idiot," I said. "Why would you want to kill yourself just because of some douchebag who betrayed you?

Especially if you have the means to bury him?"

His eyes darkened. "I don't think I could do that," he said. "It seems wrong. Dominic!" He turned in his seat and called for our server, who bolted immediately from the kitchen and over to our table. Malcolm spoke to him in French and Dominic's eyes darted over to me, taking in my soup-stained clothes. He clucked his tongue and hurried over to the bar where he retrieved a damp napkin before bustling back over to me where he began to solicitously dab at my clothes. Malcolm's eyes sparkled as he watched.

I was not amused. "Hey!" I said. "I'll do that!" I snatched the napkin from Dominic's hand and he made a huffy sound at me before saying something to Malcolm, who laughed, before disappearing again. "What the hell, man?" I demanded, gingerly cleaning bisque off myself. "I only let one guy invade Sadie's bubble right now. No fucking touchy."

"I'm sorry," Malcolm said. "I wanted to see what you would do."

"Why?" I snapped. "So you could change the subject from your stupid plan?"

"Well, it was more that I wanted to see what Dominic had to say about you. He's seen many women come through here. He thinks you're a keeper, by the way." He waved his hand. "And anyway, I don't think my plan is stupid. It was just a logical conclusion for me."

The complete nonchalance with which he was treating this made me feel cold inside. "Yeah." I glared at him. "That makes it *worse.*" I'd dealt with people who threatened suicide before. Malcolm wasn't anything like those people, which scared me, because the people who threaten to commit suicide and the people who actually do it are usually two very different types of people. He might actually mean it. In fact, I didn't have any reason to believe that he *didn't* mean it at all because he had been, so far, completely and candidly honest with me. If I asked the right questions, of course.

I had a horrible feeling that if Malcolm Ward had decided to kill himself, then he would do it without any sort of pomp and circumstance. No dramatic death threats, no leaping from a bridge into rush hour traffic, no televised gun to the head. He'd just... do it.

Drama bomb, I thought. Except it wasn't. He sat across from me, swirling a mouthful of wine and watching me carefully, as though he hadn't expected I would react with horror at the idea of his self-inflicted death.

"What the hell is wrong with you?" I said. "Why didn't you tell me this before?"

He shrugged. "It's not really the sort of thing you confess on a first date, is it? Happy to meet you, by the way, the moment before our eyes met across a crowded room I had resolved to kill myself that night."

I worked my mouth soundlessly. "That *night*? As in, last Friday?"

"Oh yes," he said. "It would have landed me in the papers on Sunday and everyone would talk about it Monday. There'd be a great hullabaloo and everyone would be quite happy to talk about it. I figured it was the least I could do for all the people I screwed over to make myself so rich."

I couldn't believe what I was hearing. Setting my elbows on the table in front of me, I buried my hands in my hair, staring sightlessly at my barely touched meal. I just couldn't wrap my head around this, that *anyone* could be so meticulous in the planning of their death. I mean... killing himself courteously on a Friday so everyone could be talking about it on Monday? As if he wanted his suicide to have the greatest positive impact on the world? It was weird. Awful. It made me sick to think about. In fact, the shellfish in my wine-basted stomach was starting to turn on me with this news. Well, as long as we were being honest, I might as well put it out there.

"I think I'm going to be sick," I said.

"If you are," Malcolm replied, "please be sick into your soup bowl. These floors are very old and it would be a shame to have to replace them."

I almost told him thank you for the sympathy, but that seemed silly to say to a man who had just confessed he wanted to kill himself because his oldest, closest friend had betrayed him. Everything seemed silly, except now every encounter with him took on a different significance in my head. The auction, the art, the freaking movers... had he made arrangements to have his house packed up to make sure no one would be inconvenienced by his death? Just... got the ball rolling on the particulars afterward? What was going on here?

"So..." I shook my head. "You were going to kill yourself before you met me, and I've convinced you to live?"

"You have... stayed my execution," Malcolm said after a moment, which sounded downright ominous. I didn't like it one bit. That was definitely not a life affirmation.

"How long?" I said.

He scooped the last bit of bisque from his bowl

and ladled it into his mouth before swallowing thoughtfully. "What do you mean?" he said. "How long have I been planning my exit, or how long have you delayed it?"

"Delayed it," I said. I had to know how much time I had to convince him not to do it, though even as I felt moved toward him, moved to help him, Felicia's words came back to me: *You always fall for the broken ones. Don't get in the trap of trying to fix him.*

God. I had no idea what to do. Everything depended on his answer.

He seemed to ponder the question as Dominic came out and removed our soup bowls, replacing them with large rectangular plates. Three delicate portions of food had been spooned artfully onto them in a neat little row. "I suppose," he said, "that I will hold off killing myself until I have finished my masterpiece."

I felt like crying. I felt like leaping across the table and tackling him to the floor where I would beat the ever-loving snot out of him.

"You're a shithead," I told him. "You really are."

"I'm sorry you feel that way," he replied, and he did sound genuinely sorry. "I was hoping we could learn a bit more about each other on this trip--I think it's very important for me to understand you before I can complete my masterpiece--but if you are just going to hurl invective at me we could cut the trip short and I could turn myself into the authorities."

"And then kill yourself," I said.

He shrugged.

"That's manipulative. You are being a manipulative asshole."

A flash of pain crossed his face. "I'm sorry. I don't

mean to be. I am only trying to be honest with you. You are free to leave at any time. I will happily send you back to the States on the next plane out of Dubrovnik."

"You should just gift your private jet to me," I said crankily. "Since you aren't going to be using it any more, that is."

To my surprise, he smiled at that. "Yes, I suppose that's true. But I doubt you could afford the upkeep on it."

I passed a hand over my face as he began to eat his meal. Savory scents wafted across the table to me, and my mouth watered. "All right," I said. "Fine. So you're going to kill yourself, even though it's really stupid. What's all this business with seducing me and doing all the art and shit?"

He chewed thoughtfully. "I don't know," he said at last. "I enjoy your company. I like to be around you. You... make things more vivid. I told you that in that whole room of people, you were the only one who was alive, remember?"

I nodded. I remembered.

"It's that. I want to borrow your warmth for a while. You warm me up. I don't feel so cold when you are around. And you submit to me so readily... it has been a long time since I felt in control of my life. The company runs itself, the press runs away with stories on me, my own trusted people are not to be trusted, and my emotions..." He trailed off. "Well, let's just say that I am not used to having my emotions run away from me, though I believe I have been able to effectively let them go. Betrayal does strange things to a man. But you reminded me what it's like to have something under my control. With you, I can indulge in a bit of pleasure. You are alive, and you make me feel alive. And the things we create..." He sighed. "I don't know. The photographs are just bits and bytes. Your painted body didn't last. Our sculpture will last until it breaks. And yet for some reason I don't feel as if that is the thing I am striving for. I am impermanent, and I want my art to be permanent, a reminder to the world that I was here... but it all feels empty, somehow."

I wanted to reach across the table and take his hand in mine. No man had ever spoken so frankly and candidly with me before, except one man, and he didn't count.

"You have to figure out what you're trying to say first," I said.

His eyes darkened. "I'm afraid I don't have anything to say. A lifetime of grabbing for every dollar, reaching for things that are reachless... Perhaps it's just turtles all the way down. A hole in the middle of me that I keep trying to fill with sex or philosophy, possessions and money and fine wine." He lifted his wine glass and took a sip as though to emphasize this point. "I'm afraid I am just empty, Sadie. I was hoping art could help me find what it was I wanted to leave behind, but maybe there isn't anything to leave." Then he smiled. "If I could figure out how to express *that* in art, I'd have my masterpiece."

Yeah, right. We both knew he was going to get arrested and go to prison before that ever happened.

"I'm sorry," I said. "I'm having a hard time processing this."

"I know," he said gently. "I didn't want to bring it up. It's not your burden to bear, but, well... I feel my hand was forced. Don is good at that."

"So why'd you give control of your company over to him?"

"I wanted to help him. We both tried to outdo each other in business, and I suppose I won in that regard. After he'd lost everything I offered him a job with me. Comfortable, good benefits, pay to make the richest man green with envy, but most importantly something to do. His failure was just bad luck; he's a brilliant businessman."

He stared at his wine glass. "He was always my closest friend, and about a year and a half ago I'd decided that I'd worked myself to death enough for a while and that I needed an extended vacation. I left Don in charge... it went organically from there." He sighed and put a forkful of asparagus tips in his mouth. He had already cleared one portion of food—the seafood dish—and was starting on the middle dish, a delicate slice of some hapless farm animal. From the green sauce on it, I had to deduce it was lamb. He carved a slice, then, noticing I was watching, gestured to my plate. "Please, eat," he said. "You'll get sick if you don't have something in your stomach after all that wine."

Too late, I wanted to tell him, but I didn't. "So... what do you want me to do with this information?"

He looked surprised. "I don't want you to do anything with it. I told you under duress, as you might recall. Why, do you feel the need to do something about it?"

"Of course!" I said. "Who wouldn't?"

His mouth twisted. "Well, plenty of people. I wouldn't blame you if you wanted to cut and run right now. I'm wanted by the FBI, I am a self-admitted empty shell of a human being, and there is very little I have to offer you. If I were in your situation, a lovely young woman with a good job and a sense of self and purpose, I would cut myself off so fast I wouldn't even pack my toothbrush."

Well, I thought, *that just makes me sad*. "You just cut off people who become a problem?"

He shook his head. "Of course. That's human nature. Connections become anchors. Love becomes a burden. I wouldn't want to be an inconvenience to you."

Jesus Christ. What had happened to this guy to make him this way? Was this why he always seemed just a little disconnected, a little apart from the world? I had to help him somehow. I knew, of course, that probably be the best thing for me to do *was* cut and run because I couldn't save someone who didn't want to save themselves. I knew that much. But I just don't learn. That's a problem I have.

"Don't be a shithead," I advised him. "I'm not going to cut and run."

"Oh?" he said. "Then you'll stay? Enjoy fine wine and good sex and the high life with me for a little while? 'Gather ye rosebuds while ye may?'"

God, he really was kind of a shithead. But there was hope for him. I'd seen it in him, glimpsed it under his distant exterior, in his moments of candor. I didn't want him to die, and if the only person who knew his plan was me, I had to try, right?

I always tried. I'd taken care of my mom. I'd taken care of Felicia. I took care of all my broken boyfriends, too. I wouldn't be me if I didn't take care of everyone around me.

I set my shoulders. "No," I said. "I'm not gathering any rosebuds. Obviously what I'm going to do is convince you *not* to kill yourself. Duh."

That got his attention. He sat up ever so slightly straighter in his chair. "Oh?" he asked. "Is that a challenge?" His eyes took on a predatory gleam, the same gleam he got that first night we met, when I had explained to him the protocols of artists.

Ruthlessly I stabbed a slice of lamb while I glared at him from across the table. "Not everything is a fucking challenge, you goddamn weirdo."

"Oh." He placed his hand over his chest. "You wound me, Madame."

I saw what he was doing. He was acting like some kind of comic relief character in a movie to keep me at a distance. I wasn't going to let him get away with it any more. Just because he had gobs of money and had shrugged off all earthly attachments and was looking to upgrade to the afterlife and I was still paying down student debt and hadn't given my spiritual life a single thought since that really bad 'shroom trip my junior year in college didn't mean he could just mess with me and keep me at arms length, as if he were somehow *better* than me, more *enlightened.*

I liked Malcolm Ward. I especially liked the glimpses of the passionate man beneath the cool, distant, ironic facade he put up for the world. When we fucked, he lost his armor. He wanted me to submit to him, let him do what he wanted with me just to feel less at odds, less out of control? Well that was just fine with me. I'd slip under that hard shell and find his tender parts and remind him just how much he *should* be feeling.

Rage. Pain. Betrayal.

The thing was, those things weren't *bad.* They just *were*. And by the way, they made damn good art. And after they were done, there were other things to feel, like a lust for life, or a lust for me. Only when could feel could he express himself through art, and when he did I was certain he would remember why he had held on to this life for so long already.

I squared my shoulders. "I'll help you finish your masterpiece," I said.

That seemed to knock him off balance. "You will?" he said. "But I thought you wanted me to stick around, although god knows why. You'd probably be better off without having to deal with me."

"Yeah," I said. "I probably would. But I'm really bad at doing things that are good for me."

"Oh?" He smiled. "Are you?"

I felt like he was mocking me. "Yeah. I am. You want to know what I ate for lunch last Friday? Half a block of store brand cheddar cheese because it was the only thing I had in the house and I didn't even have time to stop for food while I was organizing that stupid auction. I do shit that's terrible for me all the time. Store brand cheese gets the job done, so that's what I eat."

I realized he was staring at me in vague horror. He'd probably never had to eat store brand cheese in his life. "Hey," I said, "don't judge me. A cheese-lunch is pretty delicious."

"But not," he said, "nutritionally sound."

I rolled my eyes. "Exactly. But like I said, I'm good at doing things that are bad for me. So don't worry about me. I'm the best at surviving on Cheez Whiz and street vendor hot dogs."

Malcolm looked pained. "Are you comparing me to street vendor hot dogs?" he asked.

"Nutritionally," I told him. "Don't worry, you're

hung better. My point is that you don't *need* to be nutritionally sound, uh, emotionally speaking. You're still delicious." This metaphor had gone bad places. I tried to salvage it. "I'll survive somehow."

He watched me for a long few seconds, his dark eyes contemplative. "Yes," he said after a moment. "I suspect you always do."

"It's a talent," I told him. "I'll totally teach it to you." Triumphantly I speared a tip of asparagus and shoved it into my mouth, where it melted in a delicious mush of butter and salt. I chewed it with relish before swallowing.

Malcolm was still watching me with that pensive, thoughtful expression on his face. "So..." he said at last. "You are going to try to convince me to not kill myself?"

"I am," I said. "It would be a total waste of a perfectly good person if you were to go through with it."

"I was going to donate all my organs and my body to science," he replied. "That wouldn't have been a waste at all."

"Yeah, well, you'll still be using them for a while so tell the scientists to cancel the party."

He smiled a bit at that. "You are a strange woman," he said. "I think that's why I like you so much."

"You *charmer*."

He appeared to reach a decision. "Very well, you may attempt to convince me not to kill myself."

I rolled my eyes. "How gracious of you—" I began, but abruptly his spine straightened and his chin lifted.

"Don't interrupt," he commanded.

Ah. The billionaire businessman again. A glimpse of who he had been before he had lost his closest friend and his company, all that he had lived for. The man in control. Suddenly I wondered if this was such a good idea. Well, fine, *more* of a bad idea than it was already. But I shut my mouth. I could play the role he wanted.

He seemed pleased by my acquiescence. "Good. If we do this, then I must ask for things in return from you."

I gulped. "What kind of things?"

He smiled. "Nothing you haven't already given me. Submission. Conversation. Your body. Your mind." He pinned me with those startling eyes, dark and almost sinister in the low ambient light. "Your thoughts. Your memories."

Hooboy. But fine, whatever. I'd poured it all out before. What did I care if he knew things about me? He'd already opened himself up wider than I ever would have to a person I barely knew. "Okay," I said.

"I mean it, Sadie. I want to know all about you."

I nodded. "I understand. I mean, I don't know *why*, I don't think I'm that interesting, but I'll do it. From now on, I'm an open book to you."

He tilted his head. "Do you really not know why I find you so fascinating?" he asked. "Why I envy you so much?"

My mouth dropped open. "Envy me?" I said. In a hundred million years *that* would never, ever have occurred to me.

He nodded slightly. "Envy you," he repeated. "Part of me wants to break you, you make me so jealous. Part of me just wants to hold you and make sure nothing touches you again. Keep you just the way you are."

His words left me feeling queer and messed up inside, defensive. "You can't break me," I blurted without thinking. "I won't let you."

Silence descended on our table, and I licked my lips again. His intense stare made me nervous, but I refused to show it. Well, mostly. Beneath the table, my hands fiddled with my napkin, twisting and turning it, rhythmically pressing it into a ball and letting it spring back.

"I'll see which side wins out," he said at last.

"Okay," I told him. "Then I guess we're both going to try our best."

He smiled. "Yes, we will. Now why don't you eat? You'll feel better after you do."

With a sigh, I finally acquiesced to his urging and dug in again. The food was delicious, and for a while we ate in silence. My mind whirled, revolving around the bombshells that had just been dropped onto my mental landscape. I had been worried my life was becoming boring, but now it was far too exciting for my own good. I already had second thoughts about this; Malcolm Ward needed therapy, not an affair, but as it was this was probably the best he was going to get.

After I had finished my main course, I set my fork and knife down and dabbed at my lips with my napkin. He was right, a bit of food had done me a world of good, and my thoughts were beginning to calm from the turmoil of his revelations and my own planning. "So," I said at last, "what do you want to do now?

He smiled and polished off his wine. To my admittedly-drunken eyes, he didn't seem at all inebriated. "I think we should board my boat and head out into international waters," he said. "Shut off our cell phones, cloister ourselves away where no one will bother us for a while. Float around on the sea. Make art. Make love."

Make love. The very words sent a delicious stab of heat through me as I remembered the passion of our previous fuck sessions. I wanted very badly to sleep with him again. I felt addicted to him. And I was already here. Already a party to his flight. The only thing I had to lose was my sanity. It'd been a while since I'd done that, though the older I got the less the idea appealed to me.

But he had said I was alive, and he *made* me feel alive. I'd been drifting along for a while, taking care of business, taking care of Felicia and her numerous problems. Maybe I *was* just a fixer at heart.

You really have no business trying, I told myself. *This is a fool's game, and you are not a fool.*

If only I could convince myself of that fact, my life would be a lot easier.

"I imagine this is much like becoming involved with someone who is terminally ill," Malcolm said, interrupting my thoughts. "But all things end. That is the way of the world."

I reached across the table and grabbed his hand, and it was cool and dry in my hot palm, as though he were already halfway to dead. "I don't want this to end just yet," I said. "Let's go sailing."

11

Malcolm didn't waste any time. After our final course—a warm chocolate soufflé—he drew a small pad of paper from his back pocket and wrote something down—in French, of course—before carefully selecting an enormous wade of bills from the depths of his wallet, wrapping them in the piece of paper, then placing the whole burrito on the table. He put a heavy glass on top of them, to keep the half-folded stacks from popping open again.

Hush money, I thought to myself. Money to pay for the meal, money to keep Dominic from spilling the beans to the FBI. Or would it be the CIA, since we were out of U. S. jurisdiction? I had no idea. The famous infighting between departments was probably why we weren't already on a prison plane back to the states.

Smoothly, Malcolm stood, and I sensed a change in him. A purpose. I couldn't help but let my eyes wander over his body, and I noted, before it was obscured by the fall of his coat, that his cock was hard and straining against his trousers. My breath caught.

He looked down at me, his face cool but his eyes burning. "I have to make a few quick phone calls. I think you should go to the ladies room and remove your panties," he suggested mildly, but I could tell from the hard edge beneath his voice that it was more of a command than a suggestion.

Well, I'd agreed to this. I nodded and stood up, tottering back to the bathroom again, toting my purse. When I reached it, I took out my cell phone and turned it off so it couldn't be used to track us, then I hiked up my skirt and slid my panties down my legs. The crotch was already wet with anticipation, and I stuffed them into my purse for safekeeping.

The wine was wearing off, and I was starting to get a headache, but it didn't matter. I stood in the middle of the tiny bathroom and smoothed my skirt over my generous hips, adjusted my bra over my modest breasts, and tried to look presentable. Civilized, even. Not like a tramp from Jersey who was about to get fucked good and hard.

The very thought sent a rush of heat between my legs, and I had to take a few deep breaths to cool the flush from my cheeks.

Throwing my shoulders back, I left the bathroom and re-entered the dining room.

Malcolm was behind the bar, talking on the phone in what I recognized as Japanese. I wondered who he was calling, but decided it didn't matter. He was *making arrangements*. That was what he did. That was how the moneyed world operated, I had learned. You *made arrangements*, and things happened, just the way you wanted them to. I gathered my coat from the chair where I had left it and noted the stack of bills was already gone.

After another minute, Malcolm hung up the phone. He turned to me. "Put your coat on," he said. "We're going for a walk."

That much was obvious, but something in the way he said it made me think the particular walk we were going to go on would be a bit longer than the walk we'd taken to get here. I nodded and shrugged into my coat. Malcolm put his broad, warm hand on my back and, to my surprise, ushered me into the kitchen.

It was small, but very modern. Slick steel gleamed, brushed and burnished to a fine shine. The great sink was full of dishes, and Dominic was standing over it, washing them with a curious intensity that I only realized was deliberate when we slipped past him and out a back door into an alleyway. He hadn't looked at us, I realized, because he was pretending to not know where we had gone.

Did Malcolm think the police were already on their way? I realized that his cell phone was still back at the apartment. If it had been tracked, Don would know Malcolm's haunts in Dubrovnik. It was obviously a place he came to often, or often enough to have an apartment here. My heart picked up the pace and a queer feeling spread through my belly, a tight anticipation not unlike desire. The thought of being on the run from the feds in a foreign country, a handsome billionaire at my side—well, I'm not totally immune to the thrill of sex and danger. Malcolm took my hand and led me out into the dark, medieval night.

Together we wove through the back alleys of old Dubrovnik, my hand clutched in his, though neither of us said a word. Would we even make it to the boat? I wondered. Or did Malcolm think we had enough time to go back to the flat and get our things? All those clothes, just wasted. I had the important things I needed in my possession, but I felt a pang at all those warm clothes newly bought languishing in a flat, never to be worn.

Oh well. It wouldn't be the first time I'd fled and left everything behind.

After what seemed like a hundred twists and turns, Malcolm led me up a narrow staircase and into a higher alleyway. Above us the clouds had parted, letting the moon shine down for a few moments, and the ghostly light bathed the curiously quiet city. Far away I could hear the occasional car in the city outside the walls, but here it was quiet. The chilly ocean breeze whistling past my ears was the predominant sound. We came to a halt, and all the hair on the back of my neck stood on end.

Two white and black scooters were parked in the alleyway next to a door leading into the building we'd just scaled. *Policija* was emblazoned on the sides. Malcolm turned to me, and I was gobsmacked to see him smile.

"They're in here, watching the street outside my apartment," he whispered. "Let's see how good you are at submitting to me now."

My whole body tensed, and to my utter shock he unbuttoned his fine coat, unzipped his pants, and freed his erection to the night air before mounting one of the scooters. Placing one hand on the back and one on the handlebars to brace himself, he smiled at me.

"Suck my cock, Sadie."

I'm not ashamed to admit I was quietly freaking

out. This was... well, this was serious. What if they came back? What if someone saw us? His hot, hard shaft thrust at me from his trousers, and I felt a blazing, melting heat twine its way through my core. It was terrifying, and unbearably arousing. Like fucking your boyfriend in your parents' bed, when they could come home at any moment. Except way, way more dangerous.

My eyes met his, and he smirked. He didn't think I would do it.

Maybe we were more alike than I'd thought, because I found I couldn't back down from a challenge either.

I stepped forward and wrapped my hand around his cock.

The hiss of breath between his teeth was all I needed to spur me on. Acutely aware of how exposed we were to whoever might decide to walk down the alleyway, or peek from between the curtains above us, I let my hands glide over his thighs and bent down, my hair falling around my face, shielding me from his gaze.

His cock thrust up at me. I'd wanted to taste it since he first touched me and made me come. Now was my chance. I extended my tongue and gave it a soft, tentative lick, swiping the tip of my tongue against the soft slit, lapping up the sweet precum beaded there.

Malcolm hissed again. "Jesus," he muttered, and I smiled. Another chink in his armor. *Feel it,* I wanted to say to him. *You want to leave this behind?* But I didn't. Instead I opened my mouth as wide as I could and swallowed his cock whole.

His hips bucked, thrusting down my throat, and I

gulped, savoring the dark, earthy taste of his skin, the heaviness of his cock lying against my tongue. I wanted him to lose himself in the sensation, wanted him to feel as alive as he thought I was. I sucked hard and pulled back, and his pelvis followed me, as though he couldn't bear to give up the heat of my mouth and the tight seal of my lips.

Loosely I looped my fingers around his shaft and picked up a quick rhythm, giving just enough friction to tease him as I sucked and licked the soft head of his cock. I must have been doing something right because he groaned and nearly fell off the scooter as he tried to reach my mouth.

I denied him, pulling back and back the further forward he thrust, until he was standing up and I was kneeling in the street. Cold cobblestones bit into my knees, but the heat rolling from Malcolm was enough to keep me warm.

Abruptly he reached down and pulled me to my feet. His breath was hot and fast, and he shoved me up against the wall of the building behind me, trapping me in the dangerous curve of his body as he curled around me. His hands scrabbled, clumsy, at the hem of my skirt before lifting it up over my hips and ratcheting my thigh up over his hip. His cock probed my pussy, seeking entrance, and his lips and teeth found my throat as he slid home.

Stars exploded across my vision as the sudden sensation of being filled to the brim took me over. I gasped, suddenly lost. Legs turning to water, I sagged against the cold wall, trapped between it and the inferno of Malcolm as he began to thrust his hips, grinding his pelvis against my clit, lifting my whole body from the ground and slamming into me.

I had to bite my lip to keep from crying out. One strong arm held my ass in the air as the other raked over me, fingertips digging into my back, nails scoring down my thigh. The tight, hot center of me ached and quivered and I struggled, pinned to the wall, my hands on his shoulders either pulling him closer or pushing him away. I couldn't tell. The cold air caressed my flaming cheeks, and I couldn't help but moan softly.

"Shh," he said, and the fingers of his free hand found their way between my lips and into my mouth.

He tasted good. Salty. Clean. I sucked hard on his fingertips and he grunted, a strangled thing deep in his chest that I felt more than heard. My cries were muffled by his hand, and I bit down lightly, scraping my teeth over his flesh, my hands bracing myself on his shoulders as his thrusts became harder and faster, more wild and uncontrolled. He bit my nipple lightly through my sweater, and I squirmed and mewled around his hand, my legs locking high and tight around his waist. Any second I felt like I was going to fall, but each time I felt myself slipping his thrusting hips caught me and pushed me back up, filling me up far better than I had ever been filled before.

Our gasps echoed in the empty alleyway, the sound of the soles of Malcolm's fine shoes scraping over the gritty cobblestones with each rock of his hips loud against the silence. Around his pumping cock, I felt my body curl up and squeeze, a powerful orgasm building fast and tight inside me. My hands found his hair, dug in, gripped him hard, and he growled around my breast and nipped me again. Sharp little sparks of pain flashed and danced across my body, and I clung to him like a woman drowning.

"Fuck," I whispered. "Fuck me, Malcolm."

He shuddered at the words, his hips hammering into me even faster, and suddenly we were coming together, hot and hard. Cum pumped into me and I felt my body suck it in as I came around him, quivering and tightening, milking his cock for all I was worth. My toes curled and my head banged against the wall behind me, but it was inconsequential compared to the intensity of the orgasm rocketing through me.

Malcolm's knees buckled and we staggered. Stone scrapped across my back against the fine wool of my coat, and I held my breath as the spasms of pleasure spread over my body, rippling over my limbs and sending my head spinning.

Malcolm was done before I was, and he pulled out suddenly, abruptly, leaving me to sink against the wall, a tiny trail of cum leaking from my pumping core as I struggled to stay upright. A quick kiss to the forehead and his hand was around mine, pulling me up, and then we were walking briskly down the street as I tried to keep my footing, the rubbing of my thighs over my slick, swollen pussy lips an almost unbearable sensation. My face burned against the cool night air, and I barely had enough sense to keep myself from speaking. Wherever we were going, it wasn't back to the flat.

Again we wended through the back alleys, heading down, down, down to the sea, and Malcolm's hand was hot around mine. I couldn't help but feel a little pleased by his warmth—no longer half dead, I had woken him up, given him something to feel—but as our pace picked up I realized he was nervous. The twisted streets flashed by me, and before I knew it we were on the docks, hidden inside a dark alleyway, watching the harbor.

"My boat's coming," Malcolm said, his voice hoarse. "We'll run out to meet it. I don't think the police are watching the dock. I gave orders to the skipper before we even landed in Dubrovnik, and Dominic has arranged for him to meet us here. Don't worry, it's well stocked and provisioned, with art supplies as well as food." He smiled. "Perhaps we will find the perfect medium for my masterpiece out on the sea."

I could barely think straight. Slippery cum was running down my thigh, and I only had enough brain cells untouched by blazing pleasure to hope it didn't run into my high-heeled boots. That'd make things awfully squishy down there...

"I should call Felicia," I whispered suddenly. "She's going to be worried about me."

"No," he said, "don't turn your phone back on. In fact, you should throw it away."

"I need it," I said. "I won't turn it on, but I'm taking it with me."

In the dark, he smiled at me. "You can't cling to things forever, Sadie," Malcolm said. "All things fade."

"That's dumb. I'm not the one who's planning on killing herself, so I'm going to need it regardless. Is that some of your Buddhist wisdom?"

"Not mine, no," he said, his smile deepening, "but that doesn't make it any less true. Desire is the root of suffering, as the Buddha teaches us. Holding onto that which should be let go is the root of our suffering."

"But does the root of our suffering include a list of

contacts twenty miles long that I can't possibly remember on my own?" I asked.

He laughed quietly. I heard the hum of a boat motor in the distance "It most definitely does."

I regarded him thoughtfully as he turned and watched the harbor. The moon still shone, but wispy clouds had begun to shroud it, dimming the light. Feeble lampposts beamed out in the dark, barely touching the great, hungry blackness of the ocean. I could hardly make out his face in the dark, but the set of his jaw was pensive. A man who still desired things. He desired to board that boat. He desired to fuck me until we both couldn't walk. He was a hypocrite, and I wondered if he knew it. "Hey," I whispered.

He turned and looked at me quizzically in the dim light of the moon. "Yes?"

"Just wondering. What are you clinging to that causes you so much suffering that you want to kill yourself?"

Immediately I knew I'd struck a nerve. His body tensed and his brow furrowed slightly, and I could tell he perhaps hadn't thought of it that way. To him, taking that fatal, final step *was* letting go simply because he couldn't—or didn't want—to see the alternatives. He'd said his decision was a logical one, and while I doubted that was entirely true, perhaps, just maybe, if he'd reasoned himself into it, he could reason himself out of it.

After all, most people don't just off themselves because it's the most convenient way out of their problems. Under his calm exterior, I knew he must be terribly hurt by his friend's betrayal. Why he clung to *that* attachment was the root of his problems. It stood to reason.

"I..." he said, staring off into the distance. "I'm not sure." His voice wavered, and I could tell I had startled him, perhaps even frightened him. "We should get ready to walk to the boat."

He backed up ever so slightly, as though he were wary of me, and I realized that he had trapped me against the wall again, holding me up. My knees, still weak from my orgasm, could barely support my weight, but I tried anyway as he released the support he had been giving me. Malcolm shot me one last look that I couldn't quite decipher, then took a step back and frowned out at the harbor. Cool sea wind blew his hair back from his face, and I wanted to run my fingers through it.

In the harbor I saw the white bulk of a yacht pull up to the dock, and Malcolm took my hand. "Let's go."

We walked quickly and briskly, but didn't run. The smell of the sea filled my head, made me dizzy, and I kept waiting to hear the shout of the police, telling us to stop in the name of the law or whatever it is they say in Croatia, but though I strained to hear, no shouts came. If we had been in a movie it would have been a mad dash, we would be separated, darting through the streets, trying to reach the docks in time, but as it was Malcolm was too sharp, too ahead of the game to be caught like that, which just made his little FBI predicament all the more perplexing to me. We made it to the boat without incident and boarded.

It was huge. Three decks and a sleek design that made me think of space age flying cars. The boat rolled beneath my feet and it took all my concentration not to fall over as Malcolm led me past a silent, uniformed captain, only a shadow barely touched by yellow lamplight, who nodded at us before setting about doing whatever it was that was needed to reel the gangplank in. The dark was so encompassing that I barely got a glimpse of the deck—ghostly chairs, a couch, a coffee table—before Malcolm led me inside.

It was even more ridiculous inside. Gorgeous, perfectly designed, luxurious... everything one might expect from a billionaire playboy who wanted nothing more than to party with fifty of his closest friends in international waters. The sitting room—or whatever it was—had been constructed in cream trim and cherry wood paneling. A comfortable place to gather and chat, or throw a cocktail party. So elegant. So high-society. So exhausting.

"Would you like a drink, Sadie?" Malcolm asked me as he crossed the room to the bar and the hum of the motors picked up. I glanced out the window and saw the lights of Dubrovnik retreating.

This was really happening. We were on the run from the law.

"Yes," I said. "I could really use a drink."

His eyes flickered to me. "Scotch?"

I waved my hand. "Yeah. Sure. Okay."

He selected a few cubes of ice from a well-concealed freezer and poured two glasses of Scotch on the rocks. Crossing back to me, he held it out and I took it, braving a sip.

Ugh. Scotch tastes like shit. But it was a drink, so I just had to deal with it.

Malcolm was already turning toward the couch, and as I fought the Scotch down, I watched as he sprawled out, throwing one leg up onto the cushions and taking a long, deliberate drink from his glass as he stared me in the eye.

I felt the silence called for some commentary.

"So," I said. "Here we are."

He nodded. "This is true." He yawned, like a lion with his pride, surveying the land around him. The master of his domain.

I looked around. The room was gorgeous, decorated in tones of taupe and white and gold, perfectly elegant and turned out like a hotel room. "So I guess my job's going to be pretty easy, then," I said.

"Oh?" he asked. "How do you mean?"

I rolled my eyes. Did he really not get it? "I mean, why would you want to leave all this behind?" I gestured around me. "I mean, shit, if I had a yacht, I'd just spend all my time on it throwing parties."

"Would you? Would they be like the party you organized for the auction?"

I glanced at him sharply, but his head was tilted to the side, and he seemed merely curious. "No," I said. "We'd be out in international waters. We'd totally get drunk and high and shove the deck chairs into the sea."

He arched a brow at that. "Those deck chairs are awfully expensive," he said.

"Really? They're deck chairs. How expensive can they be?"

"Oh," he said, "three thousand dollars at least."

I choked and coughed on my drink. Alcohol burned in my nose. "What?" I exclaimed. "You could buy, like, thirty deck chairs for that cost!"

"Ah," he said, "but then they would not be three thousand dollar deck chairs and I'd be a laughingstock of the yachting club." He smiled while he said it and I scowled.

"Are you joking with me? Do you actually belong to a yacht club?"

His smile widened. "Of course I don't. The chairs came with the boat. I just bought it and it came with all these fine things in it, it seemed silly to change it."

That sort of thinking was totally foreign to me. "What, you mean you didn't want to make it your own or whatever?"

He shrugged. "I *own* it," he said. "It's already my own."

"Uh-huh," I said. "And what do you use it for?"

He shrugged again. "Getaways," he said. "In the summer it is a fine thing to cruise around the islands off the coast of Croatia. They are beautiful and it is very warm and relaxing."

"Yeah," I said. "About that... why Croatia? It's hardly the place I'd expect a rich guy to go."

"Oh? Why?"

"Because..." I trailed off. "Well, because it's not the French Riviera or... or a private island in the Bahamas or something." I had no idea where rich people went for fun.

"I used to frequent the livelier of European countries," he replied. "But you grow out of that thing when you get older, I think."

"So now you just want to float around in a boat?"

"And start a farm in the French countryside. I would dearly love to own some sheep."

"And yet," I said, "you won't be able to do any of that once you kick the bucket."

Ah. An abrupt turn of conversation, sprung like a trap. I'm so clever.

His lips tightened. "I know that," he said. His words were clipped. "Some things are just dreams, after all."

"Yeah," I said, "but for you they could be reality. You're fucking *rich*. You have one problem and it's a person. Do you know how many people would kill to have your problems? They don't go around offing themselves the first time someone betrays them."

I took a sip of my drink, watching him from the corner of my eye to gauge his reaction. His handsome face, so many sharp planes, became sharper at the suggestion that his problems were trivial. Which, you know, they kind of were. Not *to him,* obviously, but compared to being unable to eat, or keep the heat on, or stop drinking or shooting up or afford cancer treatments or any number of problems that people faced every damn day, his problem was a few angry emails, some public snubbings, and a humiliating episode of *Judge Judy* away from being satisfactorily resolved.

It made me kind of angry, now that I thought about it. He just wanted to throw all this away for no good reason. He had the money to buy a shrink. To literally put a shrink on-call twenty-four seven, and he just wanted to take the easy way out instead of facing his issues.

What a cock. I glared at my drink, swirling it around so that it splashed over its few ice cubes, then drained it. It burned and warmed me up, and my cheeks heated with it.

"Would you like to know how I met Dominic?" Malcolm asked me suddenly.

I jumped, and then looked at him, surprised. Why would he bring up our restaurateur? I doubted I would see him again as long as I lived. Still, anything to get him off his stupid suicidal high-horse. "Uh," I said. "Sure."

He smiled, but it lacked warmth. "That was the right answer," he said, and I had the impression I had passed some sort of test. Malcolm slid off the bed and stood up, shoving his hands into his pockets. Leisurely he began to pace, but I was attuned enough by now to his moods that I realized he was quite agitated. What he was about to share was personal. I set my drink down, lowered myself into one of the plush, luxurious armchairs, and turned my full attention on him.

He continued to pace. "I met Dominic in Paris," he began, "where he was staying after the war. He worked as a bartender in an... exclusive club."

Sex club, I thought.

"We got to talking one night, and I learned that he had come to France to flee the war in his old home. You remember the war?"

"I know there was *a* war. I was kind of young."

He laughed. A bitter sound. "Of course. I don't remember it very much myself. It didn't involve me, and I was only a teenager. But when the Soviet Union collapsed, Yugoslavia split apart in a civil war and went back to its component pieces. Dominic lost everything. He had to flee his hometown—I forget where it was—and his daughter was raped and his mother was *disappeared* because she lived in the wrong village. The war devastated the countryside. Dominic was Croat living in Serbian territory. He had to leave. He left everything behind and fled to France, and he was barely scraping by there. I asked him what he would do if he had unlimited money and could go back to Croatia and he told me he would buy a cafe in Dubrovnic and become a famous chef. So I bankrolled him."

He trailed off, though he didn't stop pacing. His eyes took on a faraway look, as though he were gazing into some other time and place. I waited for him to finish the story, but he said nothing. At last I frowned. "And?"

Malcolm paused and glanced at me, as if he had forgotten I was there. Then he smiled. "*And,*" he told me, "he's not a famous chef yet, but he's living a better life now. He doesn't have to serve alcohol to degenerates like me."

Oh yeah. That had been a sex club. I tried not to get sidetracked by curiosity. "I already know you can be generous," I said. "Why are you telling me this?"

He raised his eyebrows. "That wasn't the point of the story. The point was that I *know* my problems are paltry in the grand scheme of things. I will never lose my home to an invading army. My neighbors will never turn on me and shell my city." He paused in his pacing and pinned me with his dark cherry wood eyes, the same color, I realized, as the wood paneling of the interior of this yacht. Our eyes locked to each other, he stalked across the floor to me. "I understand, Sadie," he said. "I will never be *disappeared* by a militia and dragged into the woods where I'll be shot in the back of the head and left to rot in the fallen leaves. I will never be an anonymous skeleton in the forest. I *know* that."

He'd already anticipated this line of attack. Hell, it had probably been the very first thing he had told himself if he ever tried to talk himself out of his dumb plan. I felt cold inside, as though someone had slipped ice beneath my skin. "So?" I said. He loomed over the chair, staring down at me. Then he sighed and tapped his chest.

"I'm still hollow in here. Knowing and feeling are two different things. I *know* my struggles are nothing. Betrayal by my own dear brother? What does it matter? The things that cause me pain... they change nothing. There is nothing here *to* change."

Reaching down, he stroked my face. "I'm afraid you have set yourself up for an impossible task, Sadie."

I tried not to show my trepidation. I was starting to believe him. But there wasn't anything I could do about it now. I'd vowed to try my best to reach the person under the armor. I *knew* he was there. But he was right—knowing and feeling are two different things. If I couldn't reach his heart—and there had to be something there, otherwise he wouldn't have felt any pain at all—then I could never draw out the man I truly wanted to know.

I could never talk him out of killing himself, I realized. But earnest words are never the only thing in a woman's arsenal.

I could also be flippant.

"Don't worry about me," I said. "You forget. I was an artist before I was a personal assistant. I'm like a world expert at banging my head against a wall."

A half-smile graced his lips. "Is that so? I wasn't aware art was so difficult."

"That's 'cause you're doing it wrong," I replied. "You have to dig deep."

"There's nowhere to dig," he said.

"Fine," I said. "Then show the world how shallow you are. You have to dig really deep to demonstrate that."

"Really?" he said.

"Really," I replied. "Because there is nothing harder than making a piece of art that someone can just look at and say, 'yeah, that says absolutely nothing.'"

He pursed his lips. "What about abstract art?"

"You'd better believe that says something," I told him. "For a lot of abstract artists, it was a rebellion against fascism, or a comment on modern life. Nothing makes much sense after a war so huge it ripped everyone up and changed the entire world. There was a lot of commentary on breaking free of old strictures and shit like that that didn't make any sense in a senseless world."

He blinked. "Oh. So you're saying that I somehow have to make art that means *less* than saying 'everything is meaningless?'"

The joke was on him. All art says something, even if you think it doesn't, because it's a conversation between the artist and the audience, and the only way to be utterly meaningless was to never make the attempt at all.

I wasn't about to tell him that, though. I didn't want him deciding it was impossible and offing himself right then and there. He had *something* to say, and I wanted him to figure out what it was. His desire to create was just a sign that he wasn't too far gone, because to speak and be heard is an affirmation, and when he understood that I knew he would see things differently.

I smiled. "You are certainly welcome to try," I told him.

Confusion passed over his features. "All right, I

know you said not everything is a challenge, but that sounds like a challenge."

I grinned. "Fine. *That* was a challenge," I said. "You think you're so great at everything? Prove it."

He regarded me, wordless, for a few moments. "All right," he said. "I will." Then he reached down and took my hand, drawing me to my feet. "But now, I believe it is time for you to uphold *your* part of our bargain."

I followed him to the bedroom, past a spiral staircase and down a tiny hallway. When he opened the door I had to bite my lip to keep from gasping in astonishment. He led me inside, then dropped my hand and stood back, allowing me to take it in.

I stared at the room. Sumptuous. Decadent. Delicious. Rows of windows displaying the darkness outside. A desk on one side of the room, a couch on the other. A flat-screen TV at one end.

And a four-poster bed at the other.

"I'm afraid I wasn't entirely truthful when I said I didn't make any changes to the interior of the boat," Malcolm admitted from behind me. "The bed is my own personal touch."

Really? A four-poster bed? On a yacht?

Then it hit me. Of course he'd have a four-poster bed on his yacht, I realized. *The better to tie you up, my dear.*

His hand alighted on my back. Hot and insistent, he guided me to the bed. "Stand here," he commanded. "I'm going to bind you."

I stiffened, and he felt it. Gently, he turned me around and put his hands on my shoulders, meeting my eyes with his. He searched my face for a moment, looking for something, and I couldn't have said if he found it or not.

"I've poured myself out to you, Sadie," he said finally. "Trust me. Give me this one last fling."

Anger boiled up in me. One last fling? He was so selfish. But if he persisted in thinking that he was going to kick the bucket, then fine. I'd give him his fling. I'd fling him so hard he'd have to stay. Or... come back. Like a boomerang.

Not the best metaphor, but it would have to do.

"All right," I said, and the smile that broke over his features was beatific.

He took his own sweet time setting things up. The ropes he used were stored in one of the dresser drawers, and I watched as he drew them out, long and sinuous. Black. Velvet. At least they weren't red.

"Take off your clothes."

Wordlessly, I did as he commanded. First my coat pooled to the floor. Then my top and my bra. My shoes next, and finally my skirt. I still wore no panties. His cum had dried, sticky, on the inside of my thighs.

"Lie down. Spread your legs and arms," he instructed. His eyes on me were hot, not detached like they'd been when he'd been taking out the length of red ribbon in his own bedroom, and I felt an answering rush of heat as I obeyed. The comforter was down, cool and soft, and I found myself hoping, vaguely, that I didn't ruin it by being messy. Stretching my arms above my head and spreading my legs out, I stared at the ceiling and waited for him to begin.

With calm, deliberate movements, Malcolm moved to the wall where he turned the lights off, throwing the room into darkness, cutting off my sense of sight.

Beneath me the sea rolled and rocked, and I found I was so tired I wondered if I wasn't going to fall asleep before we actually did anything.

I needn't have worried. The sound of Malcolm's clothes rustled as he moved around the bed, a presence so potent that I would have known it anywhere, listed toward it at any time. Cotton and linen and wool scraped over my ears, and for a strange, terrifying moment it felt as though they were being dragged over my naked brain. I bit my lip as I heard him tie the first rope to the post near my right hand and waited for him to take my wrist.

He didn't.

Instead he moved, one by one, to the other posts around the bed, securing one end of the ropes to the bed posts before moving on to the next. When he finally had the fourth one in place, he took a step back.

The room was almost pitch dark. The lights of the city had completely retreated.

"Beg me to tie you up," he said.

His voice fell flat and hard into the space between us, and I swallowed with difficulty. But if this was what it took, fine.

"Please, Malcolm," I whispered. "Tie me up."

"Louder."

"Tie me up. Please."

"Louder. With feeling, Sadie."

It was almost corny... and yet it gave me a delicious thrill to hear him order me around. Usually I was the one doing the ordering.

"Please, Malcolm, tie me up. Twist me up and tie me up and fuck me, please, please--"

He snatched my wrist from the bed, and in only a

few quick movements my hand was bound and he was moving on to the next one. Swiftly, with practiced hands, he bound me thoroughly, but not uncomfortably, and when at last I was fully spread and immobilized, I couldn't hide my arousal any longer. My mouth was dry as I panted in anticipation.

"I'm going to make you come, Sadie," Malcolm told me, and it was so matter-of-fact I wanted to laugh.

"Why?" I said. "I feel like I'm getting away with something, because I never get to give you--Ah!"

I shrieked at the sudden lash across my nipples. Sharp. Swift. Something that whistled through the air. A riding crop, I realized. Something for beating horses.

I should have felt insulted. But instead, I just moaned at the pain as it raced through my body, transmuting into pleasure.

"Silence," Malcolm said. "I am going to make you come." He paused. "And," he added, and I could just see the faint smile on his face, "If you make any noise at all, except for when I ask you questions, I will delay your orgasm by one minute.":

"So I have to be silent?" I asked.

The riding crop lashed over my nipples again, and it took all I had not to squeak with pleasure. "No talking," he told me. "You have bought yourself a minute of agony."

I bit my lip and said nothing.

He moved to the wall where something clicked open. A tiny glow illuminated his face, and he adjusted something. The heater, I realized when it kicked on and he shut it again, leaving us in blackness again.

Warm air caressed my skin, my sore nipples, my pussy so wet it was already coated with the juices of my core. I stared up into the dark and listened as Malcolm began to shuck his clothing.

I heard the fall of his blazer, the grate of his zipper, the whisper of his trousers as they slid past his hips and to the ground. He stepped out of his pants, removing his hard leather shoes as he did so, and his sigh of relief was like a fresh breeze.

When at last the bed dipped with his weight, I was hot and ready for him. The heat of his body was a balm on my own burning desire, and he laid against me, over me, every inch of his hard, naked body rubbing against mine. Where our skin met, we melded, and I lost myself. Soft lips found my ear, teased me with breath and teeth. His muscled arms, his broad chest, his trim hips and hard thighs slid against my body, a perfect male specimen. The contrast between his body and mine, a beautiful man and... well... *me,* made my cheeks heat in the dark in something akin to embarrassment.

I told myself it was merely a pang of regret rooted in aesthetic sensibility. In the contrast between beauty and decay, I came out on the wrong side of the equation.

Malcolm rocked his hips into me, his cock heavy and hot pressed against my belly. Then he removed himself, planting hot, damp kisses down my throat and breasts, trailing over my ribcage and stomach, until he reached my exposed pussy. Warm breath puffed over it, and my hips rocked involuntarily toward him.

He settled himself down between my legs, looping an arm casually over one splayed thigh before cupping the inside of the other in his hand and placing the pad of his thumb on my soft, slick cunt. Then, with slow, deliberate movements, he began to glide his thumb against my labia and clit, and my eyes rolled back in my head in bliss.

For what seemed like forever, he slipped and slid the pad of his finger over me, exploring my folds and crevices, slowly, inexorably driving me wild. My head tossed with each ripple of pleasure that spiraled through me, and it was pain to stay silent as he sweetly coaxed ecstasy from my body.

After a while, he switched his focus and began to move with more purpose, more intent. Gently he smeared my juices over my pussy and asshole, and I quivered and ached in anticipation. When he finally slipped his pinky finger past the tight ring of muscle of my puckered entrance, I gulped and licked my lips. Then another finger—I couldn't tell which one—slid into my pussy, an easy, swift entry. His thumb alighted on my clit, and I remembered how he had stroked me to orgasm in just this way our very first time. The memory alone caused a moan to well in my chest, and I was only able to bite it back at the last second.

Gently, without hurry, he began to play with my clit, and my already sensitized flesh hummed and buzzed with delight. It was hard, so hard to remember not to groan or speak, and when his other hand alighted on my leg, smoothing its way up my thigh, over my hipbone to my ribs, I thought nothing of it other than how good and warm he felt.

"Tell me about your phoenix."

My eyes shot open. I hadn't realized I'd closed them. Glancing down, I tried to find his eyes, but the room had become pitch black. Even so, I felt him tracing the outline of the phoenix tattoo on my side with the tip of his finger as though the room were as bright as day. How was he doing it?

The photos, I realized. My phoenix was one of the bigger ones, all gorgeous, garish colors, rainbows and flowers and fire licking up the left side of my ribcage from a pile of bones and dead wood on my hip. It was stunning. Of course he'd remembered it.

I licked my lips and he flicked his thumbnail over my clit, making my hips jump into his hand. "What... what do you want to know?" I asked.

"Did you design it?" The pad of his thumb soothed the aching nub at the apex of my pussy, and I tried not to melt into incoherence.

"Mm, yes... I... I designed all my tattoos," I managed to get out.

"And why did you choose a phoenix?"

Really? My brain scrabbled for an answer that wasn't too pat, but in the end I had to settle. I was just too distracted. "A phoenix is a... a symbol of rebirth," I said as his thumb began to circle faster and I felt my core begin to tighten. He really knew the perfect ways to play my body, as though I were an instrument.

"And why did you choose that particular symbol of rebirth?" he asked me casually. My orgasm built, a swell in the ocean about to become a tsunami.

"Um..." I ran my tongue over my teeth as bliss buffeted my mind. "Because... because everything you were burns away, and you come out new..."

"Mmm," he murmured. His hand slid over the place where the tattoo lay, soft and hot, and I shivered under it even as he stroked my clit harder and faster, until I was coiling up, aching and ready to come—

—and he paused.

My building orgasm faded. I couldn't help myself; I cried out with the loss.

"Another minute," he said, and it took all my strength not to scream in frustration. When the mounting pleasure had faded, he began again, expertly plying my body, and this time the orgasm built faster and harder and I had to bite the inside of my cheek to keep from shrieking.

Then his hand moved up to just beneath my right breast and he traced the tattoo there, and as he did, his fingers found the jagged scar hidden beneath the ink and followed it tenderly. But he didn't ask about the scar. "Tell me about your sparrow," he said instead.

My mouth fell open. The sparrow was so small compared to my other tats that it was a wonder he remembered it at all. But then his finger ghosted over the sparrow's beak—exactly where it was—before retreating and stroking against its breast and in a sudden flash of insight I realized he had memorized every tattoo of mine.

The thought shocked me, stunned me.

"Ah... uh... a sparrow... they say the gods mark the fall of a single sparrow..." My voice was a whisper.

"I see," he said. His thumb moved faster and faster, until I was on the brink again, and again he stopped. This time I kept my wits enough about me that I was able to stifle the moan of frustration. It died in my chest, strangled before it was born.

Malcolm waited for my quivering body to subside. "Good," he murmured. "Well done." His thumb resumed its pace and I thrashed and strained against my bonds as he traced his hand up to my throat and the tattoo winding over it. Words this time.

"And this one?" he asked. "What does it say? The script is so elaborate I could hardly make it out." And his fingers trailed over the scar beneath it. The red smile I was supposed to wear down to the grave.

"It says, 'Might as well live.'" I told him, my voice so soft I could barely hear it.

He gave a low, quiet laugh. "Dorothy Parker," he said, and with a flick of his thumbnail I was coming, hard and aching around his fingers, my body lost in ecstasy as I yanked against the ropes, but inside everything was tumbled and torn, rent asunder and filled with pain and anger.

He knew my tattoos. Every single one. I was raw and exposed. He'd seen the scars beneath them, and he knew they were important in some way. We were dancing around them, around their significance, and it frightened me. But all he did was wait for my orgasm to pass before moving on to the next. Gently he stroked each one in the dark and asked me, as he circled my clit with his thumb, what each one meant to me.

"The leaping koi fish?" His hand stroking the inside of my upper arm.

Breaking free.

"The cherry tree shedding its blossoms?" My shoulder, the wafting petals spiraling across my chest.

Impermanence.

"The spider? The hand of Fatima? The vulture?"

Infinity. Protection from evil. Cleansing.

And beneath each one, he found the scar, running his hands over it as he brought me to orgasm again and again.

When at last he had received a response for each tattoo and was satisfied, he untied me and he fucked me, gently, as though I were fragile. My exhausted body wrapped around him, clung to him, and we rocked with the ocean and I came around him again and again until at last he found his release and we fell asleep on the swell and fall of the sea.

12

Time at sea takes on a new meaning. The hours stretch out into days, and a single night can yawn as wide as a week. The sun comes. The sun goes. The water passes by.

We sailed south.

Malcolm and I joined together again and again, and the sea blurred the edges of our time, until it was hard for me to say if we'd been drifting on the water for a day or a hundred days. We met and coupled constantly, and when we weren't fucking Malcolm tried to capture me in art, searching for the elusive thing I carried within me that he thought would reveal the secrets of the universe to him. And when he grew frustrated, angry, enraged at his own inability to speak without words he would throw his sketch pad away, toss his canvas to the ground, squash the small clay statuette he had been fashioning and launch himself at me, wherever I happened to be, and he would force me down to the ground, up against a wall, into the strangest positions, and we would fuck again until we were sore and raw.

ꕥ

"When am I going to stop falling over?"

"When you get your sea legs. You will become accustomed to the rocking of the ship soon. You will be able to walk on the deck as if it were dry land. You simply need practice."

"Practice makes perfect, I guess."

"Not, it seems, when we are talking about pastels."

"I told you, they are a pain in the ass. Stop trying to use them."

"But the colors..."

"Color says shit. Work in black and white if you want to tell everyone life is meaningless."

"Not life. *My* life. My life is meaningless."

"Only if you use pastels."

ꕥ

I wore his clothes, mine having been left behind in our flight. The sun was warm and the boat was heated well, so I wore his underwear. Malcolm had literally fifty pairs of boxers on board, and they mostly fit me due to my ass being roughly twice as huge as my waist. At the very least they didn't immediately fall down. His shirts hung on me like smocks.

"You have a lot of underwear," I said as I modeled it for him. "What's the deal?"

"I used to have a lot of guests on this boat," he said. "Underwear was often misplaced."

I winced. "Misplaced?"

He smiled at me. In his hands he was slowly

shaping a lump of clay into something that might have been my likeness, if my parents had been Ewoks. "When you are on a boat and get lost in the moment, sometimes the sea wind sweeps by and carries your fine silk boxers out to sea. Quite a few guests lost their unmentionables that way, even after I told them it took only a moment to weigh them down." He raised his brows. "Since we are going to be in short supply of everything, I expect you to remember that tidbit."

I cocked a hip and put my hand on it. "Seriously?" I said. "Thanks for the tip, mom."

He didn't smile at that. Instead his face went still as he pushed and pulled at the lump of clay, his brows drawing down into a frown. "My mother wouldn't have thought twice about throwing such expensive things away," he said at last. "She wanted the world to be disposable. I recommend you not be like her."

Touched a nerve. A deep one. "Don't worry," I said. "I once wore a pair of gym shorts as pajamas for five straight years and didn't throw them out until they literally fell apart in the wash."

That coaxed a little smirk from him. "Oh?" he said.

"They were like Swiss cheese."

Putting the little lump of clay down, he leaned back on the couch and tilted his head, studying me. "I would have liked to see that," he said.

"It was the least sexy thing in the universe," I assured him.

"On you, anything is sexy," he said. I tried to ignore the blush that rampaged across my face at his words. "Come here, Sadie. I like to see you in my clothes."

I swallowed and walked toward him. My bare feet sank into the plush carpet, and when I reached him I crawled onto the couch and straddled his thighs. "Yeah?" I said. "We have the same size butt. That's totally sexy."

"It is sexy," he insisted. His hands found said butt and squeezed, massaging my ample ass cheeks, and suddenly I swear I thought my ass might actually be sexy too.

"Oh," I murmured.

Reaching up, Malcolm pulled me down into a kiss. His teeth nibbled at my lips, grazed over my jaw, teased my throat, and all the while his hands squeezed and kneaded, pulling me close until his cock, hard and straining, pressed into the soft hot space between my legs. He rubbed me over himself until I couldn't take it any more and pulled him off the couch. We landed on the floor with a teeth-jarring thud, and he tore his own boxers off me and fucked me as I lay beneath him in his white linen shirt, my hands holding his hips in place as he took his pleasure and gave back to me in return.

❧

"What are you painting?"

"The sea."

"I hate to break it to you, but that's been done a million times before. I thought you wanted to say something totally new."

"I'm working on it."

"I can see that... hey, wait. That's me. That's the sea in the shape of me."

"You can tell?"

"I'd recognize that pear shape anywhere."

"You are as beautiful and strong as the sea."

"Then you're hardly saying nothing with this painting."

"...I might still have things left to say. Let me say them first, before I can no longer speak. I thought you weren't in a hurry to silence me."

"I thought you *were*."

"...As tumultuous as the sea, too. I cannot predict you."

"Neither can I sometimes."

"Kiss me, Sadie."

"What will I get out of it?"

"This... and... *this...*"

"*...Oh.*"

One day I tried to make waffles. It did not go well.

"I burned the waffles," I told Malcolm when he came to investigate the smoke.

"I see that." He stared at the blackened corpses of several failed waffles. "I could smell it, too."

"Sorry," I said. "I'm a really lousy housewife."

"Boatwife," he said. "You are a lousy boatwife."

"Yeah. That."

He ran his finger over my chin and raised a brow. "Even more of a lousy boatwife because you don't know I hate waffles."

I stared at him, incredulous. "Then why do you have a waffle iron?" I asked. "It's just sitting here, begging to be used."

"Every kitchen should have a waffle iron," he said.

"Even if you hate waffles?"

"Especially if you hate waffles. Every time I see it, it reminds me of how lucky I am to not be eating waffles right now."

I stared at the black waffle discs. "I suppose we could play Frisbee with them."

"Or just throw them into the sea."

"That was the eventual goal, yes." I put my hands on my hips and blew my hair out of my face. "Well, what do you want to eat instead?" We were well-provisioned with dry and canned goods, but pre-processed crap was getting awfully old. The waffles, at least, would have been fresh made.

Malcolm grabbed me by the hips. "I can think of one thing I'd like to eat," he said and lifted me onto the counter top before sliding the boxers down my legs and letting them pool on the floor.

He knelt down and began to lick my pussy, quick and sharp. I gasped, my head lolling. "I... I think this violates some sort of health regulation..."

He paused. "Good thing we're in international waters, then." His smile was wicked, and I didn't object when he returned to his task.

"So how did you become so fucking rich? This boat is still blowing my mind."

"My father made me get rich."

"Haha! Oh, you're serious."

"I am. Hold still, you are going to mess up the exposure."

"But my nose itches!"

"Suffer for art."

"You. *You* are the one who's supposed to suffer,

not your model."

"Is that so? You see, my father taught me that in business it doesn't matter who is hurt. We all enter with the same expectations. Kill or be killed. If you get killed you might as well lie down and die in the street."

"Jesus Christ. That's fucked up."

"Is it? It's held true for most of my time in business, and it's made me quite a lot of money. Hold still."

"The itch has moved to my boobs now!"

"I will lavish them with attention when we are done if only you will hold still for one more minute."

"That attention had better be good."

"I promise it will be."

"I am entering into this agreement with the expectation to get screwed over now."

"I wouldn't blame you. I have crushed many an enemy under my heel and heard the lamentations of their interns. But for you, I think I must make an exception. Though we are at war, with two disparate goals, I believe I may fraternize with the enemy as long as I don't let my guard down. You will not convince me to change my course, Sadie. I see what you are doing."

"I'm not doing anything. And *shit.* I'm really depressed now. Do you really think of every encounter as a war?"

"Of course. What else could it be?"

"Creative. Collaboration. Lo—Sex isn't a competition."

"...It is if you do it right. And shit, this isn't it either."

"The photograph?"

"What a mess."

"Forget it. Come her and lavish attention on me."

ॐ

"Where did you go?" he asked me one day, and I realized I had been staring at the waves. I couldn't have said how long I had been watching them, and when I turned to look at Malcolm, their patterns and swirls continued to spiral across my vision.

"I don't know," I said. "I just stopped thinking for a while." I smiled while I said it. "Feels good."

"I wouldn't know," he said, walking up behind me and slipping his arms around my waist, snugging me in close. I felt the swell of his erection against my ass. "My mind has started to run away with me, too, and I have never been able to meditate."

"Mm," I said. I rubbed my ass cheeks over his cock, and he sighed, grinding into me. "It's not all it's cracked up to be," I told him. "You start thinking about nothing and the next thing you know your ramen is boiling over or someone's cat just threw themselves under the wheels of your car."

"Perhaps you shouldn't meditate while driving." His hands were slipping under the waistband of the boxers I wore, smoothing over my thighs, dipping into my pussy.

"It's just too easy when your head is empty," I joked.

His hands stilled. "Why do you always do that?" he asked me.

I frowned. "Do what?"

"Put yourself down."

I ground against his hands, trying to encourage

him to continue, but he was steadfast. "I mean it, Sadie. You have a low opinion of yourself."

My lips thinned. "It makes it easier," I said finally.

"Easier to do what?"

I shrugged. "Deal with the disappointment I feel when I look in the mirror."

Behind me I felt him shake his head. "How am I going to convince you you're amazing?" he sighed.

I could think of one way, but I didn't want to say it out loud. I was trying not to push the issue of the fact that we were living on borrowed time, whether he decided to end it all or not. "I don't know," I said. "Pay me to think I'm amazing? I can do a lot for the right incentive."

His chest rumbled in a laugh. "You and most of the rest of the world. But I think even if I did, that you would just *tell* me you thought you were amazing, rather than actually change."

I shrugged. "How would you tell the difference?"

His lips brushed against my ear, and I shivered down to my toes. "I would be able to tell."

He took me from behind, there on the deck, plundering my core first until I came around him, then withdrawing and placing his cock against the tight hole of my ass. I stiffened, but when I didn't tell him no, he pressed inside, filling me up unbearably, and as he thrust into my ass I closed my eyes and thought of nothing.

"I never see the captain. What does he do all day, jack off?"

"He tells me he's writing a book."

"About what?"

"I'm not sure. Maybe about jacking off?"

"That's gross. Don't be gross. You're rich, you should be classy."

"You were the one who introduced the subject."

"Yeah, but you should be classier than me. I'm just a working girl in a rich man's world."

"I'm just a rich man on a boat with a beautiful woman who makes him think of soft, dirty things. How else should I behave?"

"Mysterious. Enigmatic."

"I am that, too. Mysteriously and enigmatically aroused by your perfect ass. No, *inspired* by your perfect ass."

"Maybe you should do a piece of art on my ass instead of my whole body."

"It's certainly something to think about. Perhaps I should write a sonnet on it instead. Sixteen perfect lines, eight for one cheek and eight for the other, and yet only a pale shadow of the real thing."

"My ass is too big for only sixteen lines. Maybe you should write an epic on it instead."

"I could. Perhaps I should write it on the skin, as I did on the plane. But I fear it might take too long and you would get bored."

"Why, because it's so big?"

"Because I'd be writing one-handed."

"See? Gross."

"Come here and see how gross it is."

"I... Oh."

"Turn over. I will write my ode to your body with mine."

"*...oh.*"

One day, in frustration, he broke all his pencils. Deliberately, methodically, I watched him snap each one in half and throw them into the sea. The rage on his face was shocking, overwhelming. For the first time I was actually nervous of his temper, of the temper of the billionaire, the ruthless businessman who had carried the person inside of him to such a hopeless, terrible place in life.

"It's not right," he growled to the ocean. "It's *never* right. I can't get it *right!*" With one last heave, he tossed the box into the water. Made of cardboard, it floated for a moment before floating away, slowly sinking, until it had whirled and eddied beneath the surface in the wake of the boat. He stood at the railing, gripping it in white knuckled hands, and breathed deeply, struggling to get his fury under control.

I'd been posing for him. When he'd abruptly screamed with frustration and thrown the sketchbook in a rage it had skidded across the deck to my feet. I would not look at someone else's work without permission, but now I could not help it. The salty sea wind caught the pages and flipped and fluttered them, back and forth.

Stunning sketches flashed before me, each one shocking in the life it exuded. Slowly I knelt down and watched the images fly by. Me as a butterfly. Me as a mermaid, swimming in the sea, my hair floating around me. Me as Ophelia. Me lying on the couch in the sitting room, snoozing in the sun like a cat. Me arching, twisting in the throes of ecstasy. Me, me, me, and every one almost technically perfect.

But he was right. Something was missing. I couldn't put my finger on it.

"Have you taken classes before?" I said.

My voice jerked him out of his enraged stupor and he glanced at me, his eyes cold. "No," he said. "I told you, I am good at everything." A hand ran through his hair, fingers tangling. "Except *this!*"

He turned and stalked toward me, and I saw immediately that he meant to toss the sketchbook into the sea as well. I did what I rarely did now and defied him. Wrapping my arms around it, I curled over, protecting it with my body. His bare feet came to rest beneath my eyes as he loomed over me.

"Give me the book, Sadie."

"Don't throw it away."

"I can't get it right. Sketching isn't *it.*"

"Isn't *what?*"

"My masterpiece. I will never make a masterpiece with... with pencils and paper!" Anger burst out of him, raw and humiliated. "Perfection is impossible with imperfect materials!" He knelt down in front of me and put his hand on the sketchbook as he tried to tug it from my grasp.

I was too interested in what he had said to protest, and he took it from me. "Perfection?" I said, sitting up as he took the book and coldly, precisely put it in order before closing it. "Why does it need to be perfect?"

His cherry wood eyes met mine, and I shivered, they were so hard and cold. "What is the point if it isn't perfect? I must leave behind perfection. I lived my life perfectly, and my masterpiece must reflect that."

If you lived your life perfectly, I wanted to say, *then why are you so miserable?*

But I didn't. Instead I just said, "Perfection isn't the goal of art. You'll drive yourself crazy if that's what you want."

"I should be the *first,*" he said. "The first to reach that goal. I'll live forever if I could just—get it—*right!*"

And as he spoke he stood and flung the sketchbook overboard.

Like a dying bird it flew through the air, its pages struggling to catch the wind like broken wings. Then it fell to the sea and sank beneath the waves.

"You're really drunk, Malcolm."

"I certainly hope so."

"No, I'm serious. I'm worried about you. You haven't been eating and now you're downing the scotch like water. You're half way to dead."

"I've been worse."

"Yeah, I have, too. Coming back isn't fun at all."

"Your throat."

"...Yes. My throat."

"Someone slit your throat."

"Yes, they did."

"Then why am I the one who's drunk instead of you?"

"Because you are acting like a child. Get up. I'm putting some food in you."

"Not waffles. Anything but waffles."

"No, not waffles."

"Good, I love waffles."

"You told me you hated waffles!"

"I told you that so you would feel better about

murdering perfectly good waffles. What you do to waffles is a crime against humanity."

"You know what? Now you're getting waffles."

"No... no, don't..."

"Yeah. Bet you wish you weren't too drunk to resist my magnetic wiles now."

"I never can, anyway."

ꕥ

I made him waffles. They were atrocious.

He ate them anyway, to make me happy.

ꕥ

"Sorry about those waffles."

"They are with God now."

"If by God you mean the fish, then yeah, that's where they are."

"Even the fish, I think, will not eat bile- and Scotch-soaked burned waffle bits. Only the Lord will have pity on them."

"Yeah? You think he'll have pity on you when you kill yourself?"

"...A shot across the bow. And no. I don't deserve it."

"So to Hell, then?"

"The devil knows I'll take over. I will wander the world as a hungry ghost. Perhaps I will haunt you."

"I'll leave some waffles out for you."

ꕥ

"Tell me about your parents," he said one day as I stretched on the deck in the sun, assuming various yoga positions I'd seen once or twice. I don't have time to do yoga back home, and apparently it's harder than it looks. My hamstrings screeched in protest. Malcolm sat by, watching me intently as he attempted to capture my dynamic poses on his canvas in strokes of broad, abstract color before I switched to something new.

"Jeez. Just go straight for the Freud," I told him. "You're not very subtle."

"Why would I be subtle?" he replied. "You're on a boat in the middle of the Adriatic. There's nowhere for you to hide."

"Awfully Bond-villain of you."

He smiled at that. "I would have made an excellent Bond villain. Or an excellent Bond."

"I thought you might be Batman the first time I saw you."

His laugh boomed over the deck. "You had me pegged," he said. "Batman is a damaged megalomaniac in latex and leather." He stroked slash of color over the canvas as I tried to do downward-facing dog. I saw stars. "So anyway," he continued. "Tell me about your parents."

"What about my parents?" I asked him. "They were parents."

"Everyone's parents screwed up," he said. "It's a law of modern life. You already know a little something about my parents. How'd your parents do it?"

From my inverted position it was hard to discern his expression. "I'm not ready to tell you yet."

He didn't respond and I straightened up. The sun

beat down and the wind whistled past my ears as I tried to stand on one leg. The pitch and roll of the deck was wreaking havoc on my balance. Malcolm was quiet for a second.

"Then tell me about the least objectionable parent," he said at last.

I fell over. It was the sea, I swear. I gave up trying to yoga and lay down on the deck, staring up at the sky. The sea breeze wormed its way beneath the boxers and fine linen shirt I wore. The sun baked me.

I sighed. He'd been open with me. "I suppose my mother," I said. "She..." I trailed off. "She didn't know how to exist in this world."

"What do you mean?"

"She was kindhearted. Tender. Soft where you need to be hard sometimes. She liked to dance, and she made the most amazing chocolate cake. She always put coffee in the chocolate frosting. It was amazing. But she wasn't very with it. I had to keep the house cleaned up and in order, and I was the one who kept things organized in our home. She was kind, but scattered, so I had to pick up the slack. She liked to cook so I never really learned how... Which I guess explains my waffles..."

I could tell this wasn't what he wanted to hear about. He wasted no time getting down to the bones of it. "You speak as if she's dead," he said to me."

I closed my eyes. The sun burned red behind my eyelids. "She is."

"I'm sorry."

I shrugged. "It was a long time ago," I said.

"Does it have anything to do with your scars?"

The question rocked me, but I refused to show it. "You could say that," I told him.

He was quiet and the sound of paint slapping on canvas paused. "I've upset you," he said after a few seconds.

"It takes more than that to upset me," I told him.

Malcolm sighed. "Yes," he said. "I should have guessed that it does." He resumed painting, and I fell asleep.

When I awoke, I was warm all over, and my hand was outstretched, as it always was, reaching for the bedside table that was no longer there. Customary flash of panic, and then I remembered where I was. I looked back to where Malcolm was sitting, painting. I hadn't been asleep for long. The light had barely changed, but he was giving me a curious look.

"You do that in bed, too," he said. "You always reach for something that isn't there. What is it?"

My gun. My safety. "Nothing," I said.

"You are not like your mother," he said. "You are hard in many places." He sighed and picked up the canvas before putting his foot through it. "Start over again," he said. "Always, always I'm starting over again with you."

ꕥ

"The coffee you make is almost as atrocious as your waffles."

"What? No it isn't. I demand satisfaction."

"Satisfaction... like this?"

"*...Oh.*"

ꕥ

"So what's so great about Don?" I asked him one

day as we soaked in the hot tub. I couldn't remember how long ago we'd slipped into it and I was vaguely, distantly worried that I was somehow boiling my insides. However, beneath the luxurious pounding of the jets, my body had relaxed enough that I doubted my own ability to move.

"There's nothing particularly great about him," Malcolm replied after what seemed like a long, thoughtful pause, although perhaps he was just coming back from being asleep. "He is like a brother to me."

"How so, if he's so mediocre and you're so awesome?"

He laughed at that. "One can't choose family. Don and I met in Kindergarten, if you can believe that. His parents were very abusive. Terrible. Absolutely terrible. He still has burns on his body from the cigarette butts they put out on him."

I opened my eyes. "Holy shit. Really?" I'd heard of that sort of thing happening, but I'd never seen it in person.

"Really. They were the worst. My mother liked to take in stray animals, and she thought of Don as a stray. So he spent more and more time at our house, until he was basically moved in. My family took him in and my father took us both under his wing." His head was tilted back, soaking in the rays of the sun. I don't think he knew I was watching him, because he frowned slightly. "Although now that I think about it, that's kind of a dubious honor. My father was a little fucked up, I think."

"Oh? You *think?*"

"Yeah. I do. He taught us both about how to succeed in life, and everything we did had to be a competition against each other. I always won, but Don was more ruthless." A humorless smile passed across his face. "That's the strange thing. My father liked him more because he was willing to do whatever it took, and I always found myself on the defensive. Just like now, I suppose."

"So... he's like your brother, but the brother who's always trying to fuck you over and take the family inheritance."

Malcolm sat up and looked at me. "I suppose so."

I sat up, too, turning toward him and putting my elbow on the side of the tub. "You guys are like some kind of screwy Shakespearean family. Right down to you trusting him enough to give him control of the company."

His lips thinned. "He's like my brother."

"You are fucked up. He's a fucked up brother. You know what you do with people like that in your life? You cut them off. You never talk to them again."

His brows rose. "If I recall correctly, you acted horrified when I suggested you cut me off."

"Yeah... because you're not batshit insane and trying to destroy me." At least... I didn't think so. I didn't feel particularly under assault, and I knew what that felt like so I was pretty sure his talk of going to war with me over his ultimate fate was just that—talk. I'd never seen a guy with more unresolved business in the world, and given his perfectionist nature there was no way he was going to off himself before he set it all right. I was as good as victor in our 'battle.' "Cutting people off who become toxic, who make you feel like shit all the time? That's fine. That's *good.* Healthy."

"But..." His face was pained. "When we were younger, we'd band together against my father. We'd trick him into thinking one or the other of us had won whatever stupid challenge he'd put before us." I noted his use of the word 'stupid' to refer to challenges. "We looked out for each other. Saved each other's asses all the time. I don't know what happened..."

Again that lost look on his face, the one that came whenever I'd made him think of something uncomfortable, something so at odds with the way he had accepted the world that it caused him physical pain.

I could see it, too. A kid alone in a house with a frivolous mother and a father who thought of the world as a place to be sectioned up and sold off, piece by piece? I would have leapt on the first person who presented themselves as an ally, too, and I probably would have clung to them in exactly the same way. The only difference between Malcolm and I was that I'd never found someone as desperate as me to latch on to. I'd always been alone.

I moved across the hot tub and extended a hand to soothe the lines from Malcolm's brow, but abruptly he stood and got out of the tub.

I watched him walk away.

"I'm tired, Sadie. Nothing ever comes out right except fucking you."

"I thought you were good at everything."

"I don't think so any more."

"Then maybe you should adjust your expectations."

&

"Where are we going?" I asked one day.

"I don't know," Malcolm said. "Away."

"Surely we'll have to stop for fuel at some point."

He just smiled at that. "Surely we will," he said, and leaned in and kissed me. We were naked, lying in his bed, and his hand came up and stroked the inside of my thigh, lazily. "Have you ever seen the sculpture of the lovers?" he asked me.

"The Rodin?" I said. "Of course. I mean... in books, I guess."

He leaned in, pushing me onto my back. "It is extraordinary in person. The flesh gives way so easily in stone." And he put a hand to my breast and squeezed lightly, as though to emphasize his point.

I laughed, an old, familiar self-deprecating thing. "Oh, sure," I said, "if I had any flesh there to give way."

A scowl passed across his features and his grip tightened, sending a sharp pain shooting through me and I gasped and wiggled. "Your breasts are fine," he said. "Stop speaking so poorly of them."

I still wasn't used to submitting. I never would be. My customary rebellion welled in me. "But then I'd have to listen to other people speak poorly of them. You know, I'm just putting it out there. Laughing at yourself is a pretty good way to get other people to laugh, and then the jokes already over with." I managed to scoot back and his grip eased.

He wasn't happy with my answer. He tied my hands to the bed and lashed my breasts over and over again as he pumped his hand in my pussy, hot and hard and demanding, until I came with a scream and a tearless sob.

ೋ

And then one day Malcolm said, "We have to stop for fuel," and just like that it was over.

13

Time came back. The sun was setting on the horizon, turning the sea purple. We were sailing with purpose now, but I was still in a stupor. I couldn't have told you how long we'd been at sea, but I knew it had been a while. Sometimes the motors had cut out entirely and we drifted, but I knew we needed to get more fuel soon, or be in trouble.

"Where are we going to get it?" I asked.

Malcolm stood at the railing. We were on the highest deck, and he leaned back against it. His hair had bleached out almost white, and his face had tanned to a rich golden-brown. His fine linen shirt hung open, fluttering in the breeze over his white linen pants. He was barefoot. He looked more like an underwear model than a troubled billionaire, but the lines around his eyes that only I knew about gave him away. "I doubt we are going to even have a chance to land," he told me. "We're off the coast of Turkey and the captain has been in radio contact with the police on the land."

I raised my eyebrows. This was the first I'd heard of this. "And?"

"We'll probably be boarded by the coast guard. Don has alleged that there are large numbers of weapons aboard this boat. Protestations to the contrary are met, obviously, with suspicion." He sighed. "He really is one step ahead of me. I don't deserve to win against him."

I rubbed my eyes. I felt sleepy. Drugged. The sun had baked my brain. "That's not true," I said with a yawn. "He's only one step ahead of you because you don't want to stoop to his level."

"But that's how you win, Sadie."

I sighed. My god, he frustrated me. "It's not about winning. Stop thinking like that."

"I can't. It's a disease." He tossed his head and looked behind us at the water churned white by the engines of the yacht.

For a terrible moment I had a vision of him throwing himself into those turbulent waters and going under, never to surface again.

A hard knot tightened in my stomach and I hugged myself, sobering.

"Anyway," Malcolm said, breaking the spell. "Prepare to be boarded."

"Said the pirate to the pretty maid," I joked, though I didn't really feel it. The reality of the situation was starting to sink in. The big question hovered over us, and I was afraid to put voice to it.

I was lying on one of the deck chairs. One of the three thousand dollar deck chairs, and I realized I hated it. It was a nice deck chair, but it was just a fucking chair. In fact, I hated this boat. Malcolm talked a good game about enlightenment, but he wasn't even close to it. Giving up one's worldly possessions was supposed to be part of it. I stood up, abruptly feeling gross and confined by the tiny world of the boat, by the threat of Malcolm ending it all. How could I have hoped to convince him the world was worth hanging around in if we were on such a gaudy boat?

"It'll be thirty minutes before we're out of international waters," he said after a second. "Would you like to have one last fuck, for old time's sake?"

"Are you going to kill yourself?" I blurted.

He turned his face from the white-churned wake and stared at me. "I haven't quite decided yet," he said.

My heart suddenly felt lighter. "Is that so?"

"Of course, if I don't, that means you win..." The tone was grave, but his words were flippant. I couldn't get a read on him... but I allowed myself to hope.

I took a deep breath, sucking cool sea air into my lungs. "Malcolm Ward," I said, "you are one dumb motherfucker."

To my surprise he laughed. "Only you could make 'dumb motherfucker' sound like a term of endearment."

"It *is*, you dumb motherfucker."

"Come here."

I went to him willingly. He was so fine and good, and he made me feel things I had never thought possible. When he bent his head to mine and captured my lips in a sweet kiss, I tried not to think of it as goodbye.

We were so used to fucking by now that it came

easily, quickly. Heat built, spreading through me like a flower taking root, and my clit stood at attention as he guided me to the deck chair I'd just vacated. We had done a lot to devalue those chairs, and this time was no exception.

Grasping my hands lightly, he turned me over and held them behind my back and forced me to kneel down. The deck bit into my knees, but it was a good pain, so familiar by now that it made me gasp with anticipation of what was to come. His grip was loose on my hands, but I knew that if I attempted to break free it would tighten like a vise. A gentle binding, as severe as any chain.

His other hand went to my ass and he moved the shirt I wore up over my hips. I no longer put on his boxers—it was too much trouble to take them off when we decided to screw—so when his cock slotted snugly into my slick core it was swift and sweet. I breathed in, my face smashed into the cushions as he picked up a gentle, rocking rhythm, pumping his shaft into me, his hips smacking against my ass.

My toes curled as he leaned over me, tracing his mouth across my back, touching the tattoos there through the linen, and I closed my eyes and let him drive me over the edge. My breasts scraped over the canvas beneath my chest, rough against my nipples, and when I came it was a whole-body orgasm, every inch of skin shivering and shimmering with pleasure.

When it was over, we knelt there for a long time, sweaty, gasping, and my heart in my chest was a cold lump. When Malcolm slipped out of me, he replaced the linen shirt, and I heard him adjusting his clothing so he was decent. Making a pretty corpse, or, perhaps, a pretty prisoner?

I swallowed my hope and turned over, letting myself collapse against the deck. I leaned back against the deck chair, pulled my shaking knees to my chest, and hugged them close.

To my surprise, Malcolm did the same, copying my posture.

We sat there in silence for a few minutes.

"I hope there's no cameras," I said finally, just for something to say that wasn't *please,* or *don't,* or *I want—*

He looked at me funny from the corner of his eye. He didn't seem quite so tall when sitting next to me...

"I doubt there will be cameras," he said. "Don't resist, I'm sure they've been ordered to shoot first and ask questions later."

I bit my lip. "All right," I said. "I only meant... after... you know? When they're dragging me on my perp walk. I'm not going to make a very pretty perp."

"Yes you will," he said. "You will be amazing."

I shook my head. "You know, you already got me into bed. You can stop the sweet-talk. It kind of makes me uncomfortable, to tell you the truth."

Malcolm sat up straighter. "Why shouldn't I sweet-talk you?" he said. "Why shouldn't I try to make you feel beautiful?"

"Because I'm not really beautiful?" I said. "I have no idea what you see in me, but it can't be that. Don't worry, I have no use for illusions. I'm an *artiste—*"

"Stop it!"

The shout cut me off. It had been so loud it echoed across the water. I turned and stared at him.

His face was dark and thunderous. Dangerous. There was violence in his eyes.

"Excuse me?" I said. It was all I could think to say.

A muscle in his jaw leaped. "Fucking *stop,*" he grated out. "Stop acting so modest. It makes me sick."

My stomach clenched harder. Nausea swept over me.

Malcolm. Cool, calm, collected Malcolm. Yelling at *me*.

I hate to be yelled at.

Abruptly I stood and backed away. He followed me. "No, don't run away from this, Sadie."

"Don't yell at me," I said. "I'm just telling you how I feel."

"And it makes me sick to hear you talk about yourself that way! Why do you think I bought you at that auction? Why do you think I wanted to take your picture, use you as a piece in my art? You don't think you're worth it, but you are!"

He stalked me across the deck, and I froze as he reached out and grabbed me by the upper arms. I could have twisted away, but I didn't. He was angry. But not violent.

"Why do you value yourself so little?" he shouted at me. "Don't you understand how astonishing you are?"

"No!" I wanted to hit him. "No, I fucking don't!"

His hands around my upper arms bit into the flesh there, hard and bruising. I set my teeth, trying to suppress the urge to smash my forehead into his nose.

"Your strength," he said at last. "You are so strong. Your scars, your wounds. You cover them up, act like they are nothing. Don't you get it? I want that. I want to be like you, and I can't. You just forge ahead. How do you do it? *How*?"

Frustration balled my hands into fists. "You just

do, okay? You just *do* because if you don't you might as well give up!"

"Well, why not give up?" His face was terrible to look at, lost and afraid, as though he had never known anything beautiful at all.

I stomped my foot. "Because it's not all terrible, dammit! Why can't you see that? You lost a friend? So fucking what? It happens to everyone. You made a mistake—a thousand mistakes—but so what? So *fucking what?* Who the *fuck* doesn't? Stop feeling sorry for yourself and *do something.*"

Abruptly he let go of me. "Who gave you your scars?" he said. "Tell me. I need to know."

I clenched my teeth. I wanted to tell him it was none of his business, but I had been betrayed, too. I had been betrayed, too.

I closed my eyes and took a deep breath, reaching down inside me, searching, seeking out the threads of emotion and thought that connected me to that buried past, that life I had covered up with art and color and all things beautiful and fierce.

"It was my dad, okay?" I said at last. "He gave these to me."

Malcolm was silent. "Your father?" He sounded slow and stupid, as if he'd never heard of child abuse or schizophrenia.

He made me so angry. Perfect, pretty Malcolm Ward. The best at everything, the king of the world. But one minor setback and he'd collapsed like a house of cards. I wanted to punch him. "He was crazy. Straight up bugfuck crazy. Not like you, I mean... he was fucking nuts. He thought everyone was out to get him, thought that our house was bugged, that my mom was an alien in human skin. He thought I had evil inside me and he had to let it out."

I shoved my arm in his face. "See this tattoo? The lily? It covers the first one. I think it was the first one, anyway, because I was too young to remember. He'd slice me up and my mom would take me to the hospital, and then to the vet, and then to one of her old friends who was a nurse to get me patched up, and it was only when her friend told her she was going to call CPS that she kicked my dad out."

"Why?" he said. "Why did it take so long?"

"Because she wanted to take care of him. To *save* him..." I trailed off, the blood draining from my face.

That was exactly what I'd been doing with Malcolm. I was just like my mother...

I'd always taken care of my mother, but until now I'd never realized it was because she had spent all her time pouring her efforts into my father instead of me. A beautiful, fine woman, and she had chosen the wrong vessel for her love.

Oh my god, I thought.

Malcolm's voice brought me back to the present. "Sadie?" he said. "Sadie, are you okay?"

I shook my head. "No. No, I don't think I am."

Warmth enveloped my hand, and I looked down to see his palm covering mine. "Sadie..." he said.

"No," I told him. "No, I've told plenty of people. So she kicked him out and got a boyfriend and then... then one night he came back."

I lifted my head, exposing the tattooed scar on my throat, the one covered with the final line of Dorothy Parker's poem *Resume*. Suicide is too much trouble, she said. *Might as well live*. "Right there," I said. "That's where he tried to kill me. And he got my mom. Fucking slaughtered her like a pig. And then he killed himself."

To my shock, there were tears in my eyes. Angrily I swiped my arm over my face. All that was a long time ago. It was pointless to cry about it...

"Sadie..."

"You asked me why I'm always looking for a bedside table even when I'm asleep? What I'm always reaching for when I wake up? That's my gun. I've kept one by my bedside for years. He's dead, and I still keep it with me, because *what if he comes back?*"

And then I started to cry.

I hate to cry. But I couldn't help it.

For a long moment, interminably long, I sobbed, harsh and ugly and loud. Hideously loud. So loud that I almost didn't notice the sound of a plane passing over us and helicopters in the far distance. When I did realize what I was hearing, I cried harder. The time for choosing was here, and I couldn't stand it. If Malcolm decided to be a complete idiot, there was nothing I could do to stop him. I'd put everything I had into convincing him I was worth sticking around for, and if there was one thing then there must be other things, but now I thought that maybe I had no business telling him what to do. I was a mess. *We* were a mess.

Then Malcolm's arms snaked around me, holding me close and fast against his hard body, in the safe circle of protection that was his strength, his wealth, his kind heart buried under his father's poisonous teachings, and I cried harder.

I was just like my mother, trying to fix everyone except myself, screaming out things there were no words for in paintings that made no sense to anyone but me.

I was the damaged one. *I* was the one who should be jumping over the edge of the boat and into the hungry sea below. *I* was the one who ached and shrieked in silence, all my pain made pretty and nice with ink and color.

How *dare* he think of leaving, when I was the one who should want to go?

The sound of helicopters grew louder and louder. We were racing towards the waters off the coast of Turkey.

Finally Malcolm released me and pulled away. He stared at my face as the Turkish Coast Guard barreled toward us.

"Tears," he said at last. "Tears. I've broken you." Reaching up, he caught one before the sea wind whipped it away. "I thought... I thought I would at least feel satisfied. I wanted you to understand what it felt like to be me..."

He stared at the tiny teardrop on his hand, and I cried harder, until I couldn't even see him. "Why don't I feel satisfied?" he said finally.

I could barely find breath. "Because," I choked out, "I'm not your enemy. I'm your friend."

"Oh," he said quietly. "Oh, no."

His hands alighted on my shoulders and he drew me to him again. I cried harder, and now the thrumming sound of helicopters was so loud they drowned out the roar of the sea.

"I'm sorry," he shouted in my ear. "I'm sorry I broke you."

If I hadn't been so overwhelmed I would have kneed him right in his precious nuts. "You didn't break me, you cock!" I screamed over the helicopters. "Crying doesn't mean that at all!"

I felt his bewilderment rolling off him. "Then why would you cry?"

My hands came up of their own volition, tangling in his hair, pulling him down for a desperate, tear-stained kiss, and when I released him there was a strange sheen in his own eyes "Because," I yelled, "I do understand. I'm listening to you, Malcolm. I've been listening to you since the moment we met! Everything you say, I've heard it. I'm *listening*, you *dumb motherfucker.*"

His hands came up and cupped my face and he leaned in, our foreheads touching. From the corner of my eye I saw men in riot gear sliding down ropes to the deck of the ship. "Then listen," he said. "Listen to me."

"I am!"

He closed his eyes. "You win, Sadie. You *win.* When you get back to New York, the white vase is yours." And then we were torn apart and thrown to the deck by violent hands, and the last thing I saw as someone dragged me below was Malcolm watching me from where he lay prone, three men standing over him, their yells drowned out by the throb of the helicopters, until the whole world was chaos.

He never took his eyes from mine.

14

I cried from the moment we entered Turkish waters, and didn't stop until I was released from custody.

I don't remember much of what happened after I lost sight of Malcolm. Tears made the world blurry and unreal, and in my chest a black hole had appeared, a terrible, unbearable void that would not let me go. My very bones seemed to creak under the strain of withstanding the crushing gravity of a heart collapsed, and I sobbed out my agony.

Malcolm, who I fought so hard to save—I'd saved him. And I'd lost him. And I didn't know what to do about either of those things. My brain had been bleached by the sun, all my rational thoughts faded, leaving behind only the blinding white feeling of loss and longing. I didn't want to be separated from him. Not yet at least. It wasn't time. I wasn't *ready*.

Outside of my head, the Turkish Coast Guard was the first to deal with me, and after I sobered up and looked back on it I felt sort of sorry for them. People shouted at me in Turkish and English, demanding to know where the guns were stockpiled, but of course there were no guns. At least, I hoped not. The small part of me who still distrusted everyone, who never let her guard down, wondered, briefly, if Malcolm had been playing me the whole time and there were, in fact, stockpiled guns on board.

But if there were, they were stored in another dimension. The Coast Guard found nothing. To their credit, they covered me in blankets after it became clear I was having some sort of mental breakdown and stopped shouting at me for the same reason one doesn't shout at toddlers—it just makes them cry harder. They left me alone until we landed and the US took over.

That wasn't quite as pleasant as getting shouted at. The FBI—or CIA or *someone,* it was never quite clear to me—interrogated me several times, though they got nothing from me. Thankfully I wasn't being charged with a crime. Quite the opposite, it seemed, as Malcolm's list of sins now included kidnapping as well as fraud and embezzlement, and no one would listen to me when I told them I had been on the boat of my own free will. I may have been incoherent with grief, of course. That might have had something to do with it.

Eventually I just stopped trying to talk. *Never talk to the police.* That had been drilled into my head for ages. Good advice. I clammed up and hummed aimless tunes, whatever I could think of while staring into the distance. Acting crazy had worked for Malcolm. Maybe it could work for me too.

Then Felicia came to my rescue.

❧

It didn't even take her twelve hours to get to Turkey and take me home. She had probably been en route even before I knew that my time with Malcolm had come to an end. Money can do a lot of things, and when she showed up with a small army of lawyers, my release was quick and painless.

She didn't say anything. Just hugged me and handed me a bundle of my clothes, brought straight from my apartment, and I dressed myself before we left for the airport. The old familiar feel of jeans and a t-shirt and one of my comfortable old hoodies sliding over my arms and hiding my face from the world calmed me, and I finally stopped crying.

I hadn't been wracked with enormous sobs the *entire* time, although that I certainly had been completely incoherent with depressing regularity, but even when I was speaking or humming or forcing myself to think about something else entirely—such as how the orange blankets the Coast Guard had given me totally clashed with my skin tone—huge tears had welled up and spilled down my face. It was only when I was wrapped up in my own clothes, with my best friend, in her private car heading for home that the tears finally slowed to a stop.

A tense silence descended as I wiped my face vigorously. I could hear the horrible rattling sound my chest made every time I took a breath.

Felicia sat next to me in the back seat and watched me, her face full of sympathy and concern. I hate to be worried about. I knew she was waiting for me to say something.

I sniffled and wiped my nose on my hoodie sleeve.

A disgusting smear of snot shone on the cuff when I took my hand away. I didn't give a fuck.

"Well," I said at last. "That sucked."

Felicia sighed and shook her head. "Which part? The kidnapping or the international interrogation?"

I didn't even have the energy to shoot her a glare. "There was no kidnapping," I said wearily. "I wanted to be on that boat. You think anyone could make me do something I didn't want to?"

She shrugged. "I don't know, Sadie. Knowing you... no. But everyone has a breaking point. I thought... I thought, what if he really *was* crazy? What if he pulled a... a weapon on you?"

A knife. The words hovered above us. He could have pulled a gun, yeah. But that was never what I feared the most. Felicia knew my past. She knew me before all my scars had been hidden. Tattoos cost a lot of money. She'd helped me pay for some of them.

"No weapons," I said with a sigh. *None except emotion.* "But it was... intense."

She regarded me for a moment. "Yes, I see that. So... you went on his boat, without telling anyone, and sailed around aimlessly in international waters for shits and giggles."

I was so tired I could hardly think straight. "No, it was to get away from the police."

Her intake of breath was so sharp it hurt my ears. "So... you knew about the embezzlement and fraud when you agreed to get on his boat with him?"

I started to feel like I was being interrogated all the more. *"Yes,"* I snapped. "I mean... no. It's not like that. Malcolm's being framed. He's not embezzling his company, and he's not committing fraud, and he *definitely* didn't kidnap me."

For a moment I thought she was going to shut me down completely, but then she closed her eyes and pinched the bridge of her nose. "I believe you," she said. "At least, I believe you believe him."

I made a frustrated noise. "It's his personal assistant. Or secretary. Or whatever. That guy is the one defrauding the company. Don Cardall. Malcolm said he had proof."

"I see. If he had proof, why doesn't he just hand it over?"

"Because!" I said, annoyed. "He doesn't want to betray Don. Supposedly he's like a brother to him. He was just planning on getting caught by the feds and then *killing himself* instead of turning Don over. Don's the one who's framing him."

It had made sense when Malcolm had explained it to me. Perfect sense. But as I watched Felicia's face, I realized that it was just as crazy as I had first thought.

Was Malcolm crazy? Really crazy? Paranoid, or... or bipolar or sociopathic or something? He had to have been telling me the truth... right? He had no reason to lie.

Had he really been betrayed... or was Don the one telling the truth, exposing his corrupt boss to the world in the name of justice? And if they were like brothers why Don was only Malcolm's secretary?

I was so *tired*. I'd believed Malcolm when we were together... why was doubt creeping in now?

My doubts were reflected in Felicia's frowning. "Sadie... Why would anyone remain loyal to someone who's framing them?"

I pitched forward and buried my hands in my hair. "I don't know. Because he's almost as damaged as you?"

That was a low blow. Felicia had her problems, and they all involved remaining loyal even when there was no reason to be so. I didn't look at her.

When she spoke, her voice was quiet. "Do you really think he has proof?"

"He told me he did."

"Did he tell you where he put it or hid it or kept it?"

I sighed and shook my head. "No. Up until we were boarded I was pretty sure he was just going to off himself and it wouldn't have mattered after that." I looked out the window, wishing I wasn't listening to myself say these things. I sounded like a naïve sap that had fallen for a con man.

Then I remembered. *The vase.* He'd told me I could have the vase I had broken. But that didn't make any sense either. Why would he give *that* to me? Why not tell me where the proof was hidden with his last breath as the helicopters drowned out our voices and the men in jackboots closed in?

What the hell was Malcolm playing at?

"He said I could have something of his," I blurted. "He didn't tell me about where he kept the proof, but he told me I could have the vase I broke at the auction."

"The Qing dynasty one?" Felicia asked. "It was beautiful, but why would he give you a broken vase?"

"I have no idea. I don't even know where it is."

"In his house, maybe?"

I shook my head and it turned into a nod of sleep for a split second. I caught myself and forced myself awake. "No... I think he moved all his stuff out to storage."

"What? Why?"

I felt a faint smile on my lips. "He said it was because he'd decided to kill himself the night of the auction, but that when he laid eyes on me he decided to live for a little longer."

God. It sounded stupid when I said it. Felicia thought so, too.

"Oh, *Sadie...*"

"I *saw* all his shit getting carted out," I said. "I saw it when I went to see him... Jesus. I don't even know." I passed a hand over my face, feeling the puffiness of my eyes and lips. "How long were we gone?"

"About three weeks," she said.

Three weeks? Jesus. *Jesus.*

I leaned back and closed my eyes. "Christ, I'm tired."

"You should be," Felicia said. "You've been through a lot. Why don't you try to rest?"

I yawned. "Won't we be at the airport soon?"

"Yeah, but if you don't wake up I'll ask Ihsan here to carry you." She gestured at our driver, who was extremely hot and who gave me a smile in the rear view mirror that under any other circumstances would have been devastating and cause for a case of spontaneously combusted panties. But I just didn't feel it. I missed Malcolm.

No, more than missed him. Needed him. He'd thought I was his muse, but in a weird way he had been mine, inspiring me to step out of my life, the comfortable, safe niches I had built for myself. I liked safe. I liked comfortable. He had been neither, and yet there was a promise with him... with time... we could be something greater than what we were now...

I didn't even return the nice driver's smile, instead electing to cross my arms over my chest and slump in my seat, turning to glare out the window like a sullen teenager.

"I can walk," I told Felicia grumpily, but I'd been awake for almost twenty draining hours and I was asleep before I'd finished talking.

༻༺

I woke up on a chartered plane over the Atlantic, twisting on the couch and reaching for my gun that wasn't there. Felicia sat in one of the reclining chairs on the opposite wall of the plane, her eyes closed, her perfect, lovely face angelic in repose. The drone of the plane buzzed around me. We were alone except for each other. I sat up and looked around, trying to shake the cold feeling that stole around me, telling me to find a weapon, any weapon, but we were on a plane and weapons were few and far between. For the first time since I'd boarded Malcolm's yacht, I felt truly unsafe without it. Naked. Haunted.

What if he comes back? I'd told Malcolm. It was the first time I'd ever told anyone my deepest fear. The fear that not even death would keep the ghosts at bay. Putting it out in words didn't rob it of its power at all. It just made it creepier.

My father. The root of my problems. He used to come into my room late at night, after he'd tried to drink the voices away. Sometimes he stood by my bedside and babbled, long weird strings of words that made no sense, demon names and Bible verses. Other times he would say nothing. Just stare. And sometimes he would cut me.

Not often. Not too often. Just often enough.

To let the evil out.

I still dreamed bad dreams and woke up in cold sweats. If I'd been able to keep a dog in my apartment on my shitty schedule, I would have had the biggest, meanest dog that ever lived. I'd have fed it steaks and kept it on my bed, just in case. *Just in case.* I had a gun instead, and cold comfort it was, though it was comfort all the same.

But Malcolm... in the middle of the ocean with him, with his hands on my body, the sun warming me, the sea breeze whipping my cares away, all our problems left behind on the shore... with Malcolm my fear had faded. I retained the habit, but there had been no drive behind it.

The betrayal of my family, my father's insanity, my mother's inability—or unwillingness—to keep me safe, had faded in the bright sun, in the warm breeze. The bones of the past bleached out at sea and crumbled to ash in the fire of our mutual desire.

Now that Malcolm was gone, I wasn't safe any more. And if he had been telling the truth about his secretary, there was one more person out in the world looking to destroy, to betray. If Malcolm had been telling the truth, he wasn't safe, even in jail. Hell, I probably wasn't safe.

What if Don suspected something? What if he *did* know Malcolm knew about his betrayal? What if he thought *I* knew where Malcolm had hidden his proof of Don's malfeasance? What if *he* knew where to find the evidence? He'd known Malcolm for a lot longer than I had. If anyone guessed accurately, it would be him...

No. No, I had no proof of any of that, had no proof even that *Malcolm* had been telling the truth, either. All I knew about Don was what Malcolm had told me, and what small things I had learned while I spoke with him on the phone, and he hadn't given any indication that he thought Malcolm had figured him out. Had he?

...Shit, I'd been too drunk to remember properly. Mostly I had a vague impression of being shouted at for no good reason and treated like I didn't have two brain cells to rub together.

He's not crazy.

The words came floating up to me from the depths of my memory.

Oh. Right. Now I remembered. He'd thought I was a woman hoping to exploit a rich but vulnerable man for her own gain. Not only had he *thought* it, but he had said it out loud. Admittedly he had been under quite a bit of stress at that point, what with Malcolm allegedly skipping the country right before all his plans were to come to fruition...

I bit my lip. *He's not crazy.* That meant that Don thought Malcolm was just acting a part, whereas I was now not so sure. Where did that leave me?

Lying on my fainting couch, feeling like shit and pining for a man that I'm suddenly not certain is really real. I wanted the Malcolm I knew to be the real Malcolm. I cared about him, or the man I thought I knew. Our time together, floating on the sea—it all seemed like a dream already, something that had happened to someone else, in another time and place. Was what we shared real, or had he only been manipulating me? The snatches of our interactions in my memory could have gone either way, it seemed...

I bit my lip, hard. What did it matter? I had to choose if I was going to believe him or believe his secretary, the FBI, the CIA, the Turkish Coast Guard, and, probably by now, the press. And if I knew anything about any of those guys, I'd go with Malcolm any day.

Which left me with one option: I had to get him out of prison. I couldn't let him waste away in there. He still had to finish his Masterpiece.

And I'd seen his attempts at art. There was something *there*.

I lay on the couch and stared at the ceiling of the plane, my mind chasing itself around in circles.

I was no closer to figuring out what I should do when we reached New York and Felicia finally woke up.

"Morning, sleepyhead," I said to her as the plane began its descent and she blinked around the cabin, clearly trying to remember where she was. She shot me a glare.

"Oh, shut up, Sadie," she told me. "If you only knew how many nights of sleep I've been missing because you decided to get yourself pretend-kidnapped or whatever, off running around the world without even sending me a text, which, by the way, is totally rude because you're my personal assistant and you have a lot of vacation saved up, so you could have just *told* me you were taking your vacation days instead of letting me worry about it... You know the feds came and talked to me? They wanted to know if you'd talked to me at all about Malcolm, or if you'd left me a message or contacted me since you were kidnapped..." She trailed off. "What was my point?"

"I think you were trying to say you were tired."

"Right! I *am* tired. And you are sunburned. Don't you know that's a great way to get cancer?

I shrugged. "I'll live." It felt good to banter with

her as if nothing had happened. Being as exasperating as possible to Felicia was always one of my favorite past times, and now it made the ache in my chest and the lump in my throat recede a little.

"You're *impossible*," she told me.

Oh yeah. That was the stuff. *Feed me, Felicia.* "Sorry. I have a lot on my mind."

Her face softened. "Yeah. Sorry. There I go, making it all about me again."

I gave her a little smile. "If that bothered me, we'd have parted ways a long time ago."

She smiled back, a small, rueful thing before sitting up and stretching. "So," she said, "want to tell me what you're thinking about?"

I figured I might as well tell her the truth. "Malcolm. And the vase."

"Ah," she said. "Right. The embezzler and the broken vase."

Her words sent a stab of pain through me, unexpected and unwelcome. I shoved it away, hurt and irritated. I'd always supported her, *always,* even when she was being really stupid, and that was often. But whatever. It wasn't my job to convince her of anything. "Yes. That."

She rubbed a hand over her mouth, not looking at me. "Yeah," she said, "I've been thinking about that, too."

"While you slept?"

"Yes, actually. Specifically the vase. It was broken at the auction, right?"

Yup. That was how this whole thing had started. Just a moment of inattention and boom, you're running from the FBI on a luxury yacht in the Adriatic Sea. I'd been worried about my life getting boring. I was never, ever going to worry about that again. "That's right."

"In that case, why did he tell you that you could have a broken vase?"

I put my hands over my eyes. "I don't know," I said. "Malcolm is a troubled guy. He has issues. Maybe he thought it was symbolic." Was that part of his masterpiece? Leaving me a broken vase? Our relationship come full circle?

Ugh. I love performance art, but when it gets hard to tell the difference between art and life I sometimes wish people would be just a little *less* obtuse. I once spent a full five minutes at the end of a long, fully packed art show staring at an empty stone bench and wondering if it was an exhibition piece or just a nice bench to sit on. *Can I sit on this bench?* I had wondered. *Is it art? Can I sit on it if it's art?* I wasn't even drunk. I felt the same way now. Leave me a broken vase? Is it art? Or are you just a dumb motherfucker who I miss so much I could scream?

"You have to go get the vase," Felicia said, breaking me out of my maudlin thoughts. "He wanted you to have it."

"Fine," I said. The pressure of the descending plane was starting to weigh heavily on my head and I worked my jaw to pop my ears. "I don't know where it is though."

"Start with his house. He couldn't have had everything cleared out."

"Sure he could have."

"Fine. But we'll start with his house *anyway.*"

"Oh, you're coming now?"

She grinned at me. "Hell no. I'm just the brains of this outfit."

"Okay brainiac, tell me how I get into his house. I don't have a key."

"Don't worry about that," she said. "I have lawyers, and so does he."

I shook my head at her, but I couldn't help but smile. "Look at you. You stopped keeping it real as soon as humanly possible."

She made a face at me as the plane touched down. "Would keeping it real involve breaking and entering and getting arrested and never saving the grand paramour of your tumultuous affair?"

I wasn't even sure she'd used all the words in that sentence correctly, but, after a moment of sorting through it, I nodded. "Probably," I said as the plane finally slowed to a stop.

"Then we'll use the lawyers," she said, and at the front of the plane the pilot hopped out of the cockpit and opened the door and the wild, blustery wind of a New York March gusted inside the plane, wrapping us up in chill and cold, and underneath it the hint of spring.

I was home, but when I'd left, it had been with Malcolm. Now I was returning without him, and I suddenly realized that I had no idea when I would see him again, touch him again, talk to him again.

The hitch and ache in my chest returned with a vengeance and something must have showed in my face because Felicia asked me if I was all right.

I had no words for her. It hurt too much to think.

So I stopped.

15

Felicia promised to get the key, and I thanked her. I didn't really know if I wanted the key, or the vase, or any of this drama, but I agreed to spend the intervening time at her house.

So I buried myself in one of the guest beds at her mansion and slept like the dead. Occasionally Felicia or Anton would pop their heads in to see how I was doing or drop off take-out, telling me to keep my strength up. Even Arthur showed up once, seeming genuinely concerned for my well-being up until the moment he told me he needed me to get back on the job because he was swamped like a Long Island beach community.

In the few hours I was awake, I tried to contact Malcolm, but his bail had not been posted. His assets were frozen, and, I suspected, he didn't really want to be sprung from jail anyway. It was just the sort of thing a guy filled with self-loathing and melancholia would eat up, although if he actually went to prison I suspected the experience would begin to pall fairly quickly. His lawyers stonewalled me, and I eventually stopped trying.

Going to see him was out of the question, too, since paparazzi had surrounded both Felicia's house and my apartment. Malcolm was obviously all over the news, and as his "kidnapping victim" so was I, even though kidnapping had been dropped from his charges. Terrible photos of me beamed out across the airwaves and showed up online.

I'd been a genius at helping Felicia defeat the reporters back when she and Anton had been in and out of the tabloids for kinky sex in semi-public, but now that it was me in the spotlight I was utterly helpless. I had no idea how to protect myself. I was slow and stupid from the sun, fucked into a gentle torpor, but also ripped open and rubbed raw, and even after I'd closed the wounds the muscle underneath still needed to heal.

I turned completely inward, focusing on the ache Malcolm had left in me, slowly processing our time together. Torn apart, it felt as though as he had died, all our unspoken words still hanging between us. It was a ridiculous way to feel, but I still wandered the house like a ghost and stepped outside more times than I could count, meaning to suck down a quick cigarette in an attempt to fire my mind out of its sluggish repose, but the moment I did I would remember that I was a sudden celebrity and I would curse and dart back inside. But of course just a second was plenty of time to land me back in the celeb news cycle at least once.

But most of the time I just slept. It was easier than thinking.

On the third night I dreamed about him. We stood

naked on the deck of his boat. The sun beat down, but it was nothing in comparison to the heat of his lips on my throat, my mouth, my breasts, his hands on my body. Gently he lifted my arms, holding them out, and with a delicate touch he peeled the tattoos from my skin. Fish and spiders and fire birds slipped away from me, leaving the scars beneath exposed.

Then he lifted each tattoo to the azure sky and, one by one, the sea wind whipped them from his fingers and carried them away.

ↀ

On the morning of the fourth day I awoke and finally felt *awake.* I descended the stairs, feeling restless, and, drawn by the smell of coffee, wandered into the kitchen.

Felicia wasn't there. There was only Anton, who sat at the table in the breakfast nook reading some dumb business bullshit on his tablet. I still didn't know Anton very well, so I had to force myself into some semblance of levity. Shuffling over to the table, I cocked a hip and put a hand on it.

"I really need a cigarette," I informed him, my voice rusty with disuse. "Don't you have any secret passageways I can duck into for a smoke?

He didn't look at me right away. That's what I hate about Anton. He's just gotta make everything into some kind of dick swinging contest.

Finally he lifted his eyes to mine. Cool, calm. Unperturbed. "Of course not," he said.

"What kind of billionaire are you?" I complained. "How can a guy as rich as you not have a secret passage in his house?"

He sipped his coffee and raised a brow. "One who walks around unashamed," he said.

"What about when the revolution comes? You'll be first up against the wall while the proletariat screams for your head. You'll wish you had a secret passage then. Actually, you should put one in before the revolution happens. You'll thank me when you're ruling a drug cartel in Mexico." I surprised myself with my little rant. Apparently I was feeling a bit bitter about the world.

Anton was not amused. "And even if I *did* have a secret passage," he said, choosing to ignore my dire warnings about the imminent communist overthrow of capitalism, "I would not allow you to smoke in it. It's a filthy habit."

"You're not the boss of me," I said.

"Actually I am."

...Fuck. He was right.

We stared at each other for a moment before he looked back at his tablet and sipped his coffee again. Pulling my best sullen teenager face at his unconcerned face I turned and stalked away.

In the kitchen I poured myself some coffee and stomped around the island, as restless as one of those tigers in cages at the zoo who contract OCD from being cooped up all the time.

Anton ignored me, studying the screen in front of him, as cool and unruffled as a statue of a sphinx, and just as mysterious. It occurred to me that Anton would never let someone betray him the way Malcolm did. Why couldn't I have gotten involved with one of the billionaires who crushed people without regard for sentimentality? It would have been a lot less stressful. I wouldn't have been interrogated by the feds for starters...

But of course I wouldn't have liked Malcolm as much if it weren't for the weird humanity he kept trying to hide and purge from himself as though it were a disease. I would have thought him to be just like every other jack off rich guy.

I'm just dumb, I guess. Always had to pick the complicated ones.

Felicia chose that moment to waltz into the breakfast nook, looking radiant and thoughtful. Her eyes lit up when she spied me, though she didn't mention my recent indisposition. "Good news, Sadie," she said instead. "The lawyer talks went well. We have achieved a key." And she held up a lovely coppery key for me to inspect. It dangled from a small silver chain tethered to a realtor key fob.

I inspected it. "That's a key," I said solemnly.

"And it goes to Malcolm's house," she replied. "Now you can get in and find the vase."

"It's probably been swept under a rug or something," I said. "Works all the time in cartoons."

Felicia shot me a glare. "Can we please be serious for a moment?" Reluctantly I nodded. She entered the kitchen, reached forward, and grabbed my hand, pressing the key into it. "Good," she said. "Look, Malcolm told you he wanted you to have that vase. It must have been important to him for you to get it, so I think you should take a car and go over there and see if it's in his house."

"And if it's not?" I said. Then a thought occurred to me. "Hey, wait, if you talked to his lawyers and got the key, why didn't you just ask them to ask *him* where it is?"

A faint stain of color shone on her cheeks for a

moment. Anton had put his cup down and was watching her intently. She looked from him to me and back again, then sighed. "I thought, if he really is innocent, maybe he hid a clue in the vase."

"A clue?"

She nodded.

"In the broken vase?"

She nodded again, though this time she looked uncertain.

"A clue left behind when he was literally going to kill himself rather than expose his pseudo-brother's betrayal? Left in the hopes that someone would look in a bunch of broken vase bits and find a stack of papers a mile high proving the innocence of a dead guy?"

Felicia stomped her foot. "It could happen! And besides, it doesn't have to be paper. He could have hidden it on a disk or something."

"In the broken vase?"

"Or in the pile of broken vase bits, yes," she snapped. "So I didn't ask the lawyers directly about it. I just said you needed something from his house. They cleared it with him, and I'm assuming he told them it was fine to give you a key. So here it is."

I stared at the key in my hand.

"Look," she said after a moment. "You don't have to. But you are really broken up over this crazy guy. Go find that vase and get some closure."

Sometimes I really do have the best friend, and I don't deserve her.

"I'll call for a car," Anton said. "You'll avoid the paparazzi that way." I looked at him, but he was staring at Felicia. "My dear," he continued before I was able to say thank you, "I think we should be seen in the vicinity of Mr. Ward's house doing something terribly illicit. Surely the dogs of the press are watching Mr. Ward's house as well."

"Oh," Felicia said, "I didn't think of that." Then the blush on her face grew deeper. "What should I wear?"

I took that cue to beat a hasty retreat upstairs to get ready.

ꕥ

Freshly showered, dressed in my best giving-up-on-life clothes from back when I was just a struggling artist, and preoccupied with the sick feeling in my gut, I sat a block from Malcolm's house in the back of the car Anton had called for me.

I chewed my lip and stared at the phone in my hand, waiting impatiently for the text from Felicia to let me know she was about to be caught on camera by whatever paparazzi had been lying in wait for me. I just hoped she wouldn't be caught up in the moment and forget. Then again, maybe that would be for the best. What if the vase wasn't there? What if I found it and... then what? Who cared? Just a reminder of a sweet, dreamlike time I could never return to. Why would I want it?

But I did want it. I wanted to see it, touch it. Maybe then I could figure out why Malcolm thought it was so important that his last words to me were his insistence that I have it.

I couldn't quite decide how to feel about things, and it was making me nervous. I always know how to feel about things. Until Malcolm came along, I suppose. He set me off balance, made me speechless, shocked me with his utter candor.

I hadn't heard his voice in days. Almost a week? Yes, four days, maybe five. I hadn't called his cell phone in the hopes of hearing it, because that was pathetic and also I didn't want to get pegged by the feds again. I wished I had, though, and now, sitting in the back seat of a fine car, hidden from the world by the dark windows, a silent, discreet driver studiously ignoring me, the sudden temptation to call him was almost overwhelming.

Then the phone buzzed in my hand, and a text from Felicia flashed across my screen.

"SKJii SDOI(&h ddd Kanye i"*

Yeah. She was kind of caught in the moment. Good thing the content didn't matter.

"I'm out," I told the driver, unnecessarily. "I should be back in, like... an hour? Tops?"

The driver, whose name was Jeff, though I didn't want to use it and seem too familiar, gave me a watery smile and a deferential nod. He was old, his silver hair close-cropped to his head. He looked like an ex-Marine and for a moment I wished I could just stay in this car with him, chat and talk, be *normal.* But the ache in my chest would have given me away. I nodded back to him, shoved my phone in my hoodie pocket, and let myself out of the car.

Brisk March wind whipped around me, cutting through my old clothes as I strolled down the street, trying to look nonchalant. The hood of my sweatshirt sheltered my face from the eyes of others and the worst of the wind, and before I knew it I was approaching Malcolm's house.

It was weird. I felt as though I were approaching the house of someone recently deceased and I had to fight the impulse to walk on by, to not face the sudden, sharp change in circumstances. I watched my feet eat up the pavement as if they belonged to someone else, and when they mounted the front steps I had to bite the inside of my cheek to force myself to keep going.

I reached the door. It stood before me and I realized it was almost the same color as Malcolm's eyes. Stuffing my hand into my hoodie pocket, I drew out the key, looked at it for a second, then pushed it into the lock, turned it, and opened the door.

It gave way beneath my hand without a sound, and I stepped inside and closed it behind me.

The house was empty. That much was obvious. All of Malcolm's things were gone, cleared out to be given away regardless of worth or sentimental value, and I stood in the foyer feeling more melancholy than I though possible. Yeah, the house had been the repository of a crazy person, but it had been *his* repository. I'd never asked him why he had all that junk, and now it felt like I never would. He'd go to prison and maybe I'd write to him or visit or whatever, but it wouldn't be the same. We'd never be as open as we had out on the waves of the sea, not unless he proved his innocence.

Slowly I walked around the lower floor. The place looked tiny now that it was empty, the same way a dead body looks small after the soul has vacated the premises, and I had to forcibly remind myself that I was here for a purpose rather than just turn around and leave. I should see if the vase was here. The movers probably wouldn't have taken a pile of broken pottery. It had no worth.

Or it was priceless, I thought, and giggled sadly.

I poked around the ground floor, but found nothing, so I moved to the stairwell and climbed up the steps. The house creaked beneath my feet, groaning like an old man complaining about his tired joints. The second floor was more of the same—beautiful wood, creamy walls. A library, a music room, a long narrow game room. I peered in the closets and looked in the fireplace, but there was nothing. My heart beginning to sink, I mounted the stairs to the third floor.

Here the house became more like a home than a mansion. A honeycomb of bedrooms and bathrooms greeted me, and I started at the front, snooping around, looking in every nook and cranny I could find, but nothing greeted me until I entered what had to be the master bedroom.

It was larger than the rest and emptied out onto a terrace. The cloudy sky outside made it dim and dreary, but there was a door to the master bath that I hadn't been able to access from the hallway. I tromped to it and looked around. The light from the terrace barely made it inside, and the high, tiny windows were stained glass, giving me very little to work with. I sighed and tried the wall switch, but nothing happened. I squinted up in the darkness and saw that all the bulbs had been removed from the room.

Malcolm was a serious weirdo. I wished I didn't like him so much. Opening the door as wide as I could, I took stock.

A shower stall. A toilet closet. A bathtub and a linen closet. Nothing to do but start checking behind all the closed doors. I crossed the white tile and opened the linen closet.

And there, sitting on the shelf, was the vase.

That's the thing. It was actually there. At least, I was pretty sure it was the vase, even though there were several key differences in the vase I found and the vase I had expected to find. For one thing, it wasn't broken. For another, it was so dark in the bathroom that I could barely make it out and it didn't quite *look* like the vase that I had broken—a weird, random pattern seemed to be painted onto it—but when I reached into the closet, my heart hammering a mile a minute, cool porcelain met my fingers. Then I lifted it, tipping it toward me, and something inside it made a *clunk* sound.

Swallowing around my suddenly dry tongue, I turned it over. A small dark object slid out and fell to my feet, hitting the tiled floor with the flat slap of plastic.

He *had* left something for me. Somehow. It was like a plot twist out of a movie, which, now that I knew Malcolm, was completely predictable. Replacing the vase on the shelf, I knelt down and retrieved the object that had been hidden in it.

It was a thumb drive.

My heart started to beat faster.

Calm down, I told myself. *Don't freak out yet.* Anything could be on this drive. Anything at all. It could be the photos of me, it could be old love letters, *anything.* Getting my hopes up would be stupid.

Clutching the drive so tightly in my hand that the sharp plastic edges bit into the bones of my fingers, I sprinted out of the bathroom, wove my way through the maze of the third floor, and pounded up the stairs, hoping Malcolm had left his bedroom intact.

He had. The computer still sat at the far wall, the

screen dark but the lights still on. I prayed he hadn't left it password protected as I hurried over to it, uncapping the drive before I reached out and wiggled the mouse. To my immense relief the monitor flared to life, showing his desktop. The picture on it was one of the pictures of me that he had managed to capture—a beautiful still image of my mouth and chin, the curve of my throat, the swell of my shoulder—but I forced myself to ignore it. My fingers shook as I found a USB slot on the tower and shoved the drive in.

I waited, hopping from foot to foot until the computer *dinged,* recognizing the drive, and I clicked on it, opening up the directory.

A password dialog popped up.

I nearly shrieked with frustration, but I took a deep breath and tried to think like a dumb motherfucker.

If I were a dumb motherfucker, I postulated, *who thought life should be like a movie and this was a great romantic plot twist, what password would I put on the critical information that would keep me out of prison?*

I leaned forward and typed in "Sadie."

The dialog box disappeared and the directory filled out.

Of course.

I began to click around.

With each file opened, I felt my mouth drop wider and wider. It was all here: offshore bank accounts, spreadsheets with discrepancies highlighted, huge documents detailing the history of this or that chunk of money and Don's exact role in making it disappear... Malcolm hadn't been kidding when he'd said he had proof. He not only had proof, but he had built a whole case, as though he were an expert in corporate law. Actually, he probably thought he was, given his self-assessment of all his other talents. But mostly I was just shocked that Felicia's farfetched theory had been right. He'd left the evidence of his innocence for me in the vase, and now I held his future in my hands.

Huh, I thought. Somehow, I *wasn't* shocked that her thoughts and Malcolm's had lined up so neatly. They both liked life to be like a movie, chasing that Oscar-winning scene. They both had artistic souls.

...Still, the question remained: how had he done it? I'd broken the vase on a Friday night, and we had left on a Monday. There was no way the vase could have been repaired before we departed New York...

Then I remembered. Malcolm on the phone in the cafe in Dubrovnik, speaking in Japanese. The note left in French for the man whose life he had changed, along with a wad of bills as thick as my wrist.

He had *arranged* it. I wasn't quite sure how he'd arranged it, or what the exact arrangements had been, but he'd planned it all out. Before he even knew if he was going to die or not. He'd decided to put the pieces in place *just in case.* Just in case he decided to live and needed to something dramatic as hell to keep my life interesting.

It was such a *Malcolm* thing to do that I had to laugh. He was such a dumb motherfucker, and I loved it.

The realization brought me up short, but then I nodded.

Yeah, I thought to myself. *That's right. I love it.*

Suddenly able to breathe easily, I popped the thumb drive out of the computer and capped it, shut down all the programs, then unceremoniously pulled the plug. I hadn't brought my purse with me, the pockets of my jeans had holes in them, and the pouch of my hoodie was far too unsecured. I wavered with indecision, and then with a huff of exasperation I stuffed the drive down my underwear, where it nestled in Malcolm's favorite place. Fitting, in more ways than one, though admittedly not the most sanitary spot. But when you are as flat-chested as I am, hiding things in your cleavage is not an option.

I had to get this to his lawyers.

Head whirling with thoughts of the future, of the possibility that there *might* be a future, one in which he was alive and free, I jogged back to the stairs and took them two at a time down to the third floor. I paused on the landing, and then decided that if Malcolm wanted me to have the vase, then I should probably take the vase, too. I slipped into the hallway and started for the master bedroom.

I was so preoccupied that I almost didn't hear the front door opening, but my lizard brain heard it. The part of me that always listened for the bedroom door opening heard it. The part of me that slept with one eye open heard it.

I froze in my tracks.

"Hullo?"

A man's voice with a British accent floated up from the lower floors.

Someone else was in the house.

Old impulses rose up, telling me to run, to flee, but even as my legs twitched with the flight response, my civilized brain was trying to override it, telling me that not everything was dangerous.

Yeah, right.

Swallowing hard, I inched my way across the floor, praying it wouldn't creak under my weight, and leaned over the banister, trying to hear where the intruder was in the house.

"Hulloo?" the voice called again. "Sadie MacElroy?"

Whoever it was knew my name, knew I was here. They had to have been watching the house. The voice seemed vaguely familiar, but I couldn't place it. Very cultured, a bit nasally, and definitely at the front of the house, between me and the front door. Was there a back door? Not that I could get to it without being seen, and if there was it probably led into a closed garden...

I took a deep breath and tried to think.

There wasn't any reason I *couldn't* be here. I had a key. I had permission from Malcolm—albeit through his lawyers—to be here. So really, it was the other person who shouldn't be here. Paparazzo? Reporter? They must have been waiting for someone to show their face. Though usually they stayed within the bounds of the law and remained *outside*. So probably not paparazzo. Who, then?

I looked around, but I had no idea where the fire escape was, and even as I frantically tried to remember where it had been situated on the outside of the house the sound of heavy footsteps started up the stairs.

"I only want to talk! Miss MacElroy? Please, it's important. My name is Morris Denton, and I work for Mr. Ward..."

I bit my lip and backed up from the stairway. He was going to be here any second now. Why, oh *why* wasn't there a second stairwell? What kind of rich person's house was this? I didn't want to talk to him, but I was stuck.

He came up the stairs.

My first impression was of a man Malcolm's age, but far more staid and conservative. Malcolm dressed beautifully, but there was that irrepressible *something* about him, a humming energy beneath his skin that I now recognized as the creative force. This man looked far more like a successful businessman than Malcolm did. His dark hair was cut in a sober style instead of Malcolm's wild locks, his skin was pale and his eyes were dark and serious behind gold-rimmed glasses. His coat hung well on his lean body, and he seemed surprised to actually find me when his line of sight crested the stairs.

"Oh! Miss MacElroy. There you are..."

I took a step back, even though I knew it was futile. It showed I was weak, too. But instead of pressing his advantage, Mr. Denton suddenly looked contrite.

"I'm so sorry," he said, and he spread his hands, showing me his palms. A clear, universal gesture that told me he meant no harm, and I forced myself to relax a tiny bit, but the thumb drive in my underwear was a harsh reminder that I had a job to do. An important job. I didn't have time to talk to whoever this man was.

"Sorry," I said. "I was just leaving."

"Please!" The word erupted from him and he took a step forward, startling me. The edge in my blood came back. Who was this guy, and why was he here?

I narrowed my eyes. "Yes?"

He subsided a bit. "I'm so sorry, I didn't mean to startle you. You are Sadie MacElroy, yes?"

I lifted a brow. "Who wants to know?" Not the most original of lines, but I felt that, given the circumstances, it was a legitimate one.

He seemed to relax. "My apologies. My name is Morris Denton. I'm the Chief Technical Officer of Warden Industries. I've worked with Mr. Ward for a number of years and it's my belief that he is innocent of the fraud and embezzlement charges that have been leveled against him." His British accent was pleasant and lilting, and I had to fight my natural impulse to agree with him on the assumption that someone with a British accent would naturally know what they were talking about.

"How do you know who I am?" I asked him instead."

He colored. "Everyone knows who you are. As Mr. Ward's current paramour and alleged kidnapping victim—" He held up a hand as I opened my mouth to protest. "—which it is obvious you were not, you are in a very privileged position and I have been frantic to reach you. You are well protected by your employer at the moment, but I have to admit I asked someone to watch the house and let me know if you showed up... I thought if you did, I might be able to enlist your help."

Oh, really? I wasn't quite buying it. This guy had to be an undercover reporter or something. "Help with what?"

"With finding evidence of Mr. Ward's innocence, of course."

"Why would you think I would know anything about that?"

His brow furrowed. "I've watched Mr. Ward grow increasingly erratic over the past half year. It was clear something was bothering him. Fleeing the country with a young woman is only the culmination of his behavior, and it is not entirely unlikely that he may have taken you into his confidence."

"I wasn't," I lied.

His face fell. "But... perhaps, as someone who knew his personal habits, you might have a guess?" I stared at him and he held his hands out, a gesture of vulnerability. "I admire Mr. Ward very much. He has been like a mentor to me. Please, help me?"

My eyes narrowed, but his face remained placid, pleading.

"You say your name is Morris Denton?" I said at last. "And you're the CTO of Malcolm's company?"

He nodded.

"Then I'm going to have to see some photo ID," I told him, and crossed my arms.

I mean, come on. I'm not fucking *stupid.*

A flash of something crossed his face, but almost immediately it was eclipsed by a relieved smile. "Of course," he said. He opened his fine coat and dug into the inside pocket, taking out his wallet. Opening it, he selected a card and handed it to me. I plucked it from his fingers and studied it.

That was a mistake. The first thing people do when they look at a license is study the face. It's right there. *Is that the right face?* we ask ourselves.

Yes, it was the right face. Dark hair, dark eyes, nondescript, thick brows, glasses. A nice face. The face in front of me. The right face.

My eyes drifted over to the information, and that was when my blood suddenly slowed to a sluggish crawl in my veins.

Right face. But not the right name.

I stared at the license. The name *Donald Cardall* stared back up at me.

I went numb. My instincts that this man was not who he said he was had been right, but in the wrong direction. But of course it was Don. Of course it was. It wouldn't be just like a movie if it weren't.

A click brought me back to reality and I looked up.

Might have to reevaluate the 'not stupid' part, I thought, staring at the gun Don Cardall now held casually aimed at my heart.

16

So there I was on the third floor of Malcolm Ward's house, totally defenseless with a gun trained on me by Malcolm's once bosom brother turned mortal enemy, Don Cardall, which, now that I thought about it, was totally a Mafia name.

Holy shit, I thought. *Holy shit, holy shit, holy shit.* I have to admit, I was really surprised. This guy was going to kill me. You don't just pull a gun on someone and expect them to stay quiet about it. And Jesus. I hadn't expected a fucking *gun.* I hadn't expected to get fucking *murdered.*

I mean, now that I was face to face with him and saw the tiny flame of desperation in his eyes, it made total sense to me. This was a guy who had everything to lose if I somehow managed to spill the beans. I suppose I should have been thankful that he came along to do the job himself—whack me good, just to make sure I didn't talk, see?—but it was kind of hard to feel anything positive when you're about to die.

I had to distract him somehow. Keep him from

killing me long enough to formulate a plan. I'd taken self defense classes. They were all useless in this situation, of course, but I knew how to kick at least.

Reaching out he plucked his license from my hand and put it back in his pocket, all the while watching me with a wary air, clearly waiting for me to react. I was still stuck in my deer-in-the-headlights mode. *Distract,* I told myself. *Distract!*

So I did what I do best. I told him he was an idiot.

I mean, say what you like about me, but I'm really good at that.

"Why didn't you just send goons to kill me?" I snapped at him, proud that my voice didn't shake. "What kind of shrewd business dude are you if you don't know how to delegate?"

Right away I knew that was a mistake. His lips tightened and his eyes narrowed. "Who would I trust?" he demanded, and now his voice was completely familiar to me, the voice I'd heard over the phone, without any accent at all. "There is no one to trust. This is something I have to do myself, to be absolutely sure it's handled. Now, tell me where Malcolm has hidden the files."

I struggled to maintain nonchalance. "Beats me." I shrugged. "They could be anywhere."

His eyes gleamed. "So there *are* files."

Shit. All right. I had a problem with keeping my mouth shut. Maybe I *was* fucking stupid.

"Where are all of Malcolm's things? What has he done to this house? Why is it empty?" The barrel of the gun wavered slightly as he peered around, clearly unhappy with the stripped interior.

I needed to get him out of the house. Somewhere in public. "He had it all moved to a warehouse," I said. "He told me he was giving it all away."

Don looked surprised at that. "Give it away? Why?"

I raised an eyebrow. "Beats me," I said.

"Rest assured, I will if you do not cooperate."

Threats. This fucking guy was a real shithead. First he called me a gold digger and yelled at me on an international phone call, and now he was threatening to beat me, in addition to probably killing me.

Maybe I could use the fact that he was a shithead against him, though. He was smart, shrewd, ruthless—I knew all that from Malcolm's descriptions and my own interactions with him, but contrary to what most people think, being a shithead is a pretty big weakness, and it's the best weakness to exploit because shitheads never think of it as a weakness.

I fought to keep my chin from lifting defiantly and instead tried to look scared. It wasn't hard. I *was* scared. But I wasn't going to go down without a fight. Malcolm said he admired that in me. I wouldn't let him down.

Don looked mollified. "Very well. Do you know where the warehouse is?"

Sullenly I shook my head and he sighed, as though he dealt with idiots like me every day and it was beginning to wear on his great soul. Reaching into his pants pocket he pulled out a phone and turned it on. He must have dialed this number frequently because he only had to hit a single spot on the screen before bringing it to his ear and listening for the voice at the other end.

"Rick?" he said after a moment. "Yes. I need to know where all of Malcolm's personal effects are located. Yes, he moved them. Find out."

We stared at each other for a long moment while the man at the other end of the line did whatever it was he needed to do to find Malcolm's secret stash of worthless shit. I tried not to think about the fact that one of Malcolm's lawyers was named Rick. The implications were dreadful.

On the other end of the line Rick came back and Don nodded. "Yes, thank you." He hit the end button, stuffed the phone back in his pocket, then tilted his head and regarded me. "Let's go," he said.

I balked. "What?" I said. "Why do I have to go? I don't know anything!" Feigning ignorance of course. I knew lots, but I hoped that if I acted like he might let me go his opinion of my intelligence would sink even lower, if that were possible.

My ruse worked. Contempt passed over his face and I saw that he had to fight rolling his eyes.

What a shithead.

"You are coming with me because I don't believe you. You must have come here looking for the evidence." His eyes narrowed. "Turn out your pockets."

I glared at him as I did so, my heart in my mouth. If he strip-searched me it was all over...

He watched, eyes bright, as I turned the pockets of my jeans out, showing him the holes in them. Then he walked toward me, his fine shoes loud on the wooden floor, and stuck his free hand into the pouch of my sweatshirt. His fingers were large, ungentle, and my stomach turned at the feel of them groping me through the thick fabric. He found my phone, took it and then, without warning, he lifted the hem of my sweatshirt and slipped his hand underneath.

I couldn't help myself. I squeaked and tried to

squirm away. "What the *fuck,* man?" I demanded. No one touches me without my consent. No one. "Hands off, pervert!"

He seemed startled by my outburst. His gun hand was so close to me I thought I might be able to knock it out of his grip, but if I missed...

He took a step back, and the moment was lost. *Fuck.*

"Show me your chest," he said, cool and collected again.

"No," I told him.

He lifted the gun.

Panic rose. "You shoot me and you'll never find the evidence," I blurted, then cursed myself.

"Oh?" he said. "I thought you didn't know where it was?"

I ground my teeth. "I might have an inkling."

"Here?" he said.

I shook my head.

"The warehouse, then."

I didn't respond at all.

He gave another exasperated sigh, then shoved his gun into his coat pocket, keeping it trained on me, and grabbed my arm.

Old feelings rose up inside me. Fear. Despair. Desperation. *The sting of the blade...*

"Don't be too afraid," he said to me, patronizingly. "If you lead me to the evidence, I will pay you handsomely."

He really did think I was an idiot. Fine. I could play that role. "How... how much?"

He smiled. "A million dollars?" he said. He pulled me roughly toward the stairs and pushed me down the first riser. I felt the presence of the gun trained on my back. "Let's go," he snapped when I didn't move.

I licked my lips. There was no way I could run fast enough to outrace a bullet. I clomped down the stairs, stomping on the steps as if the existence of trees personally offended me and I wanted to dance on their graves. "Twenty million dollars," I said when I reached the bottom.

"You think you can bargain?" Don asked me as we turned on the second floor and started down to the first. "You think you are in a position to bargain?"

"I think you won't miss twenty million dollars," I said.

"Perhaps not. But you would miss your head. Think of it that way. A million dollars... or your head."

We reached the bottom of the stairs and I gave him my best glower. He just laughed at me, and then took a step forward. He was tall, like Malcolm, and his presence far more oppressive. Dark eyes glared down at me from behind the lenses of his fine glasses. He could have been a college professor, or someone's father if it weren't for the air of menace he carried.

Well, maybe he could have been *someone's* father...

I shoved the thought away, but it was already there, worming into my subconscious. He was going to hurt me, just like my father used to do, and it made me afraid. He saw it in me, too, and a humorless smile grazed over his lips.

"Perhaps," he mused, "if you show me what Malcolm thought was so wonderful about you, I'll double that sum." And he reached out and ran a finger over my cheek.

Everything in me rebelled. He repulsed me. But I couldn't let him see that. Instead I let my mouth drop open, shocked. "Are you... are you saying you'd pay me a million dollars to wrap you up in a tarp and beat you with a rubber chicken?" I asked.

The finger on my cheek paused. "What?" he said, then he realized I was making fun of him, and his dark brows drew down. "Don't mock me," he told me, his voice low and dangerous. He stepped back again and opened the front door. "Let's go."

The lump in his coat pocket was still aimed at me. I had no choice.

I went.

ꕥ

The warehouse where Malcolm had hidden all his things was north, in the Bronx.

I had quietly entered the private car Don had brought with him, but the privacy screen was up between the back seat and the front, so I couldn't even see the driver. So much for silently pleading for his help with my eyes in the rear view mirror. Don sat next to me in the back seat, the gun trained on me, and I tried to plaster myself to the door, keeping as much distance between us as possible.

Now the silence between us was tense as we headed north. I watched the residential streets change and morph from the grand houses of Malcolm's neighborhood into more staid apartments. We crossed the river into the Bronx and I gritted my teeth. The further we drove the less chance I had to survive. I'd told the driver I'd be back in an hour. I'd burned only thirty minutes of that. By the time he realized something was wrong, I'd be dead.

Industrial buildings began to creep into the

landscape. Graffiti and run-down projects became the background floating past the window. My only consolation was that the sleek black car we were in was going to stick out like a sore thumb. Someone would definitely notice it. Not that that was going to do me much good... but maybe it would make Don nervous.

We finally found the warehouse. It was a small, squat building painted yellow and covered in tags. It had its own industrial charm, but I was shocked all of Malcolm's stuff could fit into it. His house was huge. Then again, I wouldn't have put it past Malcolm to pick it precisely because of its certain gritty artistry. Rich people love that shit.

I wondered if I'd have a chance to make a break for it when we got out of the car, but my door was locked from the inside, and I had to slide across the seat after Don to get out. He never let the gun waver from my body, though he kept it concealed in his coat at all times.

"Walk," he commanded me.

I bit my lip, shoving my hands in my hoodie, and walked. I didn't see very many other people, and they were all minding their own business. If I screamed for help, would he shoot me? It didn't seem likely, but then again he was a rich white man and I was... well, I was me. I was white, but not rich, and I was dressed in my poor clothes. If he shot me, there'd probably be reasonable doubt. Someone would think I looked just suspicious enough, that the light was gray enough, that I'd been just threatening enough to let him off the hook. It dawned on me that if he shot me in the warehouse, he would claim he found me here, stealing Malcolm's shit.

People would believe it, too.

If it had been possible, I would have hated Don Cardall even more with that realization.

He nudged me up to the garage entry. There was a keypad next to it and he gestured toward it.

"You put in the code," he said.

Getting my fingerprints on it, I thought. I input the numbers he rattled off, and the deep click of the door unlocking indicated that the combination had been correct.

"Open it," he commanded me.

I shot him a glare. Just to fuck with him, I pretended to struggle with it. *I'm just a dumb girl,* I thought at him, hoping to beam it psychically into his brain. *I'm so weak. Now hurry up and make a mistake, you ass.* After much theatrical grunting I finally slide the door open and we stepped inside. Don turned on the overhead lights and closed the door after us.

The warehouse spread out in front of me, ugly and stark in the fluorescent lights hanging from the ceiling. All boxed up and arranged by type, Malcolm's amalgam of junk and treasure seemed a lot smaller than it had in his house. Again I was reminded of the things someone leaves behind after they die, and a weird sadness swept through me, cutting into the low-grade hum of adrenaline in my veins.

If I died here, my worldly effects would barely fill a closet. My friends would barely fill three pews. I worked too hard, was too bitter, burned too many bridges. A lump rose in my throat.

Stupid emotions, I thought to myself. *Don't need you messing things up right now, thanks.*

"Where are the files?" Don's voice behind me cut through my self-pitying melancholia. I had to think fast.

"I'm... I'm not sure," I said. "He didn't actually tell me *where,* exactly..."

"Oh? If you aren't going to be of help to me then I'm afraid you won't be earning those one million dollars." The rustle of his hand drawing out of his coat, exposing his gun, sent a bolt of fear through me.

"No!" I said. "I *kind of* know where they are."

He was silent for a moment. "Well?"

I turned around and looked him in the eye. I wanted to make myself as human as possible to him, but the person that peered back at me was cold and hard as a reptile. "It's... I think they're hidden in or on one of his statues."

I was gambling here. I had no idea if he had any statues. I'd only seen the bust by the student of Rodin, but I was willing to bet he had more.

My gamble paid off. An expression of exasperation passed over Don's face. "Damn," he said. "I don't suppose you'd know which statue in particular?"

I tried to look contrite and shook my head.

He sighed and checked his watch. "Fine," he said. "If you do not know where they are, you must find them, and do so in the next quarter hour, or I will shoot you."

"What?" I cried. "That's not fair! I have no idea where they are!" I gestured at the boxes around me. "How the fuck am I supposed to find them in all... all *this* in fifteen minutes?"

He shrugged. "The clock is ticking, Miss MacElroy. I suggest you hurry."

Enraged, I whirled away from him, my mind racing. *If I'd been hired to move a crazy rich guy's stuff, what would I do?* I'd label everything for starters, and I'd organize it in the warehouse. But would the movers hired have done that? There was only one way to find out.

Hands sweating, heart pounding, I darted away from Don. I heard him curse behind me as he made haste to follow, and I silently swore that the warehouse wasn't as terribly cluttered as Malcolm's house had been. I could have hidden, maybe... except there was only one way out. I decided to ignore what-ifs and could-have-beens for the moment and concentrate on forming a plan.

The harsh lights overhead gave the whole warehouse a weird, surreal quality. My orientation was thrown off and I found myself bumping into things as my panicked thoughts chased each other in and out of the labyrinths in my head. I jogged on, through the mountains of boxes and furniture, clipping corners with my hip, scraping my arm over rolled up rugs. My anxious eyes swept over the packages surrounding us, some piled high and neat, others lumped together haphazardly. The only saving grace was that each one was labeled quite clearly, and I found that there was a sort of order as I scurried between the groups while Don, larger and more ungainly than me, squeezed through the narrow aisles.

Here were the *Dolls (Living Room)* and there were the *Accordions (Library)*. Collectibles. My hands floated out from my sides, brushing over the scratchy cardboard as I searched for the art section. I passed through a maze of bookcases, then through their neatly organized guts *(fiction, fiction, atlases, history...)* Large squares wrapped in brown paper—paintings, the descriptions of each floating across the surface of the paper like a pale ghost of the image inside—told me I was getting warmer. I shuffled through the phantom gallery, squeezing between *Fox Hunt* and *Nude Homosexual Couple,* making a beeline for the huge, shapeless lumps wrapped in paper and bubble wrap. Those would be the sculptures.

The chilly air caressed my cheeks as I stopped, breathing hard with fear and adrenaline. I heard Don behind me, his fine shoes scraping over the dirty concrete, and I hoped they had become scuffed to hell and back. As I had thought, Malcolm had quite a few sculptures, but not as many as I had feared. Good. I just... just had to figure out what I was going to do now...

I stepped forward and dug my fingers into the tight wrapping of one large lump. My fingernails tore at the plastic and tape as behind me Don caught his breath and said, "Ten minutes."

Fuck you, I thought. What was I going to do? I tugged and swore until the wrapping had fallen away completely and I ran my hands over a large, abstract sculpture made of welded bits of farm equipment. Rusty corners caught my numb flesh, and I gritted my teeth. Was there something here I could use as a weapon? How would I even get close enough to use it?

"Shit!" I said. Tears gathered at the corner of my eyes.

"Eight minutes."

I whirled around, breathing hard. So many sculptures, and I had no idea what to do with them. I'd bought all the time I could...

I reached for another one, hoping it would give me some kind of inspiration, but the packaging came away easily, revealing a ceramic vase painted with naked ladies. I looked inside it, for appearances, but of course there was nothing in it. The thumb drive between my legs poked and prodded me awkwardly. I moved on, ripping wrapping from sculptures and curios, sticking my hands through the gaps, making a show of looking, my mind racing. *If I were a shithead,* I thought giddily, despairingly, *what would I be thinking right now?*

I'd probably be enjoying my frustration... but I'd be frustrated myself. Without knowing where that evidence had gone, I would be forever looking over my shoulder, forever wondering when I would be caught out.

My hands mechanically ripped away the plastic covering another sculpture, and my breath caught.

The Rodin.

I'd thought it was by a student of Rodin when I'd first seen it, but now, close up, my hands actually *on* it, I realized it was the work of the master himself, and my lungs hitched as I had a tiny, artistic orgasm that had nothing to do with the circumstances I currently found myself in.

It wasn't beautiful. In fact, it was pretty weird looking, a bust of an old man all pushed and pulled and warped until the weariness of the world rolled off it, but that was the mark of Rodin. The celebration of the real, of the run down, of the tired and beaten. I loved it. It spoke to me and for a tiny split second the world ground to a halt. The cold air fell away, the high, tight panic in my chest withdrew, the noise of the street outside and Don's impatient sighs faded as I took a tiny moment to enjoy this piece that I'd admired since I'd first seen it.

A ghost of a thought grazed against my brain.

Malcolm saw something in me like I saw something in this sculpture. Something strong. Beautiful despite its flaws. Or maybe because of its flaws.

Something *expressive.*

And heavy, I thought. It wasn't the traditional bronze of a Rodin, but it was plaster. God. I didn't want to do this. I really didn't. I had to, though.

I'd found the bust sitting on the ground, so I hunched my body around it as I tore the paper and bubble wrap away. I gasped, feigning surprise, and behind me Don's shoes ground over the concrete as he stood up straighter and took notice.

I ran my fingers over the sculpture. "I..." I hesitated. "I think I found something. It's here, I think." I remembered then how I'd grunted and acted weak as I'd lifted the door, and I did so again. A great groan burst out of me as I struggled to lift the plaster sculpture. My baggy artist's clothes made me look smaller than I was, and I stopped trying to lift it, breathing hard, though it was from fear more than effort. "Help me," I panted. "I think there's something under it."

The footsteps behind me were hurried, and my stomach drew tighter and harder. He was buying it, but there was no joy in me about that. Not yet. I was so close. My hands were slippery on the plaster, and I frantically wiped them on my jeans. I'd need a strong grip when the time came.

"What's wrong?" he said. He was only a few steps behind me. I felt the oppressive presence of the gun like a weight in the world.

I licked my lips. "I need you to help me lift it," I said.

He laughed. "You must think I'm stupid if you

think I'm going to put down this gun."

"But I only have five minutes," I replied. My voice was starting to shake. If I didn't get him at least *close* to me, I was fucking dead.

"Try again. Just shove it over if you have to."

Real outrage surged through me. "No! This is a *Rodin,* it's priceless. It'll break if I push it over."

He sighed, but it was impatient. "Here," he said, reaching down for the head with one huge hand, and there, peeking from the sleeve of his jacket, was a small shiny scar, the size of a cigarette.

Time stopped and I stared at that wrist.

Scarred, just like me.

This man, I remembered. *He's just like me.* Abused. Knocked around. The world had failed him, too. But I would never kill anyone for any amount of money. Why would he?

And then, gently, the question turned on its head.

Why wouldn't *I?*

I didn't have to be good. He didn't have to be bad. And yet here we were. Was that part of what Malcolm saw in me, the alternate path Don could have taken? Where the wounds turned rage inward instead of outward? Where the disappointment and the fear and the sadness came out in stunted art and a bitter tongue rather than ruthlessness and cruelty?

And then I had no more time to think about it, because his hand was almost on the sculpture, and I thought to myself: *What the fuck does it matter?*

It didn't.

So I brained him with the Rodin.

I heaved. I was not weak like he thought I was, and the plaster lifted from the floor with just enough effort to give it a deadly heft. He tried to back away, but his greed for the evidence had unbalanced him. He was leaning forward, couldn't correct his course in time. The bust swung up and out at the end of my arms, flew gracefully through the air in a beautiful, aesthetically pleasing arc, and slammed into Don's head with a crunch that sounded like the singing of avenging angels.

I'm not a poet, I'm a painter. But it was art.

Then the statue cracked in two, and the gun went off.

White hot pain speared through my side. I couldn't breathe. The lights shone in my eyes, searing hot. The ceiling, I realized.

I was on the ground, on my back. In slow motion I lifted my head. Don lay across my crumpled lower body, groaning. A dent in his skull was filling with blood. The stench of copper hung around us.

I've been shot, I thought.

Then: *Get up.*

A heavy weight lay on my chest and shoulder. A piece of the Rodin. For some reason I felt its loss far more than the bullet in my side. With a limp hand I shoved it off me, onto the ground, and I heard it chip. Teeth clenched, pain ripping through me like wildfire, I rolled over, dragging my legs from beneath Don's body. Something shone in front of me, and I squinted, trying to see clearly.

The gun.

I lunged for it, but something was off. My balance. My brain. I couldn't think straight, couldn't see straight. At my feet I heard Don gasp, realizing what I was doing, and without thinking I kicked out, sharp and hard. Another crunch and he howled with pain and collapsed to the ground. One last lunge and the gun was in my hand.

It felt good. A heavy, solid weight. Safety. Vengeance. I could kill Don right now, if I wanted to.

I heaved myself to my feet instead.

Agony engulfed me. I couldn't feel myself think. I pressed my left hand to my side, trying to staunch the flow of blood with the thick fabric of my hoodie, but there was a lot of it. Sticky, hot, but rapidly cooling. The skin of my face was clammy, cold, wet. I stumbled forward, the gun in my right hand, and crashed through the discarded debris of Malcolm's life.

I walked like the dead. Shambling. Unable to think. I hurt. I don't know how I made it to the front of the warehouse, but I did. I somehow found it in the maze, and when I fell against the door the metal slats clattered so loudly I thought I would fall apart.

I had to bend down to reach the handle. I had to let go of my side.

Dizziness overwhelmed me as I removed my left hand and wrapped it around the handle. I watched from inside my head, trying to figure out what was wrong when I couldn't get a grip.

Red, I thought. *Blood,* I thought. My hand fell from the door, limp against my jeans, and with supreme effort I wiped it clean and tried again.

Metal screamed, and so did I.

It was almost impossible. It hadn't been heavy before, I had just been pretending, but now it weighed a million pounds. But I had to get out. I *had* to. I had to get to Malcolm, prove his innocence, or all of this was for nothing.

Red blood gushed from my side. Ruined muscles screamed in pain, unable to do what I asked of them.

I panted. My mouth was dry. I wanted water.

Focus. Focus. Squat. Lift with the legs, not the torso. *Oh god.*

Three feet. That's as far as I was able to lift it. It was enough. I fell to my hands and knees and crawled under the door, into the blinding gray light of the windy March day.

The sound of a car door opening. Wind whipped over my clammy face. I was going to be sick, but I forced myself to look up. The black car we'd taken here loomed like a hulking black beast in the street. On the far side, the driver was getting out, his mouth hard and set, his eyes glowering at me as though I were a naughty puppy. He was huge, enormous, a giant unfolding toward me.

If he gets me, I thought, *it'll be all over.*

I lifted the gun and fired.

A look of surprise flashed across his face, as though I'd just grown a clown nose. Then, silently, he folded up and slumped over.

I didn't even bother to check if he was alive. I crawled along the narrow sidewalk. A chain link fence on one side of me, and I reached out and pulled myself to my feet before I staggered onward.

A corner. There were always people at a corner. Stores. Human beings. I had to get to a corner. If I could get away from Don, I would be okay.

Well. Malcolm would be okay.

Help me, I begged silently, and then I was stumbling down a long tunnel toward two men. Dark faces, dressed like me. They were staring. They'd heard the gunshot, and as I staggered toward them they backed up. I realized they were afraid of me.

I looked down and saw the gun still in my hand. I

dropped it. Mercifully it just fell to the concrete and didn't go off. I looked up again, peering down the tunnel.

They were still there. Not running. *Thank you.*

I reached out, but my vision was blurring, the world tilting. The wind nipped and bit at me, cold against my skin, but nothing compared to the dark void opening up inside me, blooming like a black rose.

I remember their faces. One looked scared, the other horrified as he lunged forward to catch me, but, as though from far away, I saw myself hit the pavement, crumpling, and then I closed my eyes and turned inward and fell into the blackness.

ೋ 17 ೋ

When I opened my eyes again, I was in a hospital. White and cream and blue and sterile. Felicia sat by my bed, staring at her phone, a line of worry between her brows as she restlessly scanned the screen. I wanted to ask her what was wrong, but a bone deep exhaustion filled me and my mouth was dry as desert sand.

I wheezed, but it wasn't even loud enough to catch her attention. I let my eyes close.

ೋ

I woke again, this time as nurse bent over me, her perfume overwhelming my nose. My stomach heaved and I choked on vomit. She took one look at me and slammed a button on the wall.

Doctors and nurses and interns flooded the room. Tubes fed down my throat, sucking the vomit out. This time I felt pain, but it was far away, happening to someone else.

It must suck to be that chick, I thought, and fell asleep again before they even finished clearing my airway.

When I finally woke up for real, Malcolm was there.

If I could have commanded my lungs to sigh in relief, I would have, but the pain that had been at bay suddenly reared up and struck, and I could hardly breathe.

Malcolm noticed my eyes opening almost immediately, and in a flash he was at my side, his large, sweet hands running over my forehead, stroking down my cheeks, his thumbs running against my temples as he leaned over the hospital bed and kissed my brow, soft and gentle, over and over again.

Warmth spread through me, chasing away the pain. *Malcolm,* I thought. *Malcolm, you're free.* I must have done it somehow. They must have found the files. He must have proved his innocence.

I did it, I wanted to say. *I freed you.* But I couldn't talk. My mouth had the sticky, bone dry feel of too much morphine, and I tried to lick my lips to wet them. It didn't matter. It was like my tongue was plastic.

"Wait, don't strain yourself," Malcolm said. His voice rumbled through me, the sound painful in my head, but burrowing deep into my aching heart, and I subsided, willing, at last, to let him do what he wanted, completely and totally. I closed my eyes, and I drifted into a snap of sleep before I felt the sting of cold on my lips and I opened them again.

Malcolm stared down at me, his face so tender I

thought I would shatter. I need to be handled roughly to survive. Be kind to me, and I break.

His warm hand landed on my throat, his thumb coaxing my chin down, and when I opened my mouth he slipped a chip of ice into it. It hit like a balm from heaven.

Patiently, Malcolm fed me ice until I fell asleep again.

ೋ

That was how it went for a while. I would wake, and Malcolm would be there. With each waking I felt a little stronger. Doctors and nurses came and went. Felicia and Anton fluttered in and out. Friends appeared and disappeared.

But Malcolm was always there, slipping ice onto my tongue like a sacrament, and with every kiss he pressed to my brow I crumbled a little inside, my armor breaking under his tender assault. I learned later that it was only about twelve hours between my vomiting incident and the first time I was able to speak, but it felt like a year. Ten years. A lifetime.

So after a lifetime I opened my eyes and saw him curled over the edge of my bed, sleeping. He looked exhausted, the same way I'd seen him when we'd first met, when he'd resolved to die, except now the dark circles under his eyes were almost black with the beautiful tan he had obtained on the sea. His shaggy blond hair, now sun-bleached and far messier than it had been when we first met, fell across his forehead, and I had the urge to reach out and brush it from his eyes.

I got as far as lifting a hand before I realized it was

stuffed full of needles and tubes, and I remembered I'd been shot.

Damn.

I drew breath, meaning to say something, but I started coughing. It hurt like hell. I gasped as I coughed, feeling as if I was going to rip apart at the seams, and Malcolm woke up at the first expulsion.

"Sadie?" he said, panic coloring his voice. He sat up immediately and moved to the head of the bed, his beautiful artists' hands reaching for me.

I stopped coughing and gave him a weak smile.

"Hey," I said.

"Sadie," he replied, and his cherry wood eyes filled with tears. He started shaking his head, leaving me confused. Was he upset I was awake?

I couldn't even get beyond the next thought. I felt like complete ass. It was hard to rally my brain into a coherent pattern, and when I tried to lift my head the room dipped and swirled around me.

Warm hands landed on my shoulders. "Shh, shh," Malcolm murmured. "Just lay back and rest."

"I got shot," I said.

His face became lined with concern. "I know," he said. "Shit, I'm so sorry, Sadie. It's all my fault. I shouldn't have been so stupid..."

I felt my brows moving into some position or other—probably frowning—but I was still high enough on morphine that I could hardly tell what my face was doing. My confusion must have showed, though, because he drew his lip through his teeth, clearly upset.

"I mean I treated it as a game" he tried to clarify. "I didn't think Don would be *that* ruthless. I have no idea how he thought he could get away with it, but people backed into corners do crazy things. I should have known he would do whatever it took. I played with your life, all of your life, just to feel something other than emptiness or pain. I'm so selfish... I understand if you won't ever forgive me."

He is *crazy*, I thought to myself, vaguely amused. It wasn't like I hadn't known what I was doing, trying to throw myself in front of a man hell-bent on self-destruction. I'd done it before, and got a lot less out of it for my trouble. But there was something special in Malcolm, and I felt an answering spark in me when we were together. Those days on the boat, dancing closer and closer together, had been some of the sweetest of my life, and I couldn't have born the thought of never having that again. So I'd fought hard to save it, and now that was done and Malcolm was here beside me.

Worth. It.

"Sadie?" He seemed to be waiting to hear his fate.

I gave him a little half-shrug, more that I couldn't really move rather than out of any insolence on my part. "Nobody's perfect," I rasped at him.

"But... I'm so sorry..."

I managed a tiny smile. "Just don't do it again."

The sheen of tears disappeared and he smiled at me. A real smile. It took my breath away. Then he lowered his face and buried it in my shoulder.

"You need to rest, Sadie. You have to recover."

I licked my lips. "Don?" I managed to say.

"In jail, as is his driver and one of my lawyers... I couldn't trust my legal team, so I had to rely on you, and I wish I hadn't. I should have found another way..."

I shook my head, even though he couldn't see it

from where he had buried his face. "No big deal," I managed to tell him.

He lifted his head. "Yes, big deal. You could have *died.*"

I closed my eyes. His warm hands moved up my throat to my face, smoothing over my cheekbones, covering my brow. "Sadie..." he said.

I fell asleep, just happy to be with him.

ꟷ

The bullet had torn through my side, but miraculously had missed most of my major organs, though I'd been nicked in the liver. The blood loss had been the worst of it, and I learned I'd malingered for a day or so until I was able to be stabilized. It still felt totally wretched, but I got off easy. The driver of the car hadn't been quite so lucky with a bullet bursting a kidney. He'd live, but when I learned about it I felt awful. He probably hadn't known I was going to be killed.

Don, of course, got the least of it with a major concussion and a broken nose, though I guess it was lucky he was coherent because, as I guessed, he tried to tell everyone I was a thief, stealing from my disgraced lover. The thumb drive found in my underwear, of course, told a different story. I wished I could have been awake to see the doctor's faces when they found *that.* But it freed Malcolm, and though there would be an ongoing investigation into what exactly had happened I had a feeling that Felicia's lawyers would figure out a way to get any charges dropped without my intervention. I focused on getting better.

Eventually the hospital staff let me go home, although Malcolm insisted that the home I go to was his. I didn't really feel like arguing with him. I still needed a lot of help, and it was a bright, sunny day late in March when I was let out of the hospital. When we arrived at his house, Malcolm helped me hobble up the front stairs. The place was still empty, but it felt like a better empty now. The emptiness of possibility, rather than the emptiness of ending. Malcolm cradled me in his arms and carried me all the way up the stairs to the fourth floor, and I wrapped my arms around him and let him. It felt good to be carried. It felt good to be taken care of.

He installed me in his bedroom. I have to say, if you're recovering from a gunshot wound, an open room full of light in a mansion in upper Manhattan is a great place to do it. I slept in the sinfully luxurious sheets, covered in the puffy white down comforter, and Malcolm, so as not to disturb my healing wounds by sleeping in the same bed as me, hauled a mattress up the stairs and slept on the floor.

The world whirled by, but that beautiful, light-filled room was a haven. Felicia called every day, but had the good sense to stay away, and I was grateful for that. I wasn't ready for our sanctuary to be invaded yet. Malcolm and I would lay in bed and talk, or read together, or watch a movie on his iPad. His long, hard body warmed me up, and once I started physical therapy I'd be beat at the end of my sessions, and he would lie in bed next to me and stroke my hair until I fell asleep.

When I needed a bath, he would carry me down to the third floor and put me in the tub, fill it with a few inches of water, add lavender and chamomile perfumed salts, and wash me with gentle hands and soft cloths. His fingers slipped over my breasts, up my throat and down into my pussy without demanding anything, leaving me hot and aching for him, though sex—or even a soothing orgasm—was out of the question, and even the sweet tensing of sensual pleasure made my side hurt.

"Patience," he would say then, and kiss me, calming me. We were the only two people in the world, it seemed, and even if we weren't Malcolm acted like it was true. He was *there*. Gentle and attentive. Caring. Entirely *present,* entirely with me.

It was a side of him that I'd never thought I'd see, and it was sweet as the honey-spiked tea he would brew for me on the days the clouds covered the sky and the rains poured down the windows.

He was focused on me like a laser, and at the time I thought it was because he was wracked with guilt for his part in my indisposition, but I found I couldn't care less about the wound. People get shot every day and for way stupider reasons. This was one scar I was going to whip out at parties and show off. I'd totally earned it and it would make a great story. *So this one time I took a bullet for a guy who wasn't even my boyfriend...*

A few weeks passed and I was finally up and around again, stretching my legs, walking the length of his absurd bedroom, from the bed to the computer and back. It was only then that Malcolm started to take his eyes off me, as though he hadn't *really* thought my recovery was for real until he actually saw me standing on my own two feet. A tension I hadn't even known was in him disappeared.

He began to work again, lying next to me in bed or curled up on the white couch and overstuffed chairs he had dragged up the stairs one afternoon. He'd arranged them in a little semi-circle, giving us a little suite in the bedroom. I wondered what part of the house he'd cribbed them from since I'd never had a grand tour when it was full of stuff, but when I finally trusted myself to go downstairs on my own, I was shocked to find the house still empty.

"Where's all your junk?" I asked him when I came back up the stairs. He sat on the white couch, a book on his crossed legs as he wrote on a piece of paper.

"I told you," he said. "It didn't make me happy so I'm getting rid of it. I've decided that I'm not going to keep anything that doesn't make me happy."

I felt my mouth twist. "I liked the Rodin," I said. "Sorry I had to ruin it."

A faint smile graced his lips at that. "Don't worry. I've lent it to the Museé Rodin where it will be meticulously restored and displayed, then returned. I always liked that bust, but if it makes you happy then it is a definite keeper."

I couldn't help but grin at that, relieved. "That's good to know." Then he turned the piece of paper in his lap and I frowned, realizing that he wasn't writing—he was drawing. "What are you working on?" I blurted, then bit my cheek. I thought he'd given up sketching in his angry outburst on the boat.

The look he gave me could only be described as smug. "My masterpiece," he said.

"Can I see?" I asked him.

"Oh no. That would ruin it."

I scowled. "What, is it like a quantum masterpiece, where it's genius if you don't look at it and it sucks if you do?"

He laughed. "No, but that's a pretty brilliant idea

for a piece of art. I don't think I could pull that off, but I bet you could."

I blinked. "What? I haven't painted in months..."

"You don't have to paint, just make art." Delicately he placed the eraser of his pencil between his teeth. "Or perhaps you have already made such a piece? The theoretical piece of art that you *could* produce, and yet persist in not producing because you have a job and are now respectable?"

Ouch. "I'm not *that* respectable," I said.

"Fair enough," he replied. "But still. You should make art, Sadie."

He said it as though it were easy. And maybe it was. "I'll have to think about it."

"Do. I think you get sidetracked into other people too much and don't take care of yourself."

"I've been letting you take care of me, haven't I?"

The hangdog look he gave me was almost comical. "Yes, after you took a bullet for me."

"Well, yeah." I shrugged, as if that was no big deal. Brush with death? Please. The blowjob on the police moped was way more dangerous. It could have fallen over and we could have been seriously hurt. "Whatever. Are you sure I can't see it?"

He nodded.

"You won't even show it to the woman who took a bullet for you?"

He snorted and shook his head. "Especially not you, my muse. You'll just have to wait and be patient."

I don't usually pout, but I was sorely tempted to do so. If there's one way to get me all worked up about something, it's forbidding me from it. I huffed and sighed very passive-aggressively for a minute or two, then gave up and grabbed my e-reader and snuggled back into bed.

I woke up later, after the sun had gone down and the ghostly lights of the city filtered in through the windows, leaving the room eerie and beautiful. Malcolm slept like the dead on the floor next to the bed. I sat up and rubbed the sleep from my eyes, feeling hungry. Slipping off the mattress, careful not to wake him up, I padded across the floor towards the stairs. A dark square on one of the overstuffed chairs caught my attention.

The book he'd been using as a lap desk.

I stole a quick glance at him to make sure he was still asleep and tiptoed over to it. When I touched it I found the book to be large and leather bound, like a year book or a photo album, and sandwiched between its heavy pages I saw the razor thin edge of a piece of printer paper poking out.

I hooked a finger under the book's cover meaning to lift it away. Then I bit my lip and hesitated.

Would it really ruin it?

I realized I wanted to trust him. I didn't want to take that chance. I left the book where it was and crept downstairs in search of food.

ᘛᘚ

He left that book lying around where I could easily open it and peek inside, and he gave me no end of opportunities to do so. I should have gotten a medal for self-restraint. One afternoon he came up the stairs with a set of oil paints for me, a canvas and a drop cloth and told me to start expressing my 'inner pain' while he prepared for his masterpiece upstairs.

"Ain't no one want to see that shit," I told him. "Inner pain? Ugh."

"Oh, come on," he wheedled. He carried a small tackle box at his side and I was dying to know what materials were in it. You could hide a lot in a tackle box. "I bet it's a goldmine of stuff."

"Yeah, but the kind of mine that caves in and everybody dies."

He sighed and rolled his eyes at me, which was such a *me* thing to do that I almost did a double take. "Just try to enjoy yourself with the paint, okay? I must needs prepare my studio."

So dramatic.

The book containing his sketch lay on his desk and I felt its presence hovering there the entire time I listened to him banging around upstairs. Thumps and footsteps distracted me, until I finally slapped a large frowny face on the canvas and propped it up, facing the corner, to dry. I spent the rest of the afternoon pacing the floor, convincing myself that any second Malcolm would start back down the stairs and I just had to hold on a little longer. I didn't want to ruin the *surprise*, did I?

I hate surprises. But I persevered.

When Malcolm finally came back downstairs, he started straight for my own canvas, curiosity on his face.

"Don't touch it," I said. "It's a quantum masterpiece."

He smiled. "I could see it in a gallery, definitely. It's brilliant. Don't forget to sign it."

I grabbed a brush, wiped the turpentine from it, and drew *SM* across the back of the canvas in red. Malcolm nodded his approval.

"I love... it," he said.

I smiled at him, and when I woke up later that night, I saw him standing and staring at my signature on the back of it, shaking his head, as though he couldn't understand me for the life of him.

18

The next day, it was time for him to complete his masterpiece.

We spent a leisurely morning reading in bed, though I have to admit I didn't absorb a word I read. I was too anxious and excited. Malcolm helped me get dressed and took me out to lunch. There were photographs and staring eyes, but all in all it wasn't as bad as I thought it might be. I enjoyed sitting with Malcolm and holding his hand right where everyone could see it.

Check me out, bitches, I wanted to say, but I didn't because that kind of thing just got you in the papers. We ate sushi and talked about nothing for hours, and when we finally reached home I was feeling sleepy and sated.

Malcolm closed the front door behind us and locked it—the first time I could remember him doing so. Immediately I was awake again, and when Malcolm took my hand in his and led me up the stairs to the top floor of his mansion I could hardly breathe.

It was warm at the top again. The photography studio he had installed had been expanded, with more lights. The black backdrop was still there, though now it curved around itself, leaving a small cave to catch the light.

A few feet away from it lay a clean drop cloth and two pots of paint, white on the outside so I couldn't tell what color they were. Next to the drop cloth stood a full length mirror.

Malcolm led me to the drop cloth. "Allow me," he whispered, and began to take off my clothes. I swallowed and let him.

He kissed every inch of skin he revealed as he pulled my blouse from my arms, slid the bra from my chest, eased my skirt down over my thighs, helped me kick my heels off. When at last I was completely nude, he helped me sit down, and then drew a dark silk cloth from his pocket.

"Allow me," he said. It was neither a command nor a request. Just a simple statement of fact. Yes, of course I would allow him. I smiled slightly and inclined my head toward him, and he tied the blindfold around my eyes. The light of the room was eclipsed, and I lapsed into darkness.

Warm dry hands helped me lie down on the cloth, and I lay there, trembling in anticipation as to what he might do. But all that happened was the gentle *pop* of a can of body paint and a brush laid against my skin.

"Ready?" he asked.

I nodded.

He painted me.

It seemed to take forever. The brush wandered this way and that way, and I shivered beneath it, but that was all that happened. He painted my body in no particular order, sending the brush over the curves and valleys wherever the fancy seemed to take him. The warmth of the room and the soothing strokes of the brush put me in almost a trance, and when he turned me over to do my back, I nearly fell asleep on my stomach.

After a long time, his hand on my hair jolted me back to reality.

"Careful," he said as I made to sit up. "Don't disturb it too much."

I nodded and slowly drew myself to my feet, my skin caked in paint. His hands alighted on my shoulders and gently turned me. "I'm pointing you at the mirror," he told me. "Are you ready?"

I was ready. I nodded.

With a flourish, he untied the blindfold. "Now... open your eyes."

I did. My eyes caught my image in the mirror, and I inhaled sharply.

He'd painted me in a pale color that wasn't quite white, but almost. My dark hair fell over my shoulders, a stunning and glossy contrast. And all my tattoos were gone.

...Okay, not *gone,* they were just hidden beneath layers of matte paint. I had guessed that he would be doing that much at least, but what truly startled me was what he'd done to the scars underneath.

He'd painted them gold.

I couldn't stop staring. My chest hurt. I let my eyes flow over the vision of me, over the image of myself in the mirror. My body was suddenly, shockingly unfamiliar, transfigured and transformed beneath his brush. I felt as though he hadn't layered paint on, but rather swept it away, revealing the truth that lay beneath. The skin under the skin. Slowly I lifted my arms and turned, seeing every scar, the new and the old, emblazoned in gold, beautiful and bold. My fingers fluttered over them, wondering how such ugly things could be made to be so lovely. I had no idea what to say.

Malcolm had that effect on me.

He shifted behind me, and I blinked, realizing that I'd completely forgotten he was there. I glanced back at him and I saw that, in his hands, he held the vase I had broken at the auction and then found repaired in the closet. It seemed so long ago now that I almost didn't recognize it.

It was gorgeous, and now that I finally had a good look at the vase, I realized what Malcolm had done to me: the cracks made by its shattering were now filled with gold.

Malcolm cleared his throat. "The art is called *kintsugi,*" he said. His voice was hesitant, sweet, as though he didn't quite know how to go about explaining his vision to me and had to choose his words with extra care. "*Kintsugi* means 'golden joinery.' It's a method of repairing ceramics invented by the Japanese, and it embraces the concept of *wabi sabi*. Have you ever heard of it?"

Mutely I shook my head. I couldn't stop staring at the repaired vase.

"It means the beauty found in that which is impermanent and imperfect. The only sort of beauty that can ever really be, I've come to think, because nothing lasts forever." He smiled. "And nobody's flawless, so who could ever make a flawless piece of art?"

I blinked. My eyes were curiously moist. I gestured

to my body. "So this is your masterpiece?"

"As close as I'll ever get. And really, it's not *my* masterpiece. It's yours. I just helped you see it.

Weakness threatened to send me to my knees. "My masterpiece?" This foreign vessel, broken and repaired and suddenly overflowing with my soul?

He nodded. "The life of the vase is here." He brushed his hand over the porcelain, the barely visible seams of gold catching the pads of his fingers. "Your life is here." He reached out and placed those same fingers on one of the golden scars on my skin and I shuddered at the contact.

"Nothing remains untouched by time," Malcolm said. "Maybe we all start out pure, but the passage of our lives leaves us with our own unique wear and tear. Every scar and flaw is beautiful, because there will never be another one like it. You are unique. The sum of your life has led you to this moment."

There was a lump in my throat so large I could hardly breathe. I licked my lips and groped for words. "And what am I in this moment?" I whispered.

He smiled, sad and hopeful at once. "Perfect," he whispered.

Like little silver drops of my soul, now too large to be contained, tears rose and spilled from my eyes as he led me over to the dark backdrop and handed me the vase. Without needing direction from him, I held the vase against me, kissing it, caressing it, cradling it in the curve of my body. I let my inner eye be my guide, and before me and above me, in and out and all around, Malcolm snapped a hundred pictures, a thousand pictures. No, *thousands*.

I posed for what seemed like hours, thinking of a hundred new poses as I transitioned between each one—the vase in my lap, covering my pussy, my face against it, my eyes closed, the vase in my hair, my gold streaked arms reaching for it as I tossed it in the air, my whole body straining upwards—until at last Malcolm said, "Enough," and enfolded me in his arms.

Exhausted, my eyes swollen from crying, I leaned into him, and he kissed me, so sweet and soft I thought I would shatter all over again. He carried me down the stairs, just as he did when I couldn't walk on my own, and when he washed me in the bath, this time he let his hands and fingers linger on me, in places I once thought he might never touch again.

First, he ran warm water from the faucet and filled it part way before turning it off and setting me on my feet in the tub. "Kneel," he commanded.

I complied, turning my back to the faucet, my legs trembling. I bent my head in submission, giving him complete access to me, and I was rewarded with a warm gush of water over my back from a soft sponge. Gently Malcolm ran it in circles and spirals over my back, around my ribs, down over the flare of my hips. Then he abandoned the sponge entirely and used his hands.

There was an urgency to his touch this time, a swift, anxious nervousness, as though he were trembling on the precipice of remembering something very important, as though words that could change his life stood at the tip of his tongue, waiting to be said.

His hands swirled down and around the round cheeks of my ass, slipping into the valley between them, gently massaging away the paint. Again he picked up the sponge and gushed warm water over me, this time over my shoulders, so that rivulets ran down my collarbone, trickled over my breasts and fell from my nipples like raindrops from branches. The whispery caress of water flowed through me and in me, and I shuddered with desire.

Beneath me the water ran white and gold, brilliant and beautiful, milk streaked with honey. Malcolm lifted the drain and let the water run out as he turned the faucet on again, letting more warm water run out. This time he didn't turn it off, but swept it over my body, sweet and seeking. The sponge scraped against my skin, removing pigment, revealing the tattoos beneath. I felt as though he were hiding me again, and the real me, the one underneath the ink and the attitude, was a secret we shared.

I trembled as he moved his hands over my body, his fingertips scraping up my abdomen, his palms gently rubbing over my nipples, squeezing my small, perfect breasts, until the water ran clear and I panted from the heat spiraling through me. The pain in my side had subsided and now seemed far away. All that mattered was Malcolm. Long, strong fingers probed between the cheeks of my ass, and he let the tub fill with water again as he tipped me forward onto my knees and elbows. I bowed my head, letting my hair fall into the water, and as he massaged a sweet circle around my puckered entrance with one finger, I closed my eyes and gave myself over to him.

Sensation. The warmth of the water lapping at my forehead, the heat of the steam caught in the cave of my bowed body, the harshness of the iron tub biting into my knees and elbows—all of it whirled together in my head, creating a perfect moment as Malcolm gently probed me and my pussy answered his exploration with a gush of warmth and wetness. One finger pushed its way inside my ass while his other hand reached under me and cupped my breasts, rough and possessive. My mouth went dry and I had to force myself to stay still as he began to gently push and retreat into my ass while his fingers tweaked my nipples, pinching hard until I cried out. My core quivered, aching and needing, and when Malcolm transferred his mouth to my ass I groaned. He was so close, so close to where I wanted him to be...

Then the hand playing with my breasts moved down, down, down my stomach. One finger caught on my naval, dipping inside briefly before slipping out again, and he continued his trek downward. The tight ring of muscle gave way to the gentle entrance of his tongue, and he licked and thrust into me as he found my clit with thumb and forefinger and gripped it firmly. I shook and panted, my body barely able to hold on as he picked up a quick, demanding rhythm, pinching and flicking my clit while he lavished soft kisses on my asshole. The world reduced to his fingers, his mouth, his lips, my cunt, my ass, and I gritted my teeth as I felt an orgasm building in me. It had been weeks since we'd been together this way, and my body responded with hunger, with a wildness that I'd never suspected I held within me. I twisted and turned, thrashing as Malcolm played me, and when he began to scrape his fingernail over my clit the pain and pleasure became too much, sending me up and over the edge of ecstasy.

The universe contracted, and then expanded, exploding around his tongue and fingers. I shrieked, and it sounded like a wounded animal calling out. The sound echoed on the walls, in the confines of the tub, shaking the whole room with the strength of feeling Malcolm inspired in me. Over and over again waves crashed against me, threatening to take me over, but Malcolm held on to me, keeping me anchored with tongue and lips and teeth and fingers.

When at last I subsided, gasping and with tears in my eyes, he withdrew and laid a warm, fluffy towel over the top of the tub, trapping me in it. I couldn't even move, just lay there, broken and repaired, and let the steam curl around me, warming me. I heard him walk to the sink and wash up, and then he was back, pulling me out of the tub and rubbing me down. He took great care not to exacerbate my injury, but no such care with the rest of me. Swirling the cotton over my skin, he rubbed me raw until I staggered on my feet and he caught me. Lifting me up and enfolding me in the towel, he carried me back up the stairs.

He took me to his bed and set me down, towel-drying my hair and covering me with blankets before slowly disrobing himself.

I watched him. The light was low, the electrical lights of the city already flaring up against the encroaching darkness, and he seemed like a vision standing next to the bed, dreamy and unreal. First he unbuttoned his shirt—covered in streaks of gold and pale cream paint—slow and sure. One by one the buttons popped and revealed the skin beneath that I knew so well, but felt now that I was seeing for the first time. His muscled chest, the fine line that ran down his abdomen, the six-pack he sported, all were new to me as he unwrapped the prize of his body before my eyes.

When at last the shirt fluttered to the ground I

sighed and stretched out a hand, inviting him to come to me, but he didn't. He unbuckled his belt first, taking his sweet time, and the strength of his hands, barely restrained, gave me a bittersweet thrill. The whisper of the belt drawing through the loops on his pants sent a shiver up my spine, and when he popped the button of his fly I licked my lips.

He let his pants and boxers fall to the ground and stood next to the bed, naked, his erection enormous and straining, standing straight out from his body. Reaching out, I took it in my hand and drew him toward me. For once he complied, climbing onto the bed with me and straddling my chest, letting gravity and his girth stretch my lips out. My hands went around his ass and dug in, my fingernails clawing against his skin. He felt so good, so hot and fine, and I moved my head forward, gulping his cock greedily. The taste of him stirred my core again, and I thought of taking his length into my pussy, riding it until we both couldn't stand.

Above me Malcolm grabbed the headboard. It groaned under his grip as he began to thrust. He held himself back, quick and tight little nudges, but still enough for me to force myself to relax and let him rock his hips, letting his cock slide in and out of my mouth at will. The muscles under my hands were hard and trembling, and as I dug in and he began to pant, I wished we could stay like this forever.

In and out, he let his cock slide into the tight seal of my lips, and I was rewarded with tiny drops of sweet precum. I let my tongue swirl over them, licking up every last pearl until I felt him stutter and stop his stroke, clearly driven to the edge. "Sadie," he moaned, and then swung off me.

I protested wordlessly at the loss of his warmth, but he didn't leave me hanging. Instead he drew the covers up over both of us and pulled me gently on top of him.

"I don't want to hurt your side any more than it already is," he whispered. "I have to let you take over.

I shook my head. "I don't want to," I told him. "I trust you."

He smiled at that. "I know," he said. "But I don't trust me. I could be at death's door and still be fucking you. I have no control when it comes to you. I just want to... to..." His hands floated just an inch from my face, and I felt the heat rolling from his palms. Gently he outlined me in the dark and I reveled in the phantom touch of him before moving down and swiping my dripping pussy over his thick cock. Just the sensation of his cock against my slick flesh made us both gasp, as though we had never felt it before. Biting my lip, I angled my hips and began to nudge him inside.

It was harder than I thought it would be. The wound in my side screeched in protest, and more than once I had to stop, panting, and let Malcolm hold my trembling body up so I didn't sink further onto his erection before I was ready, but when I finally slid him home—all of him—I collapsed forward and buried my face in his shoulder. His arms came around me and held me. The rough texture of his pubic hair ground into my clit and his cock filled me to the brim.

He ran his hands over me, as though soothing a wild beast, and then under me he slowly drew out and thrust in.

The sweetness of it brought tears to my eyes. He wrapped me up in his body, holding me immobile as he pushed his hips against mine, his cock sliding in and out of my tight channel, the mound of his pubic bone grating over my clit, still hypersensitive from his earlier rough handling. I felt another orgasm build in me as our hips slammed together and he held me tight against him, our hearts hammering in time against our chests, as though trying to reach each other though blood and flesh and bone.

His cock swept in and out of me, and I coiled and curled over him, my mouth finding his ear. "Malcolm," I whispered. "Malcolm, Malcolm, make me come, make me come around you..."

"I will," he breathed. "Sadie, beautiful Sadie, my muse, my muse..." His hands went to my ass and gripped my cheeks tightly, suddenly moving me over him in different ways, angling up against the upper wall of my core, thrusting high and deep while my clit scraped and rubbed against him. My mouth opened and I swirled my tongue over his ear, slipping and probing into the folds, gentle and urgent, the same way he ate me out, and Malcolm lost control beneath me. His hips thrust and he thrashed, rolling in the bed under me as his cock plunged into my core, but all the while still carefully keeping me immobile so as not to hurt me. His fingers dug in, and I knew he would leave bruises, but I didn't care.

Then he thrust into me deeper and harder than ever before and I came, shuddering and shivering. Under me Malcolm called my name and I fastened my hands in his hair, pulling and tugging his head back until I revealed his throat to me. As I came I bit down and he cried out and thrust wildly beneath me, carried away, and I felt his cock coil and tighten before emptying his seed into me in short, sharp bursts.

Together we strove in the warmth of his bed, in the light of the city, and when it was over I fell asleep on top of him with his cock still inside me.

I woke in the middle of the night. We had shifted positions and Malcolm slept beside me, one arm thrown over my chest, and his breathing was deep and slow. He looked almost human in the light of the streetlamps outside, his face half-smooshed into the pillow under his head. The space between my thighs was delightfully sore and raw and sticky with his cum, and I clamped my legs together, as though I could keep that feeling with me forever. I rolled into him and kissed his forehead on an impulse.

He woke almost immediately, his cherry wood eyes black in the dim light, and I wanted to fall into them. Which was really silly, I reflected, because that'd probably hurt both parties. I must get sappy after getting laid.

No, not just getting laid...

"Hey," I said.

"Hello," he replied, all formality before tightening his arm around me and drawing me closer. The wound in my side, now unobscured by pleasure, tweaked and I winced. Malcolm froze immediately, and then moved toward me himself. I let him come. I'd spent quite a bit of time chasing after him, it seemed. It was only right that he return the favor a little bit. "How are you feeling?" he asked.

I smiled and burrowed into his shoulder. He smelled good, rich and manly and dark, and I let myself revel in his scent. "I think I'm fine," I said. An understatement.

"Good," he said. "I'm glad. I worried I might hurt you."

"Don't worry about that," I said. "I'd let you know if you did."

His mouth twisted. "I'm sure you would." Then he smiled. "And I might like it."

"If you want me to whip you and peg you, you only have to ask."

The look on his face was priceless. "I never said anything about pegging and whipping," he said.

I laughed at him. "Then what were you thinking of?"

"I was thinking more giving me a slap or something, after which I would tie you up and show you just how nice a little slapping can be."

Good grief, I was getting turned on by him talking about slapping me. The memory of our first painting session rose, when he slapped and flicked my nipples, driving me to an orgasm that nearly broke me apart, and I blushed. He saw my cheeks darken and grinned at me. "You are precious, Sadie," he said, running his hands through my hair.

For a long time we lay there, listening to the sounds of the city, far away and faint, but still active even this late at night. Finally I drew back and looked into his eyes.

"Malcolm," I murmured. "What are we? Like, boyfriend and girlfriend? Artist and muse?"

He tilted his head and looked very thoughtful. "Lovers," he said at last. "We are lovers. *The* lovers, in The Kiss" He was referring to the Rodin piece, the man and the woman caught in a passionate embrace.

"I hope not," I said. "They look really

uncomfortable in that position."

"A little discomfort never hurt anyone."

"That's... that doesn't even make any sense."

He chuckled. "Well fine, if you're looking for *sense* I'm afraid I don't have any for you. You make me lose my senses." He ran his hand down my body beneath the comforter, but when he hit a sore spot on my hip I winced. He stopped immediately. "What's wrong?"

I lifted the comforter and turned toward the window, exposing the imprint of his hand on my flank in purple and blue. "Just a bruise," I said.

"Oh. Oh, Sadie. I'm so sorry. I tried so hard to keep your side from getting re-injured and I just ended up hurting you again..."

"Don't be sorry," I said. "I like it. It's like your signature on your masterpiece. How else would anyone know it was yours?"

His shoulders relaxed at that. One hand came up and cradled my head, drawing me in for a kiss while the other soothed and smoothed over the bruise he had left behind in passion, as if he couldn't quite believe my words and wanted to make it disappear.

I *did* like it, though. Another mark on my body. Another piece of my life story.

My favorite part yet.

If you enjoyed *The Billionaire's Muse*, don't forget to pick up a copy of Felicia's story in *The Billionaire's Wife*, available now in print and ebook.

ABOUT THE AUTHOR

Ava Lore was raised by wombats and lives to corrupt the innocent. When not writing erotic romance, she spends her time thinking about writing erotic romance and drinking enough iced coffee to kill a musk ox. She lives in Texas and is the curator of one kid, one husband, one dog, one garden, and a million knitting and spinning projects.

Ava yearns for you tragically. Please email her at authoravalore@gmail.com and let her know what's on your mind!

Made in the USA
Middletown, DE
09 November 2018